Best Wi

Smoke Screen

Care Ayre.

Also, by this Author

The Mallaig Link

Breathless

Feast of the Antlion

Never too Late

Smoke Screen

By

Caro Ayre

Greenham Hall Publishing
TA21 0JJ

Smoke Screen

Copyright © Caro Ayre 2023

ISBN 978-0-9572224-7-2

Greenham Hall Publishing
Greenham
Wellington
Somerset TA21 0JJ

Writing can be a long slow process, and this book has not been an exception. So, I extend my thanks to my very patient family who have put up with my being distracted and in a world of my making, rather than being around for them.

And to all the friends who helped me make it a better book and kept me on track. You know who you are.

Chapter 1

Luke Tanner's phone buzzed in his pocket. He slowed down, pulled it out, and read the message. They needed him to clock on early. Adrenaline surged. He'd never figured out if it was fear of putting his firefighting training to good use, or the thrill of the unknown that triggered a rush of blood to course round his body.

Owen, yards ahead of him, was already turning his bike back towards the fire station. Luke assumed he'd received the same message. No words were necessary as their routine pre-shift bike ride became a race back to the station. The sound of the station bell ringing in the distance added a sense of urgency.

One pump was easing out of the building. The second would go as soon as the crew boarded.

Luke abandoned his bike against the wall and tore into the building. He pulled on his trousers and slid his feet into his boots. Owen, already fully kitted, was on his way to the door. Luke grabbed his jacket and shirt and ran to catch up. The moment he and Owen clambered onto the vehicle, the station manager raised his thumb and the engine pulled out onto the main road, with sirens blaring.

"What are we in for?" Luke shouted.

"Warehouse fire," James, the newest recruit, answered.

Luke pulled off his cycle top and searched for his regulation t-shirt. It wasn't there; he must have dropped it in the rush. He tugged the top back on and donned his bulky jacket over it and stuffed his hands into his gloves.

The tension on board was palpable with the anticipation of a tough shout ahead. Warehouse fires were notoriously tricky, making Luke regret the extra pint he'd consumed after his shift the day before.

Eye-stinging acrid smoke filled the pump long before they reached the address. The first crew already had their hoses unrolled, ready to drench the front of the building.

Flames and thick black smoke poured out of a window, licking the walls of the second floor.

"What's in there?" Luke asked the officer in charge.

"No idea. They let the storage space on the different floors to a mix of customers. No one has a clue what they store," he answered. "I want you and Owen to go around the back and check for any nasty surprises we need to be aware of."

Luke gave him the thumbs up and signalled Owen to follow him.

He led the way along the metal fencing round the side of the building, then cut down a narrow lane leading to the rear of the property. At the end, he turned off onto an overgrown path beside a ragged chain-link fence. He pushed forward through arching brambles and nettles, stepping over abandoned bottles, cans and soggy sleeping bags; evidence of rough sleepers using the space. There were no obvious breaches to the fence. Then Luke spotted a break higher in the wires, which he pointed out to Owen.

"We could try to get in here."

"Damn, I forgot the wire cutters," Owen said. "I'll go back for them." Luke turned to tell him not to bother, but Owen was already running back the way they'd come.

Luke scanned the fence again. This appeared to be the only weak spot. He heard banging and looked up. Silhouetted against a second-floor window of the blazing building was a figure hammering at the window. Luke studied the hole in the fence and wondered if he could pull himself up and use it as a foothold.

He spotted a discarded milk crate, which would give him the step up he needed. He dragged it into place, grasped the pole that supported the fence, and hoisted himself up. Wedging one foot into the hole, he swung the other leg over the top of the fence. For a second, he balanced on the top wire, then as he eased his foot out of the foothold, his grip on the post slipped. Gravity pulled him over the top. The collar flap of his jacket caught on the jagged metal support and slowed his descent, leaving him dangling with his nose pressed to the wire.

Before he had time to figure out how to release himself, he registered a loud ripping noise and hit the ground with a thud. He caught his breath and got to his feet. Still no sign of Owen. If he waited, it would be too late. The figure by the window had vanished. He sprinted across the yard to the only door on that side of the building.

Could he get it open? Would it be flimsy enough for him to force it with his body weight? He rattled the handle. Nothing happened. He tried again. No luck. He stepped back a couple of paces and ran forward, shoulder first, aiming at the height where he thought the lock would be. With a splintering crash, the door gave way, propelling him into the smoke-laden space at the bottom of a staircase. He grabbed the handrail, using it as a guide as he tore up the stairs, two steps at a time, up to the second level.

The higher he climbed, the denser the smoke became. Eventually, he stepped into a corridor with doors on either side. He figured the window was about four rooms away from the downstairs door, near to the end of the building where the blaze raged. Groping his way along the wall, counting the doors as he progressed, he entered the third. It was empty. One more, then he'd turn back. The roar of the fire above had a terrifying ferocity. He'd come this far. He couldn't leave now. He pushed the door open. The man lay slumped on the floor by the window. Luke ran over and stooped to lift him.

A deafening thud and the scary creak of failing timbers added urgency to his mission. Seconds later, the ceiling caved in. An enormous beam crashed down through the hole. Hot embers sprayed the room amid the clouds of plaster dust. The floor shook, and the blast of heat nearly knocked him off balance.

Years of training and experience kicked in. He was here with a purpose: to save a life.

He ignored the shower of embers, grabbed the man's coat, stooped lower and lifted the inert figure as near upright as possible. Then he shoved his shoulder under the sagging body, wrapped one arm around the man's legs, and straightened up.

Kicking burning debris out of the way, he staggered back to the door with the dead weight on his shoulder. Finding the stairs and getting out of this hellhole was his only focus. The thick smoke made breathing nearly impossible. He held his breath and stumbled on.

Everything seemed to happen in slow motion. How many rules had he broken by entering the building without his breathing apparatus? It didn't matter. He had done what he needed to do.

The stench of burning changed. What was it? The man's coat? No chance of checking—he had to get out of this inferno first.

Ignoring the smell, he kept going, down the corridor, down the stairs, through the disorientating thick, black smoke. He clung to the handrail to guide him to the ground level. The door he had broken through earlier was somewhere on his left, but not visible. He lurched forward, feeling his way along the wall until he touched the door jamb. He pulled the door open and almost fell into the fenced yard. Staggering under his load, he kept going as far away from the burning building as possible before he collapsed on his knees, lowering his load gently onto the weedy gravel.

Intense pain and the stink of burning flesh brought him back to his senses. It took a moment to register where it was coming from.

The area from his neck to his chest was alight. Flames licked his face. Like a slow-motion replay of a horror movie, he registered the flames were real. He was on fire. How? He looked at the man lying on the ground beside him. Smoke was coming from the man's coat. Smouldering embers had become embedded in their clothing. The ripped fastening of his jacket had enabled the glowing embers to touch his cycling top. Air had got in, setting his top alight and melting the synthetic material onto his skin. He tugged his coat off and yanked the burning top over his head, cursing at his stupidity. How could he have gone on a shout with a nylon shirt on? No time now for beating himself up. The man on the ground beside him needed his help.

Why hadn't Owen come back? What was holding him up? He rolled the man over and brushed off the burning embers. The man moaned. He was alive but struggling to breathe. Luke had run out of strength. His shoulder and chest felt as if it was still on fire, but there were no flames now, just a sickening stench of burnt flesh and melted nylon.

He retched and then muttered to his companion, "Sorry, this is as far as I can help you." He retched again. His brain went into overdrive. How the hell would Amy react? His being injured had been her worst nightmare. How would she tell the girls?

Chapter 2

Luke wondered when the fog of pain would lift, and he would find the strength to react. The clatter of a laden trolley drew closer. He waited for the swish of curtains, which would bring pain relief with an injection. People spoke to him, but he hadn't the energy to reply. The burns were deep and painful, and he trusted those around him to make the right decisions on his behalf. He didn't want to know the details; he'd rather float through this ordeal in a drug-induced haze.

The smell of burning flesh stuck with him. Sometimes a whiff of Amy's delicate perfume kicked in and she'd take his hand. He loved her so much and would attempt to respond by gently squeezing her fingers and force open his eyes. He wanted to tell her how much he loved her, and the girls. But his mouth was too dry. The fact he'd tightened his grip on her hand was enough to soften her worried expression before he drifted off again.

His waking moments became more frequent, and he knew when Amy was there from her scent. When she wasn't there, he'd lie there wondering how she would cope with him being scarred.

Sometimes, when he woke, Owen would be in the chair by his bed. And Luke knew he was waiting to reprimand him for going into a burning building alone, which he deserved. Owen was right. His pain was a constant reminder of his foolishness, and he wished he had the energy to tell Owen to skip the lectures.

Gradually, the fog lifted. The drawback being that the jumbled flashbacks had more clarity. The man clawing at a window. The chain-link fence. The locked door. An acrid smoke-filled staircase. The roar and crash of burning timber falling. Each episode was so vivid he felt as if he could touch and feel the heat. But worst of all was the revival of the stench of burning flesh that seemed to hit the back of his throat and would linger throughout the day.

On one of his more lucid days, he dared to ask the doctor the question dominating his thoughts.

"When can I go back to work?"

The surgeon raised an eyebrow. "Not for some time. Your burns are deep. You'll need more surgery. When that's done, we'll talk again. Until then, I can't possibly promise you will be fit for such a physically demanding occupation."

"When will you operate?"

"When the current grafts have healed. Follow the discharge team's instructions. They will tell you when you're ready." With that, the man turned on his heels and marched out of the room.

Amy returned later, rather remote and distracted, as if she didn't want to be there. Her perfume was different, too cloying for his liking. She fussed about at his bedside, moving his water jug and glass to one side, making the place tidy, but not easier for him, and he didn't know how to stop her fiddling.

"Can you bring the girls in?" he asked to distract her.

"Sorry. This is no place for children." Her tone was a distinct 'don't-bother-trying-to-persuade-me-otherwise' one. He wasn't ready to give up. He needed to see them.

"I could come down to the cafeteria. No need for them to come on the ward."

"Absolutely not." Sometimes Amy's stubborn reactions went too far, and this was one of those occasions. He didn't know why she was so adamant. Perhaps she would be less against the idea another day. Ten years of marriage had taught him to be patient, to win her over to his way of thinking.

Every time she came, he asked again. But nothing changed her mind.

He wasn't sure if he was imagining it, but her visits seemed to get shorter and shorter. The excuses varied, from having to pick someone up, or drop something off, work, school events, or some other vital chore she had forgotten. These came up the moment she sensed his wound was about to be dressed. He saw fear in her eyes. The realization that she couldn't cope with seeing his damaged skin hit hard. Was that what was making her behave so differently towards him? What would life be like when he went home?

Owen was more stoical. He would sit there for hours doing a crossword or reading some snippet out of the paper he brought with him.

Luke sensed the uncomplicated relationship they'd enjoyed since their schooldays had become strained. Owen was happy to talk about recent shouts, but would not discuss the warehouse fire, which resulted in Luke's injuries. If Luke brought the subject up, Owen would change the topic or find an excuse to leave.

What was it about that fire that made him reluctant to discuss it? The lack of answers niggled, and Luke tested Owen by asking about it every day.

"Did they find out what caused the fire?" he asked.

Owen shrugged, and muttered unconvincingly, "Possibly electrical. Hey, did you see the Exeter Chiefs match on TV last night?"

Next time, Luke asked, "Who headed the investigation?"

"Oh, some new chap came down from Somerset. He didn't stick around," Owen answered, and again diverted the conversation. "Did Amy tell you when she was coming in?"

"Later, I think she and Tamsin were having a spa session." Owen frowned, as if it was the first he'd heard of his wife's plan, and got up to go. Luke had never really connected with Owen's wife. He thought she was rather self-absorbed, but she had introduced him to Amy, and for that, he was grateful.

The surgeon was due on his rounds. The nurse drew the curtains around his bed and removed his dressing so they could inspect his wounds.

She chatted merrily as she worked. "This is healing well."

"Can I see?"

"Yes, I'll get a mirror."

While he waited for her to return, he peered down at his chest. Up to now, he had resisted the urge to look at the damage. He was as cowardly as Amy. The bumpy swathe of scabs that he could see were not pretty.

The mirror enabled a closer inspection of the skin round his neck. Amy's insistence that they work round his neck first had paid off. While still rather red and lumpy, it was closer to normal than the rest of his chest and shoulder area.

The nurse let him examine himself without comment. Then, judging that he was ready, explained the difference between the grafted skin and the untouched areas.

"See, now there are no oozing gaps between the newly formed scabs." The nurse pointed to a big scab in the middle of the cratered landscape of skin. "This is the worst spot where the deepest damage occurred."

When the surgeon arrived, he also pointed to the same place and said, "I presume that's the most painful area?"

Luke nodded.

"Be prepared. The pain won't go away for some time, the nerve damage is permanent. This area here," he said as he pointed towards Luke's armpit, "is where the next round of surgery will be done. The scars have tightened the skin, causing restriction of movement. The aim will be to improve your arm mobility."

"Is that why they have trussed me up like a chicken?"

"The sling helps to stop you from disturbing the scabs that have formed. Those need to heal and drop off naturally, or you will risk getting an infection in the wound. The new skin is too tight, you won't be able to lift and stretch your arm very far. Doing so could cause more damage. The aim is to let the new skin form, and then graft skin from your thigh to give this area more movement. The operation will be painful but should give enough flexibility to get you back to work. Until then you must take care to avoid infection. Nurse Brook will give you all the instructions you need to deal with this at home. As soon as she feels you're ready, you can go."

When he left, Luke asked, "What do I do about the pain?"

"Keep taking the painkillers. The nerves are so close to the surface, the slightest touch is going to trigger pain. I believe that gradually your brain learns to cope, and the sensitivity will lessen."

She talked him through the skin care regime, making him apply the creams and watching as he took those first steps of touching and caring for his damaged skin.

As he put the first dab of ointment on the least nasty looking area, his stomach lurched, but he continued. Overcoming revulsion was the price he must pay to get out of the ward. He took his time, discovering which areas were more sensitive than others. Touching one spot triggered a flashback of the fire. He pulled his hand away.

"You okay?" the nurse asked.

He didn't answer. He couldn't explain that it wasn't just the pain; touching there brought back fresh memories of the nauseating smell of his flesh burning. A smell that overpowered all the antiseptic creams he was using. He forced himself to continue applying the cream. At last, the task was over. He checked the clock on the wall. It had taken him almost an hour to cover the burn area. He looked up for reassurance.

"You've done really well."

"I'm wondering how my wife will cope," he said.

"You mustn't worry about that. I'm sure she'll deal with it. But you realize you'll have to do this three times a day, no skimping."

He nodded.

"If you have any breaks in the skin," she continued, "or you have any discharge at all, you must come back in. Please don't do the macho thing of shrugging and saying everything will be okay because all you will do is set your progress back."

"What about dressings?"

"No dressings. The best thing is getting air to the wound. Go shirtless if you can, but otherwise a soft cotton t-shirt is your best solution. Your wife brought some in for you. Here, try this on. Cotton can go through a hot wash, and you must change your shirt often. Try to do it every time you put the cream on. Good hygiene is the key to recovery."

"Understood."

"How does that feel?" she asked once she had helped slip the t-shirt over his head.

"Fine."

"Here, take a peek." She held up the mirror.

"Not bad. The scar is barely visible."

Amy would be pleased. Appearance mattered to her.

Once he had his sling back in place, the nurse continued. "The physiotherapy team will be along shortly to run you through a set of suitable exercises. Very gentle ones to start, and they'll tell you what you must avoid at all costs."

The physio work began and reality hit. If he didn't follow their instructions, he might never work again. He put on a brave face and agreed to make the effort.

It took a few more days before his discharge details were in order. They would release him from the hospital with enough medication to last him for a fortnight.

This news came with a mix of joy and fear. How the hell was he going to deal with being back at home? More importantly, how would Amy manage?

He was longing to see the girls again but was terrified over how they would react.

Amy came to collect him. She suggested dropping him off at home before going to fetch the children from school. He wasn't sure if this plan was for her benefit, a plot to keep him out of sight of her friends at the school gates, or because she thought it was what he wanted.

When she offered him a smart new coat with a high collar, along with a silky scarf for him to wear, he was sure it was the former. She wanted to keep him, and his scars, hidden from sight.

"Thanks," he said, "too hot for those. I don't need anything."

She still hadn't looked him in the eye.

"Okay, forget the coat, but at least wear the scarf." She held it out for him to take. He stepped backwards.

"Please."

He couldn't believe she would do this to him.

"Amy. Look at me." It took an age for her to turn and face him.

"I have injuries. That's something I have to live with. But no way am I going to wrap myself up in winter woollies, because you don't have the guts to look at my scars."

"Sorry, I thought you'd want to cover up." She had her eyes locked on his. He had to make her see what was visible was not stomach-churning.

"Look at my neck."

She took a deep breath, and her gaze lowered. She went pale. He knew then that to ask her to touch his scars would be a step too far.

"Not so bad?"

"No," she mumbled, but turned away from him.

"The rest are still grim, so I'll do my best to keep them covered up. All I ask in return is for you to stop treating me like some sort of freak. Deal?"

His nurse was standing in the doorway behind Amy. She stuck her thumbs in the air in a supportive gesture.

Amy wasn't smiling. "Fine, if that's the way you want it," she said, as she shoved the offending garments back into the carrier bag she'd brought them in and strode to the door.

As they walked through the endless corridors to exit the building, he half regretted the stance he had taken. How long would she hold it against him?

Chapter 3

The reality of coming home did not match his dreams. Amy stayed focused on the road, and silent on the drive back. She carried his things inside, made him a cup of tea, then shot off to fetch the children.

He wandered round the house, mug in hand, wondering how long Amy would bear a grudge over his refusal to wear the scarf. She liked to get her own way, but that was her problem, not his. He had enough issues of his own to deal with before the kids got home. First of which was to find his painkillers and apply more ointment to his shoulder. Cream applied, pills taken, and with his sling back in place, he picked a comfy spot on the rather battered old settee to wait. Buster, their rescue dog, a scruffy little hound who had ignored him up to now, padded across the room and curled up on the rug at his feet.

The prospect of the girl's reaction terrified him. He heard the car door slam. Buster jumped up and ran to the door. Should he go to greet them? No, it was safer to stay on the settee, positioned with his bad shoulder in the corner to function as a protective barrier.

Katie and Janet rushed in ahead of Amy. Their giggles made him wish he could grab them, hug them, and throw them in the air.

They skidded to a halt at his feet and stared at him as if he was an alien. He guessed they'd been primed to keep their distance, which was fine to a point, but not what he'd hoped for.

"I won't break if you come closer for a hug," he said, reaching out for the eldest Katie. Carefully wrapping his good arm around her, he gave her a kiss, and then said, "Move over, let Janet in. I've missed you both so much."

To banish their nerves, he pointed to the right side of his body and shoulder and said, "Only this area is sore, so as long as you don't touch there, you can give me a cuddle."

"Love you," Katie said and snuggled up closer while Janet stroked his hand. Amy interrupted the reunion.

"Off you go and change out of your uniforms."

The girls looked ready to protest. Luke wanted to as well, but let Amy have her way.

"Go on, hurry, do what your mum asked." Consistent parenting was something they agreed on, and this was not the moment to mess with the rules. When the girls left the room, Amy got up to go too, muttering something about unpacking the groceries.

"Can I help?"

Without a glance, she shook her head. "No, I'll sort out supper for you and the girls. I've got to go out tonight. Tamsin is going to introduce me to a developer who's looking for someone to decorate his show homes in Topsham, with an offer of an office to go with the job."

Luke followed her anyway and bit back a comment about her not wanting to spend time with him. Instead, he said, "I thought you had as much work as you wanted."

"I did, but someone has to bring in the money while you're out of action." She rummaged in the fridge, still with her back to him.

Ouch. Kick a man when he's down. But she had a point, and he knew better than to argue.

"Well, I hope it works out."

She briefly turned and looked his way, and muttered, "Thanks."

The girls reappeared, and she dragged them away to get their homework done.

Luke returned to the settee to wait for her to tire of her protective strategies. He didn't dare risk alienating her again. Once was enough for one day.

"How about taking Buster for a walk?" he suggested when the girls had done their homework.

Amy's wide-eyed expression was enough for him to know the idea horrified her.

"If you don't fancy joining us, stay and get ready to go out," he offered, knowing she was unlikely to refuse.

"Fine, supper is in the oven. It will be ready in an hour."

The girls loved going to the park and rushed off to change their shoes. Buster pulled at the leash in his excitement. It was as if he knew the destination and had decided which lamp posts to sniff on the way. The walk, while not far, proved to Luke just how unfit his stay in the hospital had left him. He settled on a bench under an ancient oak tree facing the girls' favourite play area and let Buster free. With his usual enthusiasm, Buster ran off to find a stick to get the stick throwing game started. Janet chased after him. Katie held back, clutching Luke's hand, as if she was afraid to leave him.

"Go on, what are you waiting for? I'm not going anywhere. I can't join you, but I'll enjoy watching."

His reassurance did the trick, and she ran to join her sister. They threw sticks, laughed, tumbled, did cartwheels, and occasionally huddled together in secretive conversations.

After one of these moments, they ran back to him, giving each other nervous glances and concentrating their focus on his neck.

He sat silently as they studied him. He guessed Katie, as the eldest, would be the spokesperson.

"Does it hurt a lot?" she asked.

"Yes." No point in denying it. There might be times he wouldn't be able to hide his pain. "But not as much as it did."

"Can we feel it?" He took a sharp intake of breath. He hadn't expected that, and certainly not so soon. If he wanted excuses, there were dozens to choose from, their dirty hands for a start. The ward nurse would have a fit. But none were right. Deep down, he knew this was a now or never request.

"We could wash our hands first," Katie said.

Had she been mind-reading? "Yes, that's important, good plan," he said, to gain time to get used to the idea. "Catch Buster and put his lead on first."

While they wrestled with Buster, who thought that the lead was a new toy thing to replace his stick, their regular child-minder, Charlotte, approached with her son, George, in his buggy.

"Hi," she called out to the girls. "You look as if you're having fun." They were too busy wrestling with Buster and the lead to answer. "Well, it's lovely to see you. The girls must be thrilled to have you home. Mind if I join you?"

"Not at all," Luke said, pleased that his scars didn't seem to bother her. "Thanks for all the extra help you gave Amy looking after the girls and walking Buster while I was in hospital."

"My pleasure." She smiled. "To be honest, the extra hours have been a lifesaver for me and George. I don't know how I'd have managed without the work."

Luke had never really thought about how difficult it was being a single mum and was glad that his misfortune had helped one person.

A moment later, the girls ran back, dragging a reluctant Buster behind them.

"Hi Charlotte, Daddy's going to let us touch his scar," Janet announced with a nervous giggle.

Charlotte looked at Luke for confirmation, her eyes wide in disbelief. He shrugged, as if to say he had no choice.

"We've got to wash our hands first," Katie said.

"I should think so. They're filthy." Charlotte turned to him. "Want me to supervise?"

"Yes please, I'll mind George." The three of them made their way to the toilet block, giving him a moment to prepare for the coming ordeal. George gurgled in the pushchair and rattled the toys strung across his lap. Luke envied his innocence.

His nerves jangled at the prospect of the girls touching his scar. Could he cope without flinching? He had to. He was pleased that Amy was not around. Hard to imagine how she'd react to their request. She struggled to look at, let alone want to touch his scars.

It didn't take long for them to return, brandishing spotless hands towards him, babbling on about Charlotte.

"She made us use the soap and wash them twice," Janet said, as if this was the most preposterous suggestion ever.

He acknowledged his gratitude with a smile in her direction. The two girls faced him with a mix of fear and excitement on their faces.

"Okay, who's going first?" he asked.

Katie inched closer and whispered, "Me."

Luke nodded, took her hand, inspected it, smiled, and then, holding her finger, gently placed it on his neck. He picked a spot above the scar line and slowly drew her finger down from the undamaged skin to the grafted area. Her eyes were glued to the route her finger was taking. He stayed focused on her expression. There was no revulsion. Wonderment maybe. Best of all, no fear. He released her hand, and she continued to stroke the grafted skin with light, feathery touches. Gentle enough for him to relax, but firm enough for him to know she was still touching him.

"Okay, enough, Janet's turn." Katie withdrew her hand and kissed him on the cheek and stepped out of the way to let her sister move forward.

He did the same with Janet. She let out a nervous giggle, but the tension in her face eased as she discovered the new skin was a fraction bumpier, but not too different from the rest of him. She didn't keep touching when he let go of her hand, but like her sister, gave him a quick kiss before backing off.

The jingle of the ice-cream van broke the intensity.

Too close to supper time? Perhaps, but he didn't care, and dug into his pocket for change.

Charlotte registered he didn't have money on him, and said quietly, "Let me?"

He nodded gratefully to her as she fished coins out of her bag and sent the girls off to get their treat.

"Are you okay?" she asked as soon as they were far enough away. "Allowing them to do that was brave, but so important. They've been so worried about you, and I'm sure letting them touch your scar will help."

"I'm glad you think so. I worried it might scare them witless. Amy is desperate for me to cover up."

Charlotte peered at all that was visible. "I don't see why. I've seen worse acne scars. Perhaps she thinks you'd prefer to hide it."

"No, she can't even look at me."

"I'm sorry. She'll get over her fear, now you're home."

"Maybe. But I'd better get them back or we'll be late for supper."

"I'll walk with you. Come on girls, time to go."

They set off together, Katie pushing George's buggy, Janet holding Luke's hand and Charlotte in charge of Buster, who seemed content to trail along behind them.

They waved goodbye to Charlotte and went in. Amy bustled about, eager to get their meal on the table. She had done as suggested and used the time to get ready. She looked stunning in a close fitting silky green dress he hadn't seen before, and with her coppery hair pinned up in a way that let her green enamelled fan shaped earrings draw the eye to her slender neck. The only thing that jarred was her perfume. It wasn't her usual light floral scent. This one had overpowering pachouli overtones which made his eyes water.

Now was not the time to tell her he hated that scent. He didn't have the strength to argue, or to offer to go with her. For now, he'd settle for an evening alone; the park outing had wiped him out.

Amy sent the children to wash their hands. He half expected them to object and tell her they'd washed them earlier. But they said nothing, nor did they let on they'd had an ice cream. He was grateful. He didn't want to upset Amy or deal with her making a fuss. While no one watched, he swallowed a couple of painkillers to numb the throbbing pain that intensified on the way home.

With supper on the table, he told Amy that he would read their bedtime stories, and that he'd be fine if she wanted to go, adding, "I'll probably head to bed early. I may be asleep by the time you get back."

"Are you sure?" she asked as she grabbed her bag and wrap. "I'll try not to disturb you."

When the children were in bed, Luke poured himself a glass of wine. As he sipped it, he looked round the house, wondering how difficult it would be to get back to normal.

In the following week, his relationship with the girls kept his sanity intact. They treated him as they had before. No questions asked and no restraints.

Amy got more remote. They slept in the same bed: she stuck to her side, never reaching out to touch him. She'd rise early and head out the door the moment the kids surfaced. Most days, she came home late and dashed out again for a meeting with the developer, Rupert, or a new client, or with Tamsin. He gave up waiting for her to come home. The lack of sex didn't bother him, but the loss of intimacy hurt.

With Amy working, and the girls at school, he had to occupy himself while waiting for the next round of reconstructive surgery.

He called in at the station, thinking he might discover more details about the fire that put him in hospital. The reaction he got was more unsettling than he expected. No one wanted to talk about it. He got a quick brush off every time he brought up the subject. Had his injuries made the crew uncomfortable because it reminded them how dangerous the job was? Maybe he should stay away until he was fit to work.

A couple of his watch called round to see him, leaving him with a sense of their visits being duty calls rather than out of genuine friendship. Only one, the rookie, James, seemed less reluctant to talk. "I think Owen blames himself for your injuries. If he hadn't forgotten those bolt cutters, you'd never have gone in alone."

"I hadn't thought of that, thanks. No wonder he's reluctant to talk about the shout."

"What do you want to know?

"Anything at all. I remember little about it and missed all the media coverage."

"It took us two days to douse the flames. The outer brick walls were so damaged, it only needed a slight nudge from the demolition crew to flatten the place. That's when they discovered the remains of a body. A friend of the man you saved."

Luke was stunned. Why hadn't anyone mentioned finding a body? "Any clues as to the cause of the fire?"

"Hard to tell with so little left. They considered arson to be a high probability, especially when word got out that a developer had shown an interest in the property, and negotiations were underway. Because the site was so unstable, it had to be cleared." James hesitated, then added, "I'm not sure I should tell you this, but word in the station is that you're paranoid about the fire. Supposedly, it's a common reaction to being injured."

"You're kidding. I've never heard of that before. Thanks for your honesty."

Paranoid. That was unexpected. Who had started that rumour? No matter, it would not stop him trying to uncover the truth, and find out about the man he'd saved, and the man who'd died.

Chapter 4

Luke suspected Amy was using her newfound success to avoid spending time with him. But deep down, he worried there was more to it than an inability to deal with his injuries.

He missed how things had been before. Taking matters into his own hands, he invited Owen and Tamsin over for a meal. He ordered a Chinese take-away delivery and waited to tell Amy his plan when she got home.

"Hi," she said when she hurried into the house, giving him the most cursory peck on the cheek. "I'll sort supper out, but I've got to dash. I'm meeting up with Tamsin."

"Relax. Supper's sorted," he said, holding her arm. "Tamsin and Owen are coming here tonight."

She pulled away and said, "You should have warned me."

Warned her? Surely Tamsin would have said something if they had been meeting. This was certainly not the reaction he expected.

"Did the girls do all their homework?" she asked.

The change of subject, and the distinct lack of enthusiasm about her friend coming to dinner, puzzled him.

"Yes, they've eaten and are in bed waiting for their bedtime story."

"I'll go up," she said and hurried off.

Luke laid the table with cutlery, glasses, and put out a bottle of wine. What else? He didn't want Amy to find fault with his preparations. She was so hard to read these days, and he wanted the evening to go well. Glancing round the room, he saw Janet's treasured pink bear in the corner, picked it up, and slipped up the stairs to tuck it in beside her.

He could hear Amy's voice and wondered what book she was reading. As he got closer, the words got clearer.

"No, I can't tonight. It's too tricky." Then, after a moment's silence, she added, "See you tomorrow."

Luke realized he was listening to a phone conversation coming from their room. Not wanting to let on he'd overheard anything, he tapped the door as he pushed it open. "Are the kids still awake?"

"I think so," she said, and quickly put her phone face down on the dressing table.

"Janet left her bear downstairs. I'll take it in."

On his descent to the kitchen, he noticed Amy checking the laid table, fussing about unnecessarily. He fished some painkillers out of his pocket while she fiddled, glad that her attention was elsewhere. He swilled the pills down with a glass of water and then poured out two glasses of wine. Their marriage had been less than perfect before the accident, but Amy's struggle to stay in the same room as him was wearing him down. Were his injuries so repulsive? Was that the problem? If so, how could he break that barrier? Would supper, at home with close friends, help her see he was the same man she'd married all those years ago?

When he greeted his guests, he thanked Tamsin for springing the surprise.

"Surprise?" Owen muttered.

"Oh, Amy said she and Tamsin were going out together. She didn't know you were both coming here."

Owen cocked his head to one side and gave his wife a puzzled look. She shrugged, made no comment, but gave Amy a hostile glare.

The glaring continued; but he couldn't figure out what was going on between them.

Thankfully, the food delivery arrived on time, and everyone sprang into action to spread the feast out on the table so they could enjoy it while it was still hot.

Stilted conversation about mundane things between Owen and himself prevented lengthy silences. Both women were unusually quiet. The only constant was the speed with which the wine bottle got passed around the table.

Luke, bored with talking about the weather and cars, looked across the table and said, "Come on, Tamsin, tell me more about this friend of yours, Rupert. He seems to have taken over Amy's life. I've hardly seen her since she started working on his show house."

Laden chopsticks froze between plates and mouths. Angry glances ricochet round the table.

Tamsin swallowed, took a sip of her drink, but said nothing.

Luke couldn't leave it alone. "Go on, Tamsin. After all, I believe you introduced him to her on the night I came out of the hospital."

Owen's brows angled skyward to an alarming height. Luke knew then that Rupert Patterson was more than just a client.

Tamsin took a deep breath. "Oh, I've known him for years. I thought Amy would be the best person to help with his latest development." She waved her hand towards Amy. "You're probably better able to describe him."

Luke watched for Amy's reaction.

"He's the perfect client; we share similar ideas." She stopped speaking, but the silence round the table made her continue. "He's enthusiastic, and willing to let me be innovative. And because he likes to see the plans as they develop, he's given me an office on site." She picked up her glass and took a sip before getting back to her meal.

Luke turned to Owen, hoping for something more.

Owen hesitated, then said, "He's an old flame of Tamsin's." The way he folded his arms across his chest showed that was all he intended to say. Luke wanted to press for more, but his friendship with Owen was too important to put him on the spot.

The conversation stalled. Luke was almost relieved when Amy broke the silence.

"More wine?"

She didn't wait for him to respond, but topped up his glass. He should decline her offer; he'd drunk much more than he should with the medication he was taking. But wine helped numb his senses.

"Just half a glass. I'm on days. Shift starts tomorrow," Owen said, holding his empty glass out.

Tamsin put her hand over hers. "I'm driving."

Amy put the bottle down.

"Not having any yourself?" Tamsin asked Amy in a sweetly sarcastic voice.

Amy shook her head and muttered, "I have some papers to go through later."

Luke translated that as 'I won't be going to bed at the same time as you.'

Attention turned back to their food, but with the tension so palpable, the pleasure of eating had vanished.

Luke tried to convince himself he was overreacting, but his earlier doubts had become more real. The reaction of the others at the mention of Rupert Patterson confirmed his fears.

Owen and Tamsin refused the offer of coffee. Hardly a surprise. The undercurrent of disharmony between the two women was too obvious.

When they left, Luke had two options: confront Amy, or hold back and see if she had anything she wanted to tell him. He chose the latter. Backing her into a corner was never a good plan, and he didn't want to wade in without knowing more about the man. Amy bustled about loading the dishwasher, then muttered she had work to finish. She went to her little study, which she had barely used since his return, and firmly closed the door.

No degree needed to guess that she would not emerge until long after he'd retired. He emptied the dregs of the bottle of wine into his glass, knocked back a couple more pills. Should he test her endurance? He flicked on the television. After an hour of watching a boring program about steam engines in foreign countries, he conceded defeat. He was no match for Amy and was too tired to watch another thing.

She still hadn't come up by the time he'd slathered cream on his scars and pulled on a clean t-shirt. The next morning, Amy rose earlier than usual, and was out of the door before the girls got up, without giving him a chance to speak to her.

The day passed in a blur, driven by the need to find out more about Rupert Patterson. An on-line search produced a wealth of material. Rupert, besides being a property developer, had many passions and, judging from the abundance of photos of him accepting sporting trophies, was good at whatever he turned his hand to. Whoever handled his public relations had done a thorough job. Absolutely nothing dubious came up. Disheartened at the prospect of vying for Amy's attention against such a paragon of virtue, Luke continued digging for more information about the warehouse, the site of his accident.

His colleagues' reluctance to talk about that fire bugged him. The fact he did not dare press further, and his fear of being seen as a crank, made him more determined to search on his own. His first aim was to track down the man he'd rescued and find out how he was getting on. He found a few newspaper articles about the fire, but couldn't concentrate on them. The pain level was unacceptable, and the pills were not touching it. Especially after a gruelling physio session. And the Rupert Patterson issue was messing with his ability to focus. He took his pain killer earlier than he should, but he needed it to enable him to function and collect the girls from school.

The girls were full of chat as they walked home. He got them to do their homework. The promise of playtime in the park with Buster ensured a speedy outcome.

He was very relieved to see Charlotte was there with George, who was asleep. He sat at his usual bench and Charlotte left the pushchair beside Luke and joined the girls in a game of tag. Buster raced around between them, carrying an enormous stick. After a while, Charlotte came back and sank down on the bench beside him.

"Gosh, those two have so much energy. It makes me feel so unfit," she said once she'd caught her breath.

"Well, at least you can join them," he muttered, wishing for so much more than just the ability to keep up with his kids. He was struggling with his fitness levels.

Charlotte faced him. "Are you all right?"

He wanted to lie, but there was something about her caring attitude that made him shake his head. She said nothing, but patiently waited for him to elaborate.

"Just feeling a bit overwhelmed." He could hardly accept, let alone admit, that his marriage was in shambles.

"Well, I'm available if you ever want to talk."

The offer was genuine, as was everything about Charlotte. He smiled and said, "Thanks. When's your driving test?"

"Booked for next month," she answered.

"If you're stuck, I'd be happy to look after George?"

"Thanks, but Sheena from the food bank has offered."

Before he had time to ask more, the girls ran up with the perpetual plea, "I'm hungry."

"Guess that means time for us to go," he said.

"Me too." Charlotte hugged the girls, checked she'd stowed everything away, released the brakes, and prepared to set off.

He loved how this trio treated him as normal. The girls avoided his injured side if they wanted a cuddle, but apart from that, they behaved as if nothing had made him different. And Charlotte's undemanding company provided a break from his isolation.

"Charlotte, can you do me a favour?"

She looked surprised. "Try me."

"Take the girls home? Pick up fish and chips on the way for all of you and stay until I get back. When Owen comes off his shift, I need to speak to him. I shouldn't be more than an hour. I doubt Amy will be home before then."

"Of course."

He fished some cash out of his pocket to pay for their supper. "Thanks."

The girls, delighted with the prospect of fish and chips, followed Charlotte without a fuss.

Luke headed to the pub where the crew usually went. Owen rarely skipped having a pint after a shift. Luke hadn't been for a while, but no one would think it odd if he turned up. And he needed a drink. The pills were wearing off, and it was too soon to take another.

He was certain the reason Owen had stopped dropping round to the house was because of Rupert Patterson. The escalation of tension at supper at the mention of his name had been unmissable.

Owen was a lousy poker player. He couldn't lie to save himself, so keeping his distance rather than pretend he didn't know Amy was cheating on him was his solution.

Luke might be about to lose his wife, but he was damned if he was going to lose his best friend. Owen looked wary when he walked towards him at the bar.

"Hi, Owen. Glad to catch you. I hoped you'd be here." Owen's expression showed otherwise. "I've got a couple of questions I need answers for. Can we sit over there for a minute?" He nodded towards a quiet corner table away from the team. "It won't take long. I have to get back for the kids."

That reassurance seemed to make Owen less hesitant. With drinks in hand, they moved to the table.

"Sorry about last night. I would never have suggested dinner if I had known Tamsin and Amy had fallen out."

"Tamsin took a lot of persuading," Owen said as he sat down. "She thought Amy might have got over her infatuation with Rupert and you and she were back on an even keel. But I guess that's not the case."

"To be honest, things had been tricky for some time."

"How long?" Owen asked.

Luke, surprised by the question, answered, "Since Christmas. I was spending a lot of time out on the bike and thought that was the problem."

"No. Tamsin introduced her to Rupert at a Golf Club Christmas Event."

"Not the night I left the hospital?"

"Sadly not. Tamsin wasn't happy about how things went, and they've hardly spoken to each other since then. We only came to dinner last night because you asked us. Tamsin hoped she and Amy could resolve their differences."

"I've been stupidly blind. Sorry I put you in such a tough spot."

Owen shrugged. "It was bound to happen at some point."

"True, but is Rupert Patterson the reason you've been avoiding me?"

Owen nodded.

"I thought you blamed yourself for my accident. You know I would have gone in, regardless."

"Yes, because you're a stubborn idiot, but if I'd had the cutters on me, your jacket might not have been ripped."

"You've got to stop thinking like that. It wasn't your fault."

Luke silently sipped his drink, mulling over the conversation. What an idiot he was, not to have seen the signs. That optimistic feeling that he had misinterpreted the situation was shattered.

Luke downed the rest of his drink and got to his feet, patted Owen on the back, and said, "Thanks for filling me in."

He trudged home, trying to figure out a plan of action.

Amy wasn't home. The girls had eaten and were ready for bed. When Charlotte left, he went to read the girls a story. He had just got to the end of a chapter when Amy hurried in to kiss them goodnight. She then disappeared into their bedroom and when she came back down, she had changed into an elegant dress, and dabbed more of that cloying scent on.

"Meeting Rupert?" he asked casually.

She hesitated before answering. "Yes, there are things we didn't have time to talk through today that need sorting by tomorrow."

"Fine, but tell him you'll be late in. We need to have a talk after the girls have gone to school."

"What!"

"You heard. We've things to discuss, and I want to do it in the morning."

"Fine, no need to raise your voice."

Luke hadn't been aware he had, but guessed his ultimatum might have sounded harsh.

Chapter 5

Luke spent the night trying to work out how to handle the situation, as they couldn't continue as they were.

Amy came home around midnight, she undressed in the bathroom, and slid into the bed beside him silently. He feigned sleep. He wanted the girls out of the house while they had the discussion he dreaded. But he had to face up to the truth, and the sooner the better.

In the morning, he and Amy skirted round each other warily. She was there to wave the girls off, a change to her recent routine. Luke walked them to school as he had for the last few weeks. As he left the house, he saw her move to the dining table with a coffee mug, a pad, and a pen.

Sensing she intended to treat this like a business matter, he braced himself to act accordingly. Keeping control of the discussion was vital.

On his return, he took his time making coffee. When he entered the dining room, he put his cup down and said, "Just popping upstairs for a moment." He headed to the bathroom, swallowed some painkillers, and braced himself for the chat he'd instigated.

"Amy," he said, making sure he had her full attention. "You lied about spending time with Tamsin."

"Sorry," was all she managed as she fiddled with the pen.

"Sorry that I found out?"

She bit her lip but didn't answer. So, he continued, "Or sorry for the damage done to our marriage? I assume Rupert is the reason you lied."

"I never meant to hurt you," she stammered.

"How long has it gone on?"

"Since before you got injured. Things weren't going well. You were wrapped up in your work," she muttered.

"My fault, then?"

"No, that's not what I meant."

"Did you plan to tell me?"

"Yes, but then you had your accident."

"And you couldn't kick a man when he was down. Very thoughtful of you." He took a deep breath, regretting the snipe back. It wouldn't help.

"No, it wasn't like that. I was thinking about the children."

Thinking about them would not stop them being hurt, whatever the outcome. And he had no idea what that would be. He stayed quiet for a while and then changed tack.

"Amy, I need to know something."

She nodded as if ready to answer anything he threw at her.

"Has your inability to look at me got more to do with your guilt than with my scars?"

She took a deep breath, and for the first time since he came out of the hospital, let her eyes lock with his.

"A bit of both." She swallowed and blinked back tears. She cared. That's all he needed to know.

He stared back at her and waited until she had gathered herself together.

"If I asked you to look at them now, would you?"

Her eyes widened, but she nodded. He slipped his arm out of the sling, wondering if she realized this was as hard for him as it was for her. He pulled up his t-shirt, so the full extent of his scar was visible.

She didn't turn away. He watched for signs of revulsion or horror, instead saw fascination. A tear trickled down her cheek. Enough. He eased his shirt back down and slid his arm back into the sling.

"I never thanked you for insisting they did the grafts around my neck first. You were right, it was important."

She reached out and pulled a tissue from the box on the table nearby to blow her nose.

"Sorry, I've been a coward. I'm glad you made me look. It's not nearly as bad as I imagined."

They sipped their coffee, and Luke braced himself for the next step.

"Where do we go from here?"

She chewed her lip, a sure sign he wouldn't like her answer.

"Rupert asked me to move in with him."

"And you want to?"

The blush crept up her face, telling him all he needed to know.

"Yes, but I'll never expect you to sell the house or anything," the words came tumbling out in a rush. "Your uncle left it to you, and you love the place."

He glanced around the room. Yes, he did, but it wouldn't be the same without her.

"And the girls? Where do they fit into this plan of yours?"

"Rupert is happy for them to come with me. His house is big enough."

"Have they met him?"

"No."

"How can you be certain he wants someone else's kids hanging around?"

"He says there's plenty of room for us all."

"What if they don't want to go?"

Amy gasped at this suggestion. That possibility had obviously never entered her head.

The old grandfather clock in the hall chimed, breaking the silence.

"Then they'll stay here with you." The words came out as a whisper.

It was clear he'd lost her. Leaving him was one thing, but to be prepared to walk away from her children was a measure of how much Rupert meant to her. Conceding gracefully was his only option. Making the transition easy for the girls would be his parting gift.

But resigned as he was to the inevitable, he had every intention of delaying their departure.

"Here's the deal. Nothing happens without my full agreement." She nodded.

"No talk about moving, or anything else, until I've had a chance to get to know him first. Is that clear?"

"Perfectly, and totally acceptable."

Having blurted out the ultimatum, regrets came flooding in. Was he mad? How the hell could he cope with meeting the man who was taking his wife from him? They would have nothing in common other than feelings for Amy.

"Thank you," she whispered and buried her head in her hands.

After a while, he asked, "Are you all right?"

She wiped away her tears and stared at him. "I'll be fine. What about you?"

"Shell-shocked, but I'll survive. The kids are my only concern."

"Mine too." After a while, her brow furrowed, and she added, "You could meet him today if you want. Come with me to the office, see what I'm doing, and let me introduce you."

Luke hadn't expected things to move so fast. But nothing would be gained by putting the meeting off.

"Okay."

"If I go now, I can make sure Rupert is there. Maybe we can all have lunch. Call it an icebreaker."

Who was she trying to kid? This was more like being thrown overboard in Antarctic conditions.

"Will you tell him about our discussion?"

"I warned him last night that you suspected. He said to do whatever felt right. I promise nothing happens without your agreement."

"Fine, go to the office now. I'll come later."

No further encouragement was needed. Amy grabbed her things and shot out of the door before he could change his mind.

Luke had time to mull over events. One thing was sure, to meet his rival, he needed to spruce himself up. Every picture he'd seen portrayed Rupert as a classy dresser, so casual clothing wouldn't do.

He dug into his wardrobe, unearthed a white shirt that had been too loose around the neck. It felt scratchy after weeks of wearing nothing but t-shirts. He struggled with the buttons and failed, so ditched the idea of a tie. He put on a jacket and a pair of trousers with crisp creases down the fronts, and a pair of slip-on leather shoes. The collar rubbed, but no scars peeked over the top. The reflection in the mirror did not match his inner turmoil. There was no going back. He'd agreed to meet his rival.

When Luke turned up at Amy's place of work, she took him on a quick tour of the site. Halfway round, Rupert joined them. Luke was expecting him to be cocky, but he tentatively extended his hand for Luke to shake.

"Good to meet you," he said in a quiet, well-spoken voice. It might be good for him, but for Luke there was nothing good about it at all: but he politely reciprocated.

After a cursory, slightly awkward handshake, Rupert seemed to regain his confidence and spouted on about his luck at being able to develop the site.

"So much better than the old factory that was here before."

Luke felt the tension in his jaw ease. He could manage if they kept the conversation off personal matters, and answered, "I have vague memories of the old building."

"My father had the foresight to buy the land, and now I've been lucky enough to develop it." Rupert said with pride.

A stocky, older man barged into the room. "Did I hear you talking about me?" he said, as he sidled up to Amy, placing his hand on her back in an almost possessive way.

"Yes," Rupert said, "I was telling Luke how you purchased the site."

"Ah, the lovely Amy, such an asset to the company. She's working wonders," the man said, ignoring Rupert's response, as he continued to stroke Amy's back, appearing to be oblivious of others in the room.

Luke sensed Amy's discomfort at being backed against a desk, unable to avoid the man's pawing clutches.

Rupert looked annoyed and said rather sharply, "Did you want something?"

The hand dropped. "Oh, Linda said to tell you she booked you a table for lunch. I won't be able to join you. I'm sure I've already told you that," he answered. Then, registering that there was another person in the room, fished in his pocket, pulled out a business card and, without waiting for an introduction, pressed the card into Luke's hand. "If you ever have a property to sell, call me."

Luke rarely took an instant dislike to anyone, but this man was an exception. He wanted to hand the card back, but shoved it in his pocket without even looking at it.

Luke couldn't help thinking that he was the sort who plagued people at every event he attended, doling out his cards regardless of whether or not they were wanted. The kind of brash behaviour he hated. Never mind the inappropriate way he touched women. If Rupert was anything like his father, this was going to be a rough ride for them all.

To his relief, the man left without further comment.

Rupert muttered to Amy, "I promise I didn't ask him to join us." Then continued with the tour.

The houses were modern. Glass and shiny surfaces were everywhere, the polar opposite of what Luke would ever choose for himself, but the type of house Amy loved. With the tour done, Luke was proud of the fact he'd got through it, made enough polite comments to stay civil.

"I've booked a table at Jack in the Green," Rupert said hesitantly. "I hope you'll join us. If so, we should probably leave now to avoid the lunch rush."

Luke liked that Rupert had given him the option to join them rather than assuming it was a done deal.

"Thanks. Best if I meet you there. Amy, go with Rupert."

Amy seemed disappointed. Perhaps she wanted to find out his first impressions. Too bad because he needed a brief break before sitting down to eat with her lover. Having his own transport meant he could leave if things got tricky.

The pub was one of his favourite haunts, and he was angry that Rupert had chosen it, as from now on this place would be associated with the breakdown of his marriage. Still, it had quiet corners, and he assumed rightly that Rupert would have arranged to be in one of them.

Rupert let Amy choose where to sit. She sat with her back to the wall and let them sit on either side of her, facing each other.

What the hell was he supposed to do now? Luke closed his eyes, took a deep breath. He had never experienced jealousy before, and violence wasn't something he approved of, but the unexpected urge to punch Rupert was strong. It was probably a good thing that his injuries prevented him from landing a right hook, because the temptation was there.

"Are you okay?" Amy asked, touching his arm gently.

Luke shook his head. "Not really. You can't expcct us to become friends."

Amy bit her lip. Rupert raised his hand and said, "I get that."

Luke glared at him. "I don't think you do." He was stopped from saying more by the waiter, interrupting to take their order. Luke pointed to the dish of the day, as did the others.

The brief interruption gave him a chance to get to grips with the main problem. He had to learn more about this man because his children were involved.

It seemed Rupert was as keen as him for answers and surprised him by asking the first question.

"What will you do if you don't get back into the fire service?"

Luke checked for Amy's reaction. Had she put him up to this? Her wide eyes told him she was as taken aback as he was. He hadn't allowed himself to think that far ahead, but maybe he should have. Only one answer came to mind, and he blurted it out without hesitation.

"Photojournalism."

Amy smiled. "Great idea. I loved those articles you did before."

"Before?" Rupert asked.

"Yes, when I was at college."

Crazy. He was the one who wanted information about Rupert, and if he wasn't careful, he'd end up giving more information than gaining any.

"What's your father's role in the business?" Luke asked, to deflect the conversation away from himself.

Amy butted in. "He buys the land and gets outline permissions in place. Rupert then deals with the building side of things."

"Rupert," he paused, checking that Amy registered his intent. "Tell me about your relationship with your father?"

Amy mouthed, "Sorry," and concentrated on buttering her bread roll.

Rupert seemed to struggle to find the right words. "It has its ups and downs. Working together has let us recognize each other's strengths and weaknesses."

"And what are they?" Might as well dig while he could, Luke thought.

"He has so many contacts and hears about properties coming onto the market long before I'd ever get a whisper about them. And lately, he's come to accept that I'm better at developing than he is."

"Fine, that's the positive, but what about the negative side?"

Rupert glanced at Amy as if to check if he should answer. Amy shrugged.

"I guess you'd call him domineering. He hates not having control. What about you? What was your father like?"

"He died when I was ten. My uncle became the father figure in my life."

"The one who left you the house you love so much?"

Luke was surprised Amy had told Rupert. But she'd had longer to fill the man in on his personal life than he'd had finding out about her lover.

"Yes, lots of memories attached to the place." He stopped there, remembering Amy's comment about not expecting him to sell the house. She was aware how much it meant to him; and of his reluctance to change anything. She'd tried to modernize the place. At first, they didn't have enough money to afford alterations, and later he'd put his foot down and refused to go knocking out walls and turning it into a featureless design project fit to grace a magazine spread. The work she did was fine as long as it happened in someone else's space. Rupert's development was the perfect backdrop for her skills.

The conversation faltered, and the arrival of their meal allowed them to concentrate on eating rather than talking. Rupert finished his meal first. "When can I meet the children?"

"Not yet," Luke answered firmly. He looked towards Amy. "I thought we had agreed not to rush this."

Amy shot Rupert an indignant look. "I know, I thought Rupert understood."

Luke could see she was uncomfortable. The friendly get together was not working the way she hoped, but that was her problem, not his.

Rupert looked at Amy. "It's okay. I understand, but can you make dinner tonight?" He looked at Luke. "You don't mind, do you?"

"As if you care." He turned to Amy. "Will you come home to see the children tonight?"

Amy nodded.

The waiter was hovering, ready to offer desserts or coffee. Luke had endured enough and pushed back his chair and said. "Sorry, I need to go."

Amy looked as if she wanted to say something. Instead, she put a hand on Rupert's arm, to stop him from making matters difficult.

Luke spun round and left them still sitting at the table. He needed pain relief. The tension in his shoulders was being transmitted to his chest, increasing the intensity of pain. He didn't care about not offering to pay for his meal, but hurried to the car, found a bottle of water, and snapped a pill from the blister pack, ignoring the fact that he had already had the daily prescribed dose. He was struggling to control his anger and knew he needed to avoid a further encounter with Rupert. He drove down to Exmouth, parked at the far end of the seafront, where he could sit and watch the waves pounding the beach.

He stayed until it was time to pick the girls up from school and did his best not to transmit his mood to them. Coming back from taking Buster for a walk, Luke was surprised to find that Amy had come home early to sort out their supper and to put the girls to bed.

Neither of them mentioned lunch, or Rupert. But it was obvious that she was going out again. Luke knew then what his next step had to be.

When he kissed the girls goodnight, he whispered, "I've been keeping Mummy awake at night with my snoring, so I'm going to sleep in the spare room. Just wanted to tell you in case you came looking for me in the night."

They answered cheerily, "Okay, goodnight."

He didn't tell Amy; she'd find out soon enough.

When she left, he poured himself a large whiskey and took it upstairs to have while he moved his things from their bedroom to the spare room that faced the garden. It had been his childhood room. He remembered the hours they spent scraping the walls to remove his tacky teen idol posters. Amy had turned it into a haven of peace with muted colours, with an ensuite bathroom. He'd never expected to be grateful for her efforts, but he knew he would be happier here than in the room they shared for so many years.

In the morning, Amy acknowledged the changed room status by asking if he'd slept well.

"Quite well," he replied, which was true, but he didn't mention that the whiskey had probably helped.

She had enough grace to wait a few days before she said. "I know it's difficult for you, but I need you to agree to let the girls meet Rupert. Perhaps we could all meet up in the park and take a walk together."

Luke reluctantly agreed. He had to. It was obvious Rupert was there to stay. And it wasn't fair to Amy to deny the fact. How easy it would be depended on Rupert's not pushing things.

After the initial meeting with Rupert, he occasionally joined them for walks and outings to the park. To give him credit, Rupert put in a lot of effort. He would push them on the swings until exhausted, or time them racing up the slide and down again and again. While Rupert got to bond with the girls, Luke had the role of the jealous spectator on the sidelines.

Amy's dinner dates with Rupert became the routine, and she rarely spent an evening at home. The discussion about the girls moving to Rupert's was avoided.

Then Amy wanted to spend a night away. Luke, much as he hated the idea, agreed if she told the girls she had a business trip.

Finally, when she wanted a whole long weekend away, Luke accepted it was time to prepare the girls for the inevitable move.

While they were competing as to who could suck up a strand of spaghetti the fastest, he quietly broached the subject that gave him sleepless nights.

"Do you like Rupert?" he asked.

They smiled and nodded as their spaghetti disappeared, leaving a trail of tomato sauce on their chins.

"I think your mum likes him too, rather a lot."

Katie stared at him. "Has she gone away with him?"

"Yes, just for the weekend, but I think she'd like to live with him."

It took a moment for the words to sink in. Katie, bless her, always thinking of others, said, "Won't that make you sad?"

He pretended to have to think about her question. "A bit, but I want her to be happy. Don't you?"

"Yes, but what about us?" she asked, the impact of the move dawning on her.

"Your mum will make sure there's room for you at Rupert's house, in the same way as you will always have your rooms here. Did Rupert tell you he has a swimming pool?"

Using that as a sweetener was underhand, but, having come to terms with them going, he wanted them to be happy about it, and was sure the pool would work the necessary magic.

"But Daddy, you'll be on your own."

"Not quite. Buster will be here to keep me company." Rupert's enthusiasm to get on with the girls had not stretched to embracing their beloved mad hound.

That did the trick. Moments later, they resumed their spaghetti challenge.

He had sown the seeds. It was up to Amy to take the next step.

Chapter 6

Luke struggled with the whirlwind that ensued, following his mention of Rupert's pool. Amy took the girls for a swim. Luke didn't go with them. Spending time with Amy, loving her as he did, was becoming increasingly difficult, and he didn't want to see all that Rupert had to offer. Next, the girls had a sleepover at Rupert's, then a weekend.

Luke had to get used to the idea it wouldn't stop there and braced himself for the big day when the move became more regular. The girls begged him to come and see their room, and to let them show him the pool. He helped them pack a few more of their things and drove them over.

First, he had to negotiate his way through the security gates to the compound. Buttons to press, speakers to announce their presence, and the wait for the gates to swing open. Then the girls pointed out the tall, impressive house at the end of the cul-de-sac. They jumped out of the car and ran to the door and rang the bell. Luke trailed behind with a bag full of treasures for each of them. The door opened. He'd expected Amy to be there to meet them, but instead a tall, smartly dressed woman who introduced herself as Moira Walker let them in. She didn't say what her role was, just that Rupert had told her they would be arriving. Her stiletto heels clicked on the gleaming marble floor as she guided them towards the staircase leading to the girl's room. "Rupert will be back shortly. He hoped you would stay until he gets here."

Luke thought it was rather presumptive of Rupert. And nodded that he could wait, wondering what alternative arrangement was in place if he couldn't. He noticed that the girl's giggles ceased the moment they saw the woman. They were obviously not at ease with her, and he didn't blame them. Moira Walker looked formidable, someone who like to get her way. On his agreement to stay, she click clacked her way back to the front door, letting it bang shut behind her.

Her departure lightened the mood, and the girls went back to being themselves, pulling him along to see their room. It was huge, and at first glance showed no evidence of it being a children's room. One wall comprised fitted cupboards that slid open to reveal desks, drawers, and hanging space. Their possessions were tucked out of sight, including the precious bear, who, for as long as he could remember, had always resided on Janet's pillow. The bathroom, spectacular as it might be, lacked evidence of use. Not even a toothbrush in sight. He guessed they lived in the mirrored cabinets on either side of the fancy sink. How could people live like this? He hoped the girls would soon put their own stamp on their new domain. They didn't need to be living in something that belonged in a magazine. They needed a fun space, where creativity was encouraged, not banished to a cupboard.

Inspection of the room didn't take long, so they dragged him back downstairs to see the pool. They passed through the lounge, a vast space broken only by long cream covered settees. One set positioned round a modern fireplace that opened through to what looked like a dining room with a long table with about a dozen chairs round it, and a second facing the expanse of windows looking out onto the terrace.

At the far end of the lounge, there was a door that led into the pool area. The pool was enormous. Of course, it would be. Rupert was a man who liked to impress. Katie pulled him into the vast glass ceiling pool area with more glass doors facing the same terrace as the lounge.

"Rupert taught me to dive, and Janet can swim a length. Can we show you?"

Luke had little choice. He was stuck here until Amy arrived, and letting the girls swim would pass the time better than anything he could dream up in this sterile environment.

"Do you want to swim too? There are spare swimming things in the changing room."

Luke pointed to his chest. "Thanks, but I don't think I'm ready for swimming." Katie nodded, and the pair of them ran round to the far side of the pool to the changing room. There was a comfortable looking chair that Luke sank into and waited for the fun to begin, knowing he would have to comment on every move. The diving was impressive, and he clapped enthusiastically, then allowed Janet to show her improved skill.

They stopped trying to impress him and were just having fun together, and he looked out over the well-tended rather formal layout of hedges, walls, and planters with carefully manicured rounded box shrubs in them. Then he spotted a young lad, almost cowering at the verbal assault he was getting from Moira Walker. She towered over him, waving her arms angrily. Because of the double glazing, he couldn't make out what was being said.

Katie stood beside him and said, "She doesn't like Gorka. She's always cross with him."

Janet piped up. "She gets cross with everyone."

He wanted to ask if she ever got cross with them, but thought it best not to. Or at least not while they were here. Maybe when they were relaxed at home, he could probe a bit more about what it was like to live in this no mess house.

Amy arrived and wasted no time in sending them off to get dry and dressed and added instructions about hanging their wet swimming costumes up in the right place.

Then she turned her attention to Luke. "Sorry I'm late. Would you like a tea or coffee or something before you go? Rupert won't be back for at least an hour."

Luke didn't feel comfortable in the house, whether or not Rupert was here, and he really needed to get to the chemist to pick up more painkillers. "Not today," he said. "I'll head off as soon as I've said goodbye to the girls."

Chapter 7

Luke did his best to fill his days with activity, but the lack of mobility in his arm limited his options. And the pain level was such that he found comfort in having a drink, something he controlled better when the girls were around.

He pleaded with his boss to let him come back to work, knowing only a desk job would be possible.

"Sorry, Luke, I know you have surgery scheduled. I can't have you back yet. Call me after your operation and we can discuss this again. But you'll have to pass the fitness test."

This was not the response he'd hoped for, but one he had to live with.

He turned again to the idea of photojournalism, which he suggested as an option when Rupert quizzed him about alternatives to firefighting.

He spoke to his friend Barry, the editor of a glossy magazine, and asked for his help to get started.

"If you can produce the sort of work, you did in the past, you shouldn't have a problem. Choosing your subject is the tough part. That, coupled with stunning pictures telling the story, is the key."

"Easier said than done," Luke answered.

"True. Let me set you a challenge. Pubs are closing at an alarming rate. What makes the difference between failure and success in the local area? Can you explore the topic and find an interesting angle?"

"Sure, I'll give it a go. How much time do I have?"

"The next edition is already planned, so let's say you have a month."

"Challenge accepted."

With renewed motivation, he set himself a tight schedule. Every day he would do a little work on clearing the accumulated junk in the house's annex, which his uncle had built in case he needed a carer. A hard task because of his lack of arm movement. He'd go for a work-out at the gym, doing whatever his body would allow. Then he'd focus on the story. The downside of the physical exercise was increased pain and needing more pills than the doctor prescribed. But that didn't stop him; keeping busy was vital for his mental health.

By late morning, he was ready to check out the first pub of the day. He planned to research the pubs within a five-mile walking distance of his house. With Buster on his lead, he'd set off at a brisk pace, taking photos of target pubs on the way while the light was at its best, heading to the furthest on the map. Once there, he'd have a pint, get into conversation with the landlord, and take a few interior photos, snapshots of the menu if they had one. Sometimes he'd order food. All the while, he'd be asking probing questions. Then he'd start back towards home, taking in as many pubs as he could on the way.

The plan was sound, except for the quantities of alcohol involved. Without the routine of childcare, he was free to keep exploring pubs until closing time.

The worrying aspect of the challenge was that the more pubs he visited, the less he found to excite him to write. He couldn't find the upbeat human angle the magazine would want, except maybe to name the dog friendly establishments. Instead, he had enough material to fill a guidebook, but what was the point? By the time it got published, half of them would probably have gone out of business. But he was not a quitter and, having accepted the challenge, he had to press on.

The drink dulled his creativity, but it helped take the edge off his pain and provided a distraction from his fear of the next round of surgery.

The doorbell woke him. He had a fuzzy head. An empty bottle lay on the floor beside him. The bell kept ringing. Buster was barking and scratching at the door. He had to make the noise stop. It did, for a second, then started all over again with an urgency which refused to be ignored. Buster got more frantic, especially when the person outside started banging on the door.

Luke sat up and put his feet on the floor. There was an overturned glass by his feet. He picked the glass up and put it on the table, slipped on his shoes, and went to silence the persistent noise.

Through the frosted glass he saw Amy, flanked by the girls. He ran his fingers through his hair, looked down at his crumpled clothing.

What would Amy think? He hated it mattered and braced himself for a lecture.

"Thank God, I thought you had forgotten you were having the girls tonight and tomorrow."

She bent to give Buster a quick stroke, kissed the girls on their foreheads and said, "Be good for Daddy," then turned and hurried away.

Buster chased after her, but changed his mind, and rushed back with his tail wagging, to greet the girls.

Part of him longed to run after Amy and beg her to come home. But with his head pounding and his tongue feeling fat and dry, as if he'd been licking the carpet, it was probably better not to. She stopped for a second to wave. He wanted to return the gesture, but Katie had grabbed his hand, leaving him powerless to respond. Their enthusiastic efforts were all she'd get. They kept waving until her car vanished around the corner. Two little bags were on the step beside them. He took a deep breath. How had he forgotten something so important? He needed coffee and a clear head.

Katie, having released her hold of his hand, sank down to give Buster the attention he craved. The poor little hound missed them almost as much as he did.

He watched them for a moment, then said, "Why don't you take your bags upstairs?"

He needed to treat them the same way he had in the past. Make this visit as normal as possible and prove to Amy he could manage the girls. The craving for a drink hit. But he wouldn't, not while the kids were staying.

The living room was a mess. He couldn't let them see it like that.

"While you unpack, I'll look for some biscuits."

The girls didn't need further encouragement and were already halfway up the stairs with Buster chasing after them.

It cheered him to hear their excited giggles as they reacquainted themselves with treasures in their rooms. Coming home was a bigger event for them than he'd ever anticipated, making him glad he insisted the bulk of their toys stayed here. Amy would have to provide more there and double up some of their favourite things.

Luke wanted to rush up and watch them, but first he must restore order to the living area. He reached for the empty bottle lying on the floor by the sofa and spotted another one. Had he really drunk two? He remembered opening a bottle, but not the second. He dropped them and the empty sandwich wrapper in the bin, put the glass in the dishwasher and wiped the crumbs off the table. While the kettle boiled, he tackled the pans in the sink. That done, he could relax. He made a coffee, and much as he'd have liked something stronger, he had to stay sober today.

He found a packet of biscuits. Chocolate ones. The girls would be happy with that choice. But the scary part was what to do with them for a whole day, with such a debilitating hangover.

He grabbed his phone and called Charlotte.

"Hi. Sorry to bother you. I've got the girls today, and I've a blinding headache, and need your help. Are you available?"

"Yes. No problem, I was heading to the park and I'm happy to take them. Be with you shortly," she answered in her normal cheery way.

When she arrived, she took one look at Luke and suggested that he go to bed for an hour or two. She fiddled with her phone, then looked at him and said, "How about booking them a climbing session for later?"

"Great idea, book yourself in too. I'll come and keep an eye on George."

"Are you sure?"

"Yes, you deserve a break, and I still can't climb."

A moment later, she announced she'd got a late afternoon slot. "We'll go now and let you catch up on some sleep."

He was in no condition to argue.

He didn't think he'd be able to sleep, so had a shower then lay down on the bed, consumed by guilt that he'd forgotten the girls were coming.

A feathery touch on his puckered skin woke him with a shiver. On opening his eyes, he found Janet snuggled up on the bed beside him, her little fingers skating over the surface of the rugged contours of his scars, tracing the edges. For a second, he recalled the sensation of flames licking his skin, along with the pain and the gut-wrenching stench of burning flesh. His urge to lash out was suppressed, and his body went rigid.

"Will I ever have lumpy skin, like yours?" Janet's soft voice registered, bringing his tension down. The shock of how easily he could have hurt her if he'd lashed out hit.

He took a deep breath, and gently caught her hand and lifted it off his chest, raised it to plant a kiss on it. "I hope not. Lumps are not good."

"But it's pretty."

Unsure how to respond to that, he stayed silent. His daughter had no idea how painful skin grafts could be, and what he'd undergone to reduce the scarring to this level. He'd endured it because he'd worried about their reactions.

Now he realized the appearance was unimportant. Improving his arm mobility was all that mattered.

After their climbing session, Janet asked if they could go to Rupert's house. They were going to

60

a birthday party, and she had forgotten to pack the present she had for her friend.

Luke had no desire to go there, but she was insistent. He pointed out that he didn't have a key.

"It doesn't matter. Mrs Walker will have one."

Luke agreed, thinking it better to go when there was no danger of an encounter with Rupert.

They pulled up at the closed gate. Kate said, "Press the button and ask for Mrs Walker."

A voice on the intercom demanded to know what they wanted.

Luke explained, and the gates opened, allowing him to proceed and park outside the house.

The intimidating woman emerged from the house opposite, her stiletto heels tapping rhythmically on the herringbone brick paving. She went to the house door, tapped a number into the keypad and waved a fob against a sensor.

"Make sure you pull the door closed when you leave," she instructed, and spun round on her heel and walked back across the driveway, without giving Luke a chance to thank her for her trouble.

He didn't have time to dwell on the woman because the girls dragged him inside and insisted he went up to their room. Reluctantly he let them lead him through a vast semicircle of a space with a staircase rising around the curve. This time round, he took in the details. An enormous chandelier of long light tubes hung in the well of the staircase. A wide landing wrapped around the curve with doors leading off it.

Janet decided to be the tour guide. "That's mummy's room, she said, pointing to the door nearest the top of the stairs. That's Rupert's office. These two are spare rooms, and this one is ours." She flung open the door and ushered him into their bedroom with a vast plate-glass window looking out over the manicured grounds. It was just as he remembered it. Not a toy or anything in sight to show that two little girls shared this space. The contrast to their toy littered rooms at home was a shock. He would have words with Amy about this. They shouldn't be subjected to such a sterile environment.

Katie opened a cupboard. Everything was lined up neatly. Drawers were labelled, socks, pants, shirts, etc. Shoes were lined up neatly in pairs.

He realized that this worked because they only had a small selection of clothes here. They hadn't been living here long enough to accumulate much. But how long could they keep this tidy?

Katie opened another double door cupboard, this one served as a toy cupboard and workspace. He spotted a stool in a neat slot at the bottom. Katie pulled it out and then tugged out a sliding writing surface. She picked out a card and a pen and scrawled a name on it, shoved it in an envelope and wrote on that too. Then she asked Luke to pull down a ready wrapped parcel that was on a top shelf. She found a tape dispenser, tugged off a strip of tape and stuck the card to the parcel. Then she pushed the desk flap back, and placed the stool in its allocated slot, and shut the cupboard door.

Luke took another look round the room. "Do you want to make your room at home as neat as this one?"

"NO!" they replied in unison. He smiled. Happy that they preferred to have a lived-in feel to their lives.

"It must take ages to keep it this tidy."

"Maria comes in and puts everything away when we're out." Katie explained.

No wonder Amy enjoyed living here.

Janet took his hand and dragged him back down the stairs and round to the entrance to the pool, where there was a man, with thick dark curly hair, kneeling by the edge of the water, dipping a cup into it. Luke guessed he was testing the chlorine levels.

"Who's that?"

"Antonio." Janet answered, "He never speaks."

"Only because he's Italian," Kate announced, proud to be able to supply information her sister had not grasped. "He talks to Maria. She invites him in when Mum goes out for dinner."

"I've never heard him." Janet said, her eyes wide in disbelief.

"She waits until you are asleep." Katie answered. "I know, because she always comes into our room to check. I usually pretend to be asleep. She locks our bedroom door, then lets him in through the pool door. Sometimes they go into one of the spare bedrooms."

"Why didn't you tell me?"

"Because you can't keep a secret." Katie answered. "And if you told anyone, he might get into trouble, and I think Maria really likes him."

Luke forced himself not to interrupt. This information was worrying, but he couldn't let them know. The man's thick set neck muscles were a sure sign this guy was a regular at a gym. Antonio looked up, saw Luke, and hurried away to the pool pump room. Their eyes never met. Odd. Most people would at least acknowledge his presence.

Chapter 8

Panic overwhelmed him. Hands gripped his wrists. The scream went on and on. He was the one screaming. He forced his eyes open. Antiseptic fumes overpowered his senses, knocking out the stench of burning flesh. Two masked and gowned figures hovered over him, holding him firmly but gently, pinning his limbs to the bed.

"Relax, Luke, you're safe." He registered kindly eyes and then heard another voice.

"Welcome back."

Back? Where was he? What was going on? He glanced around: hospital. Why?

"Take your time. Your operation is over. Everything went well. Doctor Harries is pleased with the graft."

He processed the words. Graft. Doctor Harries. Gradually, the pieces fell into place.

A dream. The worst so far. Vivid images of the fire haunting him. His tension eased, as did the grip on his wrists and ankles.

"Sorry," he muttered.

"No need. The drugs often cause odd reactions. We're used to it."

They might be, but he never wanted to go through that again.

The nurses bustled round him, checking his pulse, moving tubes, changing bags of liquid attached to his arm. Their smiles were a sign that all was well.

He was tired, but afraid to close his eyes in case the flashback returned. Would it haunt him forever?

A soft voice kept repeating, "Go back to sleep. You're safe here."

Safe. Would he ever feel safe again? His world had turned upside down. His marriage broken. His kids didn't need him as much. The job he loved might be taken away from him. Should he trust that voice? Maybe he didn't have a choice. It was hard to concentrate.

Light poured in through the window when he became aware of his surroundings again. He could make out the treetops swaying in the breeze. A chair creaked and papers rustled.

He turned his head to find Owen sitting by his bed, engrossed in a crossword puzzle. Silently, he watched him, wondering what compelled him to keep coming. Habit? He had been waiting last time he had surgery. A gesture of friendship? He remembered there was a time he put it down to guilt over his injuries, even though it wasn't Owen's fault.

Owen smiled when he worked out a clue and frowned when he got stuck. The moment he spotted Luke was awake, he pushed the paper aside.

"You okay?" he asked.

Luke smiled and nodded. "I think so. The painkillers haven't worn off yet."

"Amy dropped by. Asked me to call and let her know how you're doing. She wanted to stay but had to hurry back for the girls."

Luke was touched that she'd come. But Amy worked hard at keeping up appearances of being close for the girl's sake, which he sometimes struggled to reciprocate.

"Thank her for me." As he spoke, he wondered if Amy's friendship with Tamsin had been restored. "I can't believe you didn't fight to win her back," Owen said.

"Leave off."

"Why? You still love her, don't you?"

Of course, he still loved her, but there was no way he could ask her to come back when he was in such a mess, physically and mentally. He could never offer her the degree of luxury and lifestyle she seemed to crave, and that Rupert seemed to offer.

"Why don't you go home to your wife? I bet she'll be overjoyed to have you home for the evening."

"Touché." Owen got to his feet. "I can see you're back to your usual self, so I'll leave you in peace."

Luke lay there trying to work out what his usual self was. He'd like to think it was an amiable being, but knew that for the last few months since that fateful fire, he had been anything but. Grumpy and reliant on pills and booze to blot out the pain and the memories. Not likable traits at all. And that made it even more surprising that Owen spent so many hours at his bedside. Perhaps he should make more effort to show his appreciation of his friendship.

His surgeon approached the bed. Luke lay still, dreading the prospect of hearing that all had not gone well. The pain was worse now than after his earlier surgeries.

"Glad to see you're awake."

"Hard to sleep when it hurts so much."

"I'm sure it is, and I'm sorry about that. I asked them to keep you on the minimum dose of painkillers."

"Why?"

"You've become rather too dependent on them. I gather from your notes you've been drinking, too. The combination has damaged your liver. To be honest, if you don't make changes, you will end up in serious trouble."

Luke couldn't argue. But it didn't help with his current pain level.

"I need something now."

"Yes, and I will sort something out for you. The graft and the donor sites will be sore for a while yet. I followed your instructions and did as much as I could in one go to give maximum flexibility to your arm movement. The danger of numbing the pain completely is that you will overreach and undo the work done. But we also need to prevent the new graft from becoming too tight. You'll be stuck in this brace until the healing process is well underway."

Luke surveyed the pulley device from which his arm was suspended, outstretched, and elevated.

"I might be able to fix your body to the point where you can go back to work, but drug or alcohol dependence will destroy that option. Only you can decide what to do about the problem. I can point you in the right direction for help, but you must be prepared to put in the effort, which means dealing with the trauma caused by the fire. I see from your notes you rejected all previous offers of support."

"I thought I was in control."

"Sadly, that's not true. You need support. The question is, are you ready to accept it?"

"Yes."

"Good. I will sort out an alternative pain relief plan, but you have to accept the help on offer to make a full recovery."

Luke's post-operative care was intense. The team who tended to him previously were back to keep him on track as the adjustment to different pain medication kicked in. The fact that he had become addicted to drugs and booze so quickly was terrifying. It made him almost afraid to mention the pain. He had to crack the problem for the sake of the family.

The physio team drove him relentlessly to improve his core fitness, saying that his arm recovery would come later. As soon as he could remove his arm from the suspension brace, they added a long list of exercises to do several times a day. The object being to prevent the skin from tightening and reducing the benefits the surgery had gained.

When the physical team took a break, the mental health team took over. They encouraged him to talk about the fire, and this time he did. Opening up was hard, but cathartic, and allowed him to connect how he felt at the time to what was happening now.

Talking about Amy was harder. The accident and his injuries were not to blame. His marriage had been shaky long before then.

Towards the end of one session, the therapist said, "How you deal with all this is up to you. You can nurture or destroy your relationship with your kids. Bear in mind, you might only get one chance to get it right."

"I understand," he answered.

"While you're doing well here, I recommend you join our twelve-step program for people like yourself who have had drug and drink problems to overcome. But they can only help if you want to be helped."

"I do."

"Fine, I'll ask Sheena to come and talk to you. I think you'll like her."

Later that day, she appeared.

"Hi, I'm Sheena." Luke studied the woman facing him. Her bright, unnaturally red hair suited her. It was hard to decide her age. He guessed she was probably about ten years his senior. Her smile won him over.

She explained about the twelve-step program, how the meetings worked to help people break the pattern of addiction, and the role of sponsors.

"I was hooked on prescription medication too and, like you, had added booze to the mix. So, you are not alone there. Don't worry, the first meeting is the worst," she said. "I hated the idea of a group. But I promise you won't regret coming."

"I hadn't realized how dependent I had become."

"None of us do. But eventually we get that wake-up call and find a reason to break the cycle. Knowing why you want to quit is the first hurdle. There's a meeting today if you want to come. You needn't say anything if you don't want to."

Luke was as ready as he would ever be. "Okay, I'm up for it." Sheena led the way. They were first to be seated, which allowed him to survey everyone as they came in, and he was struck by the fact that not one of them looked to have a problem. Could they all have developed a drug habit? Not one fitted his mental image of a heavy drinker or drug user.

"We come in all shapes and sizes," Sheena said quietly. "Nearly everyone here had problems getting off prescription medication. Some with alcohol issues as well."

"Like me?"

"Yes," she answered.

"What about you?"

"Depression got the better of me."

"Still a problem?" he asked, then wondered why he was so interested in this woman's problems. She seemed nice enough, but he doubted he'd ever engage with her outside this room.

"The depression still comes and goes, but I've got better coping mechanisms now, thanks to this group."

The meeting continued, and Luke took the plunge and stood up to introduce himself. He learned that being busy and doing things with meaning appeared to be the key to success in most cases.

Afterward, he asked Sheena what made her take so much interest in this group of people.

"I like helping people," she answered. "I work at the food bank; it makes me feel useful. My previous job," she continued, "didn't have much impact on people's lives. What about you? What gives you a buzz?"

"Working for the fire service. And, of course, being able to care for Katie and Janet."

"The fire service certainly fits the bill as far as meaningful work goes. And your children are the best motivation of all."

"Yes, and I hope to be fit enough soon to pass the physical test required for work. When I get out of here, I'll come and check out what you do." Luke went on to tell her about his plan to search for the man he had rescued from the fire. He added, "I need to know how he's doing."

"I'm not making any promises, but I may be able to help. I'll ask around," Sheena said. "Sorry, I won't be at tomorrow's meeting. I'm helping a friend doing her driving test."

"Charlotte?" Luke said, cross that he hadn't confirmed the connection before. Sheena was the friend who was going to mind George.

"Yes. How do you know about her?"

"Babysitting, and dog sitting. Lovely girl, she's been a great help."

"You don't have to tell her we've met," Sheena said.

"It doesn't bother me. She'll be glad I'm getting help. How about you?"

"No problem. Being open about addiction is the best way to be."

Sheena's comment made him decide to be honest with Barry. He had failed with the challenge and needed to own up to the failure. He phoned to tell him.

Barry's reaction was better than expected. "I'm not surprised. I deliberately gave you a tough challenge, but never intended to trigger a drink problem."

"Don't blame yourself. I was the one overdosing on pills. Drinking just brought the problem to the forefront sooner."

"Don't be put off. One day you'll find a story worth telling. Then I'll be interested."

Chapter 9

Sheena, true to her word, through her contacts at the food bank, found Martin, the man he'd rescued, and arranged a meeting.

"Martin's glad of a chance to thank you for putting yourself at risk to save him." She pointed down road. "Great, here he comes."

Luke studied the man walking towards him. He would never have guessed that this was the person he'd carried out of the burning building. The scruffy beard had gone, and his thick mop of unruly hair was less wild than Luke's vague recollection.

Sheena introduced them, then pointed to an empty bench under a tree in the little green space across the road. "Sit there. I'll bring you both a coffee."

Martin and Luke followed her instructions and sat down to talk.

"I'm sorry to hear your friend died," Luke said. "Tell me about him."

Martin shrugged. "I didn't know Pete well. You don't on the street. Everyone has their own problems, and no one wants to dig to find out what dragged them down to that level. But Pete was okay. He looked out for others, always ready to share what little he had with someone less fortunate."

"Did he have family?"

"I guess so. Someone arranged his funeral, but I didn't go. The silly thing is that he'd been warning me for weeks that the place wasn't safe. Said it was likely to be torched."

"What?"

"There had been a dodgy character checking out the building. One of the other homeless guys who saw him hanging about warned Pete it was time to clear out. Told him the man meant trouble."

"Did you tell anyone?"

"You must be kidding. Being homeless is like being invisible."

"Could you find the guy who warned Pete about them and ask if he'd mind talking to me?"

Martin frowned, and Luke dropped the subject.

"How have things been since the fire?" he asked. The change of tactic worked as Martin smiled.

"Okay, they found me a flat. And I'm even back in touch with my family. What about you? Sheena said you were injured."

Luke brushed that comment aside. This man didn't need to know the details. Instead, they talked about how he had ended up homeless, and how having a permanent address changed his life. Luke knew this could make a worthwhile article. He let Martin ramble on for a while, then thought it best to be up front with Martin about his idea of writing about people in his predicament. He checked if he could use his story and asked if he would help by introducing him to some others in the same situation.

"If you'd asked me before when I was on the streets, I'd have said no. But having a home is what I needed, and now I'll do anything to help others get the same."

The offer was certainly heartfelt, and whatever article came out of this new friendship, Luke hoped it might make a difference to someone's life, which made the prospect exciting.

But caution set in. Go slowly. Bond with this man and build his trust. Make no promises.

They talked for over an hour. Luke offered to help Martin in any way possible. That done, he jotted down Martin's new address, and scribbled his own phone number on a scrap of paper and passed it over. "If you think of anything that might be useful, call me on this number, or ask Sheena to give me a shout."

The conversation renewed his determination to dig for more information about the warehouse fire. Who stood to gain? Who owned the property? Who was the developer involved? So far, he'd met dead ends at every turn. Ownership was buried in a string of offshore companies.

Luke divided his time between working on his fitness and minding the girls. The start of the summer break made this more of a full-time occupation.

He had to pace himself carefully with the fitness regime, because the pain levels needed more management since his medication changes. He was learning to live with the dull background pain and trying hard to delay taking his allowed medication, only taking a single tablet when he couldn't cope with the pain any longer.

Thankfully, his pain tolerance increased, as did his fitness levels. Running further and lifting weights became easier. He applied his creams as often as he could, and the tightness of the skin eased to the point where he had almost complete flexibility and he was keen to attempt the fitness test required to resume work.

The date loomed fast.

Passing the test was the first step. Regaining the confidence of the crew and adjusting to their crazy shift patterns would follow. The downside of returning to work was juggling care for the girls and that they would spend more nights with Amy than he wanted. They were happy enough, but he wasn't sure Rupert would feel the same way.

The day of his test arrived. Luke was certain he had done enough to pass, but would he be able to perform as well under pressure? He knew what to expect, and when he reached the halfway point, was sure he could manage to get to the end without faltering. One of the others doing the test had dropped out. But Luke was determined to finish.

A few days later, he was back on shift and faced dealing with a shout. The first time the alert sounded, he felt a momentary panic. Physically, he could manage anything, but what about the mental side? He breathed a sigh of relief when he heard it was a car on fire on the side of the motorway.

The next shout was to deal with an out-of-control bonfire, followed by a rescue from scaffolding that was threatening to collapse. This was a tricky task, but without the pressure of a person being in danger, these presented more of a logistical challenge than a dangerous incident that entering a burning building presented.

Three weeks on, when the station bell sounded, word quickly spread that a block of flats was on fire. His heart pounded. Was he ready? He had to be.

The crew followed a well-rehearsed routine. This steadied him. He could do this. He'd trained for this. No reason why he couldn't cope. When they arrived, he registered they were at Sheena's address.

The fire was raging. Plumes of smoke billowed out from an upper stairwell window. Luke and Owen pulled on their smoke hoods and slung their tanks onto their backs and waited for instruction.

Checks were made, radios, flashlights and helmet cameras switched on, and the order given for them to go ahead.

Luke's heart thudded, the familiar rush of adrenaline coursing through his body.

The boss checked with him. "You don't have to do this if you're not ready."

"I'm ready." He gave the thumbs up sign. Too late to back down. He must face this challenge. He turned to Owen, who was in the lead position.

"You're sure?" Owen asked, his voice muffled by the connecting microphone.

Luke understood why they asked. He nodded and waited for Owen to go ahead, happy with the change of roles. Luke had led on the last few occasions they'd gone into a fire together.

Luke wished he knew which flat Sheena lived in, not that it would change anything. There was a rescue pattern to be followed, and that is what he would do.

He had forgotten how claustrophobic and cumbersome the breathing apparatus was. A flash of panic made him question the sanity of doing this.

No, he would not back out. He stood by the steps of the building, listening to Owen telling him to stay close. They started with the ground-floor flat on the left; another team would check the flats on the right.

Luke took a deep breath and followed his friend. They pushed open the door. Checked all the rooms. No one was there. Luke spotted a parrot cage with two birds in it. He covered it and grabbed the hook at the top and hauled it outside. Owen shook his head but didn't stop Luke as he went to dump it on the lawn, but before he let go, the owner rushed over to take the cage from him, thanking him profusely. He hurried back to join Owen, who was already on his way up to the next floor.

The smoke was thicker. The hoses were in action and water ran down the stairs, making them more hazardous.

He and Owen moved up cautiously and entered the flat on the left-hand side. They found two children with their grandmother, huddled in a back room. Owen picked up the youngest child and, taking the hand of the older one, took off, without waiting for Luke and the grandmother. The old lady could barely stand. He'd need superhuman powers to get her down. He wrapped his good arm round her, and almost lifted her off her feet and half dragged her out and down to the ground level.

He nearly dropped her. His arms aching from the strain of trying to grip the woman to keep her upright.

As he caught his breath, the gremlin in his head was telling him he was a liability. That he should quit before he put someone in danger because of his weakness. But before he had time to decide, Owen tapped his shoulder and indicated it was time to go back up to the third floor. Owen's insistent tug pushed thoughts of quitting off the agenda. And drove him forward.

The rising smoke was more intense. Speed was the only thing that would save anyone left in the building. Thick black smoke filled the flat. It would be a miracle if they found anyone alive. Owen did. The family was huddled on the floor. Owen pulled the children and the mother to their feet and pushed them towards Luke.

"I'll stay and help the father. You take this lot down."

Luke didn't want to leave Owen, but followed his instructions. These people would not find their way without help. Half-way down the stairs, he handed them over to a colleague and hurried back up to help Owen.

He pushed on through the dense smoke, fighting his fear as it got thicker and thicker. Without his breathing apparatus, he would be a goner for sure.

Owen was struggling to lift the man.

"I think he's having a heart attack," Owen said. "We need to get him out."

Owen took the man's shoulders and Luke his legs, and between them they hauled him down the stairs into the care of the paramedics.

Luke tugged off his hood and collapsed on the grass to catch his breath and take in his surroundings.

More appliances had arrived on the scene and the dazzle of flashing blue lights was blinding. But the ferocity of the flames billowing out from the windows of the upper floors was astounding. Nothing seemed to make an impression. It was hard to understand how the fire had escalated in such a short space of time.

He watched the paramedics baring the man's chest, calling out for everyone to step back as they used the defibrillator on him. Luke was not sure if the man would survive, but at least he had a chance.

Owen handed him a bottle of water and sat with him for a while before saying, "Wait here. I'll go and check what needs doing."

Luke was too shattered to move, but desperately wanted to find out if Sheena was okay.

He tried to stand, but his legs wouldn't work. He sank back onto the grass. Moments later, a paramedic came over.

"Let me check you out," she said, and without waiting for an answer, called a colleague, who joined her. She clipped a monitor on his finger, then put an oxygen mask on him, and ordered him to sit where he was. He hadn't the strength to argue. He knew his pulse was racing, but he had no idea how to deal with it. Was this a panic attack? If so, he was definitely suffering from a full-blown crisis of confidence, or whatever anyone wanted to call it.

Someone handed him another bottle of water. Luke gulped the refreshing liquid down. The taste of toxic smoke filled his nostrils and hit the back of his throat, leaving it feeling raw.

He was aware that the paramedics had lifted the man onto a trolley and were loading him into the waiting ambulance.

"Will he make it?" Luke pointed towards the ambulance.

"Not sure, but they got a faint pulse going, so maybe he'll be lucky," she answered.

"You ready to go back?" Owen asked.

Luke wished he could be honest about the fear that overwhelmed him. He and Owen had worked as a pair for so long, and he felt that whatever he did would let down the side. But he knew Owen well enough not to lie, though their relationship was still rather strained since that fateful dinner.

He was saved from having to decide, as the paramedic answered for him. "I think he needs to wait a while longer."

"I'm still struggling to catch my breath." It was the truth, but not the full story.

"Don't worry, stay here. I'll tell the boss."

"Thanks."

With that, Owen moved away. Luke sat where he was, not sure if smoke inhalation was the issue, but it was a good enough excuse to avoid any risk of having to go back into the building.

As he sat there wondering how to find out about Sheena, she appeared.

"Luke, are you all right?"

"I am now. I know you're safe," he said.

"I mean, did you get hurt?"

He played down his problem. "Lightheaded. I'm fine."

"Good, I came over to find out what was happening to my neighbour." She pointed to the man they were working on in the ambulance.

"He had a heart attack, but he's stabilized," the paramedic told her.

"Thanks, I'll tell his wife where he is. Then I'll come and sit with you."

He wanted to tell her not to bother to come back, but it seemed rude. Maybe he could do with her support right now, and come to think of it, she might need his. For the first time since leaving the hospital, the need for drugs and a drink hit. A sure sign he was struggling, and he didn't want his colleagues to witness him fall apart.

For a moment, he considered just walking away. But that would be chickening out. His years of training on the job meant that option was not available. If he vanished, his colleagues might think he had gone back into the building and would put their lives at risk to find him.

Owen had given him time to pull himself together. Or, perhaps, time to find the strength to continue, or to decide if it was time to quit?

Admitting he was not fit to continue was the last thing he wanted to do. Showing weakness would end his career forever, but lives might be at risk if he didn't. Not something he wanted on his conscience.

Before he worked out what to do, his boss strode over.

"Well done," he said, as he looked at the paramedic to see if he was going to enlighten him on Luke's condition. The man didn't say anything, gave a thumbs up, to indicate he was fine. "Owen tells me you went back for him, and that he'd never have got that man out without your help. No need to rush back. We've got enough men on hand for now."

"Thanks," he answered, relieved not to be pushed into returning to the fray, or into confessing his fears about his ability to continue working.

It touched him that Owen had praised him for doing what he was trained to do. Sheena said she'd come back. He could do with her company. She had taught him how important it was not to bottle things up.

Chapter 10

As he sat there, his fears escalated. He scanned the surroundings. The fire flared up again. The crew repositioned themselves to tackle the latest hot spot. The good news was that everyone was accounted for.

A gawping mob pushed against the police cordon. He hoped some of them would take home some sense of caution and make their own homes fire safe, but he doubted they would.

He wondered how long Sheena would be. He realized that while he valued her support, on this occasion, she might need support herself. It was hard to imagine what it would be like to lose everything.

He spotted her in the distance. She looked as if she was about to have a word with Owen, but someone caught hold of his sleeve and pulled him aside, into the shadow of a tree.

Sheena changed direction and plonked herself on the wall beside him. "Here." She handed Luke a takeaway cup. "Coffee. I got them to put extra sugar in."

"Thanks," he said, grateful not just for the hot sweet drink, but more for her kindness.

"I hope you put a ton of sugar in yours, too." She nodded.

"I'm so sorry. It looks like you've lost everything. If you need somewhere to stay, you can come back to my place."

"No." Her response was firm, and he knew not to press her. Then he remembered AA discouraged sponsors from accepting gifts from other members.

"Sorry, didn't mean to sound unappreciative," she said. "Someone is organizing accommodation for us."

"Great, but if that doesn't work out, I have a bed available."

He took a sip of coffee.

"Any idea who your colleague is talking to?" she asked, pointing to the pair standing in the shadow of a tree.

Luke craned his neck to look. "No, don't think so. Why?"

"I noticed he didn't look thrilled to see the man he's with. There's something familiar about him, but I can't think where I've seen him before."

She held her hand out to take Luke's empty cup. "Are you going back to join the others?"

"I'm not sure."

She didn't say anything, but sat there waiting for an explanation.

"I had a panic attack. Maybe I should opt for a desk job." She would understand what this admission meant.

"Sorry, but whatever you do, don't make a hasty decision. Sleep on it. You may feel different by tomorrow."

He nodded, and to avoid seeing her pity, looked back to check what Owen was doing. He seemed to be arguing with the man in the shadows. "Is there a camera on your phone?" he asked.

"Yes, why?"

"Can I borrow it for a second?"

Sheena handed over her phone. He stood and faced the mass of people, set the phone to take a video and panned the crowd, slowing down to capture Owen and the man at the far end of the scene. Owen's arm gestures were agitated. Luke hoped the streetlights would provide enough light to capture their faces.

He sat down again. "Thanks," he said, as he fiddled with the phone, and sent the video to himself before handing it back.

They sat on the wall and watched the flames diminishing, and the smoke gradually being reduced to an occasional wisp that was quickly dealt with.

The paramedic came back to Luke and checked him again and gave him the all clear.

Luke turned toward Sheena. "Guess I should go back to help get the equipment stowed. I can at least do that."

"I'm glad to hear it."

"Are you going to be okay? I can stay with you if you want," he said.

"No, I'm fine. I still have my phone if you need to talk about anything."

"Remember, you can call me if you need to," he said, aware Sheena was unlikely to seek his support.

She waved as he made his way back to help the crew.

Most people were pretty shattered, but not too tired to notice his return and give him a pat on the shoulder, a nod, the occasional thumbs up, enough to show they were aware he had taken time out, but also grateful to have him back. Their support and reactions touched him.

He made an extra effort to help speed up their return to base to be debriefed.

Owen worked alongside him to help stow away the gear.

"Glad you've joined us. I was worried for a while. You did well, considering it was your first big fire since you came back."

"Thanks." Luke wanted to add this was a misplaced vote of confidence. "Who were you talking to?"

Owen gave him a wary stare. "What?"

"It looked like you were arguing with a chap over by the trees."

After a moment's hesitation, Owen said, "Oh, some drunk mouthing off."

Luke wasn't convinced, but didn't dare say so. Owen wasn't the sort to engage with drunks at a shout and certainly not get into a lengthy conversation with them.

"Are you coming to the pub?" Owen asked. "I'll shout you a lemonade."

Luke nodded. "Yes, Lemonade sounds good." It had been tough putting himself in a situation where he was surrounded by people enjoying a drink. To regain the trust of his colleagues, he'd been forced to face that demon. Tonight, would be tough, as a drink was more than appealing. But seeing Sheena had made his resolve strong.

The first few times had been difficult, but now everyone accepted he was off the booze. True, some assumed he was driving, others knew he was dealing with a problem, but he no longer cared what they thought.

The pub was used to them coming in after shifts. Owen went to the bar and ordered the drinks once they had settled at a table.

Luke turned to Owen. "Sheena lived in one of those flats."

"Sheena, your AA sponsor?" Owen said softly, as if afraid someone would overhear the mention of AA.

"Yes, she's okay. Seems that some emergency accommodation is being provided."

"Good. I thought I saw her in the distance. I'll bet she's busy organizing the other residents and making sure they're sorted."

"You're probably right. That's her forte, helping others."

Owen's mobile buzzed. He took a quick look at the screen, frowned, and downed the rest of his drink. He excused himself from the group and hurried outside to take the call.

Luke took the opportunity to ask the others at the table.

"Did anyone say how the fire started?"

"No, but the forensic team has begun their search for clues. It might have started in the outside bins, but hard to pinpoint what was in them to cause the fire to spread so fast," James said. "We'll have to wait for them to complete the investigation to find out."

"Enough talk of fires for today," Owen said on his return, clutching a fresh pint.

Owen's habit of shutting down the conversations about fires worried Luke. Half the reason for going to the pub was to talk through the shift. It triggered a flashback to previous occasions when Luke asked about the possibility of arson.

With his friendship at stake, he decided not to persevere with the subject.

The conversation turned to talk about the Exeter Rugby team's forthcoming match. All the crew were fans. Luke let them get deeply into discussions about team tactics and slipped away.

Chapter 11

After that fire, Luke had a few days' leave. He needed some thinking time.

Amy phoned and asked to meet at a coffee shop in Exeter for a chat. His heart sank, thinking that she would want to discuss divorce. He drove to Southernhay, and while he paid for his parking ticket, he noticed Rupert's flashy Range Rover pull up to drop Amy off.

"Don't let him change your mind. You know it's the right decision," Rupert called out to her as she stepped away from the vehicle. Luke realized they hadn't seen him, so he turned his back on them. The last thing he wanted to do was to talk to Rupert.

Rupert's instruction to Amy set alarm bells ringing. There was a plan afoot, which he wasn't going to like.

He took the ticket from the machine, shoved it into his pocket, and waited for Rupert to drive away before walking back to his car to display the ticket. No need to let Amy know he'd overheard Rupert's instructions.

When he dug into his pocket for the ticket, he pulled out a business card. He studied it, remembering the last occasion he'd worn the jacket. It was the day he'd met Rupert for the first time, and his father had pressed the card into his hand. Unable to find a litter bin, he shoved the card back into his pocket, put the ticket in the car, and hurried after

Amy along the pedestrian walkway to the café. She was already settling herself at a table by the window. She looked more beautiful than ever. Would he ever be able to deal with the fact she was living with someone else? He leaned in and gave her a kiss on both cheeks. The waft of familiar perfume hit him, the same one he used to buy for her. His love for her was as strong as it had ever been.

He stepped back, determined not to make a fool of himself, and checked if she'd ordered. She shook her head.

"One shot cappuccino?" he asked. "Anything else?"

She smiled. "No, just the coffee."

At the counter he spotted a luscious-looking walnut cake, the one Amy loved, so he ordered their coffees and a slice of the cake, requesting two forks and a spare plate as well.

He joined her, taking his time to settle down before getting into conversation. He wanted to hear what she had to say, and didn't want to fall into a trap, certain there was a big one waiting for him.

She asked about his return to work and seemed genuinely interested in his wellbeing. He admitted getting fit was a struggle, but the changed painkillers, and cutting out booze, helped. He glossed over the difficulties he faced at work, making his life sound perfect.

Eventually, the conversation turned to the girls.

"Sorry, you've had them more often than we planned. I hope to get organized soon, and we can go back to the routine we set up before I went in for the operation," he said.

Amy bit her lip and seemed to be struggling to find the right words to respond. He recognized the sign. Something was troubling her.

"I'm guessing I won't like what you're about to suggest," he said. If Rupert was behind it, he was sure he wouldn't. He slid the plate with the walnut sponge towards her and the empty plate and offered her a fork.

"Go on, I know you can't resist." While he was desperate to know what bombshell she was going to drop, he would not rush her.

She smiled, accepted the fork, and helped herself to a mouthful and muttered, "Thanks."

An awkward silence descended as they sipped their coffees and tucked into the sticky cake the way they always had, from the same plate. Finally, he cracked.

"What won't I like?"

Their marriage had not been perfect, but he could spot when Amy had something important to say. But the fact she'd instigated this meeting was a huge clue.

"The girls' schooling."

The three words left hanging puzzled him.

"I thought they were doing okay. Did something happen?"

"No, but I've been thinking about getting them into Blundells as weekly boarders."

He stared at her. "Blundells. Are you crazy? How the hell do you expect me to find the cash for a posh private school?" As he finished speaking, he realized he'd dived in with a negative, with no time to give the idea any merit.

"Rupert says he'll pay."

Luke pictured Rupert selling her the idea. Oh yes, boarding school would suit Rupert well.

"Let's put the finances aside. I'm surprised you ever let the thought enter your head, because if I remember rightly, you always told me going to boarding school was the worst experience of your life."

Her eyes widened, and she bit her lip. "I did, didn't I?"

"Yes, so is Rupert putting pressure on? Is he that keen to have you to himself?"

"No. How could you jump to that conclusion?" she said.

"Quite easily."

"Well, you're wrong. It wasn't like that at all. We were discussing schools, and I mentioned I had been to a private school, and his father suggested it would be good for the girls to experience the same."

"I can't believe you're letting his father influence you." Luke remembered his instant dislike of the man. Why would he be keen to get the girls out of the way? What benefit was there for him?

"I'm not, but then he produced the latest brochure and introduced me to some Blundell's parents, and I got caught up with their enthusiasm and now Rupert is obsessed with the idea."

"You struggled for years to fit in. Do you really want to inflict that on your children?"

"But boarding is so different now," she pleaded. "And it will be much easier for the girls to be in one place."

It worried him that these people could brainwash her into even considering boarding as an option.

"No, it won't. You'd be adding to their problems. It's hard enough for them switching between Rupert's house and home. Why add a third place? Who benefits, other than you and Rupert?

Lucky for him, that he can afford to get them out of the way for most of the year."

"That's not what he wants."

"Are you sure? If he doesn't want them living with you, they can come home full time." He peered at her with a 'don't push me' look. "If they board, I'd see even less of them than I do now. Is that what you want? Is this a plot to cut me out of their lives altogether?"

"Of course not."

"I suppose you've asked the girls what they want."

"No, I didn't want to say anything until I had spoken to you."

"Good, because it's not happening. At least not until they reach the 6th form. If Rupert is so keen to be rid of them, I vote we swap things round. They stay with me during the week, so they can walk to school, and join in with more after-school activities. You can have them on weekends if it suits you."

"That arrangement won't fit with your crazy shifts."

"Amy, believe me, I will make it work."

Once he decided on a plan, he would stick to it, and she was aware of his determination when he set his heart on something. Since he'd returned to work, occasionally his shifts clashed, but he always organized cover. She couldn't fault him on the stability he had provided.

She was obviously in doubt as to what to do next. Rupert and his father were likely pressing her into a decision without taking into account his opinion, or that he might make Amy doubt their motives. Planting the idea that Rupert's enthusiasm stemmed from the desire to have Amy without the children was one Amy would find hard to dismiss.

What puzzled and bothered Luke was the fact Rupert's father was actively pushing the plan. He struck Luke as a bully, and he hated that he might have any influence on his family.

"I saw Owen last week," Amy said.

Fine, she wanted to change the subject, let her.

"He's glad to be working with you again."

Owen never mentioned seeing her. But then again, why would he? No one likes being in the middle when a couple split.

"He and Tamsin are going away," she added," to visit her aunt in Scotland."

"Are they? He didn't say."

"Oh, it was a sudden decision. The old lady fell and hurt herself."

Luke nodded, pretending to be interested, but unable to clear the boarding school suggestion out of his mind. He didn't care what Owen and Tamsin were up to.

"Are things okay between you and Owen?"

"Yes, fine." No need to tell her Owen was behaving rather oddly since the revelations about her affair with Rupert.

"He said you helped Charlotte with her driving practice and have been spending time with your friend Sheena at the food bank."

For a moment, he wondered if she was jealous because he was in the company of other women. She could hardly complain if he found a replacement for her, not that these two fitted the bill. Adjusting to the fact that she'd moved on was not easy.

"How's the interior decorating world suiting you?" He pushed the plate with the remains of the cake towards her to divert the conversation.

She'd left him because they wanted different things. The desire for a fancy car, a bigger house, and the freedom to buy whatever she wanted were possible reasons. His salary, even if he rose in the ranks, would never match Rupert's spending power. But maybe she just didn't feel she could cope with his injuries.

And the biggest bonus was fulfilling her dream of setting up her own business, which, thanks to Rupert's backing, had become a reality.

"Very well. Two new clients signed up this week."

Luke smiled. "You deserve to succeed."

"And I'm happy you got your job back."

He wanted to say it was not turning out as expected and he was seriously considering asking for a desk job and possibly quitting altogether. It was an option he'd take to save the girls from boarding school.

"You know it makes sense for the girls to come back and live with me. At least think about it."

"Will Charlotte be there?"

Her question surprised him. "Charlotte? What does she have to do with this?"

"I gather she spends a lot of time around your place. The girls adore George."

"He's a great kid. And, yes, she is around quite a lot. She takes Buster out every day, and steps in to mind the girls if I'm on call, same as she did when you lived with us. Believe it or not, the girls need someone around to cook their supper. Anything wrong with that?" Amy shook her head.

"It's no different," he continued, "to Rupert's housekeeper, Mrs Walker, or the cleaner minding them while you're off at a posh dinner." He decided this wasn't the moment to tell her what the girls had let slip.

"Moira, what's wrong with her?" she said.

"I think they prefer spending time with Charlotte than with that stuck up woman, or the paid staff. Ask the girls."

Amy's startled expression showed she'd never considered the prospect that the person who ran Rupert's household might not get on with the girls.

Luke regretted he hadn't brought up the subject sooner. He had been too wrapped up in his own health and work issues. But his encounters with the woman who made the staff cower resurfaced. It had shocked him they'd needed a team to manage the place. But then, with all the glass and shiny surfaces, it made sense. Even the man raking the gravel cowered when she was around and put his head down and raked faster. And he remembered the girls telling him about the pool cleaner and the babysitter who had locked them into their room while she entertained him.

He needed to talk to the girls again before he made a fuss, until then the best he could do was to have them home more often.

"I don't want you to use the staff as babysitters. If you're going out, I'd rather they came home to me."

Amy looked as if she wanted to protest, but she glanced at her watch and said, "Okay, I'll call you later. I need to go now." She reached down to retrieve her handbag.

"Amy," he said, reaching out to hold her arm before she left, "let's not fight about what's right for the girls. We messed up our relationship, but let's not mess up their lives more than we already have."

She put her hand on his. "You're right." She took a deep breath and walked away.

Luke wasn't sure if her response was that he was right about boarding school being a crazy idea, or if she was simply agreeing that they should not fight over the children's care.

Chapter 12

As Amy walked away, he noted she'd lost weight, not that she needed to. He would never dare comment in case she took it the wrong way. She had always been touchy about the subject. Her hair, cut shorter and a shade lighter, suited her. He could have complimented her on that but had to keep personal comments off the agenda. No need to turn the meeting into a minefield.

One thing surprised him. No mention of divorce. He'd psyched himself into believing that was the purpose of the meeting and was shocked at how wrong his assumption had been.

Was he mad to have let things go on for so long without having that conversation? Deep down, he feared the finality of cutting off all ties. Divorce rarely ended amicably, and might lead to having to sell the house, destroying what semblance of normality the girls enjoyed. He didn't want to give up his uncle's legacy, which he hoped to pass to his children. There was something about deep family roots that so many of his generation didn't understand. They were in too much of a frenzy to move jobs, move house, move location to feel the benefits.

Stuck in a rut? Maybe so, but it was his rut, and he was in no hurry to leave it.

Isolation made him wish he could talk to Amy the way they used to before children and all the trappings of life got in the way.

He'd wondered why Owen hadn't been round to check on him. Even though things were odd between them of late, Owen had been so consistent with following up after a shout. Amy's information about Tamsin's aunt explained his absence.

He ordered another coffee; he had half an hour to waste before his appointment with his doctor.

He'd learned enough about himself to understand he needed to discuss his crisis of confidence after the shout. He wasn't prepared to slide down the self-destruct route again. Talking to anyone at the station would end his career in a flash. He needed help to clarify if his reactions were a continuation of delayed shock from the accident or not. And to work out if he could cope with being stuck behind a desk or take on training rather than fighting fires. He didn't think he could easily give up the job that had been his passion for so long.

He'd taken the plunge and made an appointment with Dr Marsh, who was able to see him more quickly than he expected, leaving no time for second thoughts.

Henry Marsh had been his doctor for years. "Hello, Luke, wonderful to see you," he said, as he stretched out a hand to welcome him.

"I'm not so sure it is."

"Sit down and tell me what's up."

They talked about his injuries, the surgeries, and the post-operative care, leading up to Luke's admission.

"I'm having a problem at work."

Dr Marsh nodded and leaned back in his chair, forcing Luke to continue.

"A few weeks ago, I went back on watch."

Luke waited for a reaction. All he got was a raised bushy eyebrow. What was it about this man with his silent treatment that coaxed words out?

"The first few shouts were fine, a burnt-out car, someone locked out of their house, a motor accident with smashed cars, but no injuries of concern. Then we received a call out to a block of flats. The fire had spread up the building, and we had to go in to help the residents out."

Luke faltered.

"It triggered flashbacks?" Dr Marsh prompted.

"Not exactly, but we had to go back several times. The final time we struggled to carry a large man down two flights of stairs. He was having a heart attack. We got him down and handed him over to the medics. I knew I should go back into the building for the last sweep. But I couldn't."

"Someone else went in?"

"I'm not sure. I don't think so, but my partner, Owen, covered for me. Told everyone I had inhaled smoke and wasn't fit to go back."

"Not true?"

"No. I hadn't really inhaled enough to make me unfit. I was no worse off than him. Though carrying that dead weight down the stairs left me pretty breathless."

"So, Owen, your best man, if I remember correctly, made the right decision on your behalf?"

"I suppose he did."

"That's what friends and partners should do."

"Yes, but I can't help but wonder if my weakness might put someone else at risk. When the ambulance crew checked me over and suggested I might have pulled a muscle, and offered me pain relief, I was so close to saying yes, but thankfully remembered how much trouble that had put me in before. I confess I was also hankering for a drink."

"You resisted, didn't you?"

"Yes, but it was hard."

"I am going to ask you a question, and I want you to give it a lot of thought."

"Okay."

"Are you expecting me to tell you what to do, or did you come to clarify your thoughts?"

"To clarify my thoughts."

"Fine, so let me make a suggestion." He peered over his half rim glasses. "Get yourself a desk job, while you make up your mind. I know firefighting was your main focus for your recovery. No one wants to take that away from you. But you have to ask yourself, is it still the right one?"

"You think I should quit?"

"Not at all. It was a brave and sensible decision to come and talk to me today. But you said it yourself, carrying on as you are, could put people at risk. Imagine if Owen found himself having to pull you out, because you froze."

"That's what bothered me."

"That's a good sign. You're concerned. You're thinking straight. There's nothing wrong with that. We all know how much that job means to you."

"Is it wrong to pretend nothing happened?"

"Only you can decide but stick to a desk job while you do. You said you pulled a muscle in your shoulder?"

Luke nodded.

"Fine, I'll give you a sick note to cover that. I think a week off should be enough, but if it isn't, come back to me."

"Thanks. I'll do as you suggest."

Luke left the room, knowing that Dr Marsh had given him a lifeline to hang on to his career. Probably the last one. If the extra time failed, he would be out of the fire service forever. The prospect was daunting, but something he had to face.

He found a bench in the park on the way home and sat down to call his boss.

It was easier explaining his predicament than expected. Having admitted that he'd found the last shout physically demanding and had pulled a muscle in his shoulder, he asked to be taken off the rota while he improved his stamina. A tremendous wave of relief washed over him.

"I'll do whatever jobs you want at the station for a while."

"Take the rest of the week off," his boss said kindly. "We have new recruits starting next week. You can put them through the initial training sessions."

"Perfect. I'd be pleased to take that on."

"Well, thank you for your honesty about your fitness. I was concerned but hadn't wanted to press you. I know how hard you fought to come back to work."

With the decision made and time on his hands, he went to see Barry at the magazine office to discuss an idea that might make a good story.

Making a living from photography rather than being stuck with a permanent desk job in the fire service had to be investigated. He needed flexibility and a reasonable income before he did anything stupid like resign. Both offered the chance to take care of his girls rather than send them to boarding school.

Barry, keen to escape his office, suggested lunch at a café on the edge of Cathedral Green, yards away from the gutted wreck of the Clarence Hotel.

Luke chose to sit with his back to the remains of the derelict building. It had been one of the biggest fires any of the crew had ever attended, which burned on for days as they struggled to control it. The fire, which started in an adjoining building, had spread next door through the roof and on again to the hotel. Once the ancient timbers took hold, nothing stopped the fire from spreading further. Crews from the neighbouring counties had been called in to help, and they worked in shifts before the fire was finally extinguished.

Barry, who hadn't noticed his positioning, spoke for a while about his shock at the lack of information about the redevelopment of the site. He assumed that the insurance people were arguing over who was responsible.

"I'm guessing they'll rebuild the facade to look like the original." He stared up. "Shame that they had to knock that last bit down, but safety has to come first."

Luke nodded but decided not to add anything. Barry's mention of property developers made him pull out the card from his pocket.

"Ever come across a character called Frank Patterson?" he asked as he handed him the card. Barry had an encyclopaedic memory for names.

"Don't tell me he's pressuring you to sell your property? Bit of a vulture, if all I've heard is true."

"No, I met him briefly a while back, and took an instant dislike."

"Your instincts are sound," Barry said with a smile, returning the card. "Now, tell me about the family?"

"The girls are doing well."

"And Amy?"

Barry and Amy knew each other from way back. Of course, he'd ask.

"Amy and I parted company," he said, though it hurt to admit it. "She's living out towards Exmouth." He took a deep breath and added, "She moved in with Rupert Patterson, Frank Patterson's son."

Barry's brows rose a fraction. "That sucks. Is that what made you call today?"

"No, although I failed the last challenge you set, I need to know if it is possible to earn enough as a photojournalist to pack in my current job?"

"Why? Getting too tough for you?" he asked.

"I might need to find something less physically demanding."

"Well, your photos are brilliant, but there's a lot of competition."

His glum face told Luke that Barry was about to shatter his hopes. Should he stop him now, and skip hearing the negatives, but before he could say anything, Barry continued. "We only have a couple of staffers these days, because we can pick up what we want from the web so easily. Having said that, what we like is ready-done feature articles. Pictures and text combined, with an interesting story to tell. If you can tempt me with a few of those, I might consider regular commissions."

Not so negative; Luke liked that and waited for Barry to add more.

"I'd be crazy not to warn you, the income won't be steady as a freelancer. And unless you can get yourself on the magazine payroll for a paltry salary, there's no pension attached."

The warning about the lack of pension was a timely reminder of the benefits that sticking with his current job provided.

"Sorry, I'm guessing that isn't the news you wanted to hear. But if you can produce three feature-length articles with pictures in a few weeks, on whatever topics you fancy. I'll look at them and give you my honest opinion about whether you might have success in this field. If I like any of them and choose to publish, you can decide if you want to pursue the dream."

"Thanks for your honesty and for giving me a second chance."

"Remember, I said three articles. Less than that won't do. If you can't produce that many, then it's unlikely you will succeed in this business."

Luke settled the bill and waved goodbye to Barry.

His head was buzzing with ideas. One he had been thinking about was housing for homeless people. Another focused on the fire service, though he would have to be careful, and keep it rather general, or he might find himself in trouble.

He wondered what sort of story he could create around rock climbing. The subject offered several aspects, including the pleasure the kids got at the clip and climb venue for a start. But he could also delve into the more advanced climbers' thrill of getting out on a rock face and dealing with overhangs.

And for something different, the local rugby club might be an interesting source for a story. Young men dreaming of the day they might play for a club like the Chiefs.

With his head buzzing, he was pleased that his work at the station was going to be less demanding, and probably on a more scheduled daytime routine.

The only downside was facing Owen to explain his decision to step back from the front line. Owen had been the driving force in getting him back to normal, and he hated letting his friend down. But better to do that than put someone at risk.

Chapter 13

Luke wandered through Cathedral Green while he decided on his next move. The meetings with Amy and Doctor Marsh had made him accept that an alternative career was worth considering.

A few tourists milled about, most coming over to the corner to take a picture of the old burnt-out hotel. Some stopped at the quaint black and white timbered tearoom which served at tables outside on the pavement. They were reaping the benefit of no competition at this end of the square, but would suffer once rebuilding work started. Maybe he could explore the matter.

He took out his phone and made a note. If he was going to make photojournalism a success, he needed a ton of ideas to keep up with what a magazine or paper might demand. He snapped some pictures of the burnt-out building, the tearoom, and the tourists sitting on the grass relaxing. He could always come back to take better pictures when he was ready.

Time to take positive action on an idea that Sheena might be able to help him with.

He tried her phone, which went straight to message. He needed to catch up with her now, while his head was buzzing, and he was too impatient to wait for the next AA meeting to catch up with her.

His best bet was to check if she was at the food bank. It was one of their open days, so chances were she'd be there. He headed down the street and went in. Mabel, a lovely lady in her wheelchair, greeted him. He'd met her before on a previous visit with the girls, when they dropped things off at the bank.

"Sorry, I don't have anything for you today. I was really hoping to catch up with Sheena, and she's not picking up on her phone."

"Oh, she went off to buy a charger. I don't think she'll be back today."

"Do you have her address?"

"I'll go and ask."

Luke stood and waited while she disappeared through a door at the back. A young girl came in with a baby in a sling and a buggy with a sleeping toddler on board. Luke held the door open for her. His brain switched to a different plane. What had brought this young woman to the food bank? How had she got in a position where she needed this sort of support? Yet another idea for an article. But today, his focus was on finding Sheena.

Mabel returned and told him the name of the hotel.

"Pretty grim by all accounts," she said. "Sheena says there's an alternative lined up for her, but not until tomorrow."

He thanked her and headed home to take Buster for a walk. At least Buster would benefit from his enforced week's leave.

The pair of them walked back to the rather drab hotel in a shabby area of town. The grubby foyer didn't give hope Sheena would be happy here. The gruff old man behind the desk told him he couldn't take Buster upstairs. Luke gave him the option of going to check if Sheena was in or minding the dog. The lazy option won, and Luke and Buster got permission to go up together.

Sheena hesitantly opened the door.

"I was passing by and wondered if you'd like to eat out?" he said.

"Liar, nobody in their right mind passes down this street. But I'd love to join you for a meal, best offer of the day."

"Okay, so I took a bit of a detour, but the invitation stands, but it has to be somewhere Buster is welcome."

"Anywhere would be better than this dump. I was dreading having to keep myself entertained in this place."

"It's grim."

"Beyond belief, inside and outside. Take a look at the view from the window."

Luke peered through the grimy glass at the filthy backyard which competed with the take-away shop next door for the prize for accumulating the most rubbish.

From a firefighter's point of view, this was a disaster waiting to happen. He wondered what he should do. He craned his neck to check the premises further down the street; none were any better. He took out his phone and snapped a picture.

"Our choice of venue is limited." He pointed to Buster. "Would the Mill on the Exe be okay with you? I can't think of anywhere nearer."

"Sounds perfect."

"How long will you be here?"

"They've promised to find me an alternative tomorrow."

"If that promise fails, remember my offer of a bed." Her expression was enough for him to accept his offer was unlikely to be taken up. "Even as a very temporary measure?"

She shook her head.

"Just remember, the option is there if you're desperate."

"Thanks."

Once they were at the pub and had found themselves a quiet corner seat, where Buster could curl up at their feet without being in the way, Luke went to the bar to order their meal and drinks. He still found being surrounded by such a tantalizing array of choices hard. Staying sober was a small price to pay for his sanity. He glanced over at his companion. Sheena was in her late fifties; henna was keeping her grey at bay. She was a kind, uncomplicated, 'what you see is what you get' sort of person, with a heart of gold, though he was discovering Sheena didn't let anyone learn more about her than absolutely necessary. Her support had helped him, and he'd like to return the favour.

With the order done, he joined Sheena, and this time admitted how difficult he found coming to a place like this and breaking the habit of ordering a pint or a glass of wine.

"It still gets to me too," she admitted. "I was a bit surprised when you chose a pub."

"The pub research had an upside: I discovered where the food is good, and which are dog and child friendly."

"A minefield I've never had to navigate." Her wistful expression made Luke wonder what he was missing, but decided perhaps this wasn't the moment to pry.

"To be honest, I struggled yesterday. Then thought about what you were going through, and realized if anyone was likely to be pushed to take a drink, you were a candidate. Losing everything in the fire must have hit hard."

"I confess, after seeing my hotel accommodation, the temptation was there. Fortunately, I was too shattered to go out again." She smiled. "I'm touched by your concern. It can't have been easy for you to deal with the fire at the flats so soon."

He nodded. With Sheena, he didn't have to pretend.

"More than I expected. I'm taking a desk job for a while."

"You'll hate that."

"True, but I have a mortgage, and I hope it will only be temporary."

"Mortgages are monsters," she muttered, "forcing people into impossible corners."

Luke wondered what experience she'd gone through.

"Of all the possessions destroyed, what will you miss the most?" he asked.

"Precious irreplaceable photos and paperwork I accumulated doing my family history. Most of the information can be collected again if I can summon up the energy, but the original documents are gone, and copies don't have the same pull."

"I didn't know you were into family history. What started your interest?"

She looked flustered. "Oh, something someone said started me digging."

Luke noted her reluctance to explain. This made him more aware that, while she took an interest in him, he had found out very little about her. No clues as to what had led to her becoming a sponsor; all he knew was that she'd been sober for seven years—a target that felt like a lifetime away.

He still hadn't got used to accepting he'd become dependent on drugs and alcohol so easily, or over the fear that it could take over his life again if given half a chance.

"I often think I should dig into my family history if only to pass it on to the girls."

"A good idea. If you decide to do it, I can help."

Luke then told Sheena about his idea of changing his career. He also told her about the offer Barry had made, and how tempted he was.

"Three topics sound great. You might consider a piece about AA."

"I'm not sure I've experienced enough yet. All this is a bit new to me."

"It could be tricky, but I'd be happy to help you if you decide to write it."

"Actually, what I wanted to dig into is what it is like to be made homeless by fire."

"So that's why you asked me to join you?"

"Busted. But I thought we would benefit from mutual support."

She laughed. "Don't worry, I was joking. I know it's not how you work. What I like about you is your total honesty. Of course, I'll be happy to help."

"Thanks. I was also thinking of doing something about rock climbing, and one about youngsters getting the bug by going to places like Exeter Climbing Centre, where they have an area for kids to click and climb."

"What on earth is that?"

He described the multi-coloured walls with all different shaped hand and footholds, and how the kids get clipped to a safety device, which lowers them safely to the ground if they let go of the wall.

"Half the kids love the descent more than the climb itself. My kids love it. You should come and watch one day. There's a café that serves good pizza, which is a hit with the girls. They have vast areas of walls, including some with overhangs for serious climbers to train on, and to develop stamina when outdoor climbing is too dangerous."

"Sounds amazing. Any other ideas?"

"Arsonists."

Sheena raised her eyebrows. "Interesting."

"My colleagues think I'm paranoid, but I'm convinced there's an arsonist at work."

"You'll need to be careful not to give them reason to be concerned, but if you're sure, then let me help stop you from doing anything rash."

"You'd do that for me?"

"Yes, not just because you deserve a break, but because I believe you're right about there being an arsonist at large."

"What?"

"Someone wanted the tenants out of that block and had been putting us under pressure to move. I'd received several letters offering me alternative accommodation. Three families who I thought loved the place moved out in the last few months."

"Odd."

"Exactly. Which is why I'm also keen to discover exactly how that fire started," she said.

"Well, having a desk job will make it easier to delve into old files. Maybe I can spot a pattern. And if you introduce me to your neighbours, I can hear their side of things."

Sheena nodded. "I'll see what I can organize."

Chapter 14

Luke, determined to be productive while rostered off duty, pulled out his diary to make a plan. He had three articles to write and deliver, which meant research. The two articles about climbing were contenders. They would be the easiest to research, so he booked sessions to climb for himself and for the girls.

He would need Sheena's help for the third one, about people being rehoused after a fire. She had already arranged for him to meet a few of the displaced tenants of her building, which was a good start.

To tackle the arson theory, he would need evidence before writing about that particular worm-filled can. His gut feeling was not enough, but he would not let that stop him from searching for proof. So, he set about isolating images from the video footage taken on Sheena's phone and mulled over everything he knew so far. The fire at the warehouse had been the trigger. Meeting Martin had made it more real. He needed to show these images to Martin and ask if he or his contacts could identify anyone in them. It was well known that arsonists sometimes watched the results of their efforts.

After that he went to the climbing centre. Nathan, the manager, expressed delight at the chance of extra publicity, and promised to help him both with climbing and with information about the business. They chatted for a while, and Luke let on about his struggle to regain peak fitness. Nathan let slip he was a qualified physiotherapist, though he no longer worked as one, and offered to help Luke tackle the tougher climbs. And suggested that climbing would provide exercises more beneficial than those he had been doing.

"I'll make sure you don't push yourself too hard and will help you strengthen your upper body safely. Why don't we have a session right now?"

Luke was thrilled. If sessions on the climbing wall doubled up as fitness work, he could skip lifting weights at the gym. A bonus as far as he was concerned; he hated that mindless form of exercise.

They put on the necessary harnesses, and Nathan led him to the beginner's climbing wall. Luke hadn't expected to be going back to basics, but Nathan insisted and made him climb it a few times. It was almost as easy as climbing a ladder, something he had practiced enough to pass his fitness test for work.

Then Nathan suggested he climb the same wall faster and faster against the clock, timing his ascents. The continuous climbing left him breathless, to the point he couldn't argue when Nathan insisted he take a break.

"I have a few things I need to do, but I'll introduce you to Duncan. He might be an excellent candidate to interview for your article."

He called out to a tall thin man wearing a t-shirt with the centre's logo on it. As he came nearer, Luke registered his distorted face. "Duncan, can you join us here?"

The man came over. "Hi, what can I do for you?"

"I'd like you to meet Luke. He's working on regaining fitness and considering writing an article about our range of activities. I wondered if you would mind helping him. I think he would be interested to hear how climbing helped your recovery."

"Recovery?" Luke said.

"I had a massive stroke. No one thought I would get back on my feet again, let alone climb, or find employment as a part-time instructor here." One side of his face curved into a huge grin. The other half never moved. "What happened to you?"

Luke explained about his injuries, and as he did so realized this single introduction presented a storyline with more impact than he'd expected. This could easily be an additional article to add to his growing list.

"Why don't you both take a break for an hour, have a coffee and chat? Then, if you're not too sore, and you want to try the next level, Duncan can work with you."

Nathan sat with them for a few minutes as they all discussed an article about the benefits of climbing for injury recovery, and whether he would find enough to write about. He would have his own first-hand experience to draw on, and with Duncan willing to add his story it might be enough for the article, But Duncan offered to put him in touch with other people who had found similar joy from climbing against the odds.

Nathan agreed it was a great idea. As far as he was concerned, all publicity was welcome and said it was fine for Luke to take photos, as long as all the people in them signed a disclaimer, with extra emphasis on the importance of asking parents' permission before taking pictures of their children.

"Some people are quite rightly touchy about this. So do be careful."

"Don't worry, I'll be extra diligent," Luke answered quickly, grateful for the timely reminder.

Permissions presented a real stumbling block. He wanted to thank Nathan for the advice, but held back, as it would only show how inexperienced he was as a reporter.

They talked for over an hour. Luke was grateful Nathan had stopped him when he had. His arm muscles were tight, and he decided it was foolish to continue. He'd save the next level for the following day.

Nathan suggested some flex and stretch exercises to ease the tightness, and Duncan fixed a time to work with him at his next session when he would willingly answer any more questions that Luke might think of in the interim. There was so much to learn, and he saw how unrealistic it was to think these articles would be easy to produce. But it didn't dampen his enthusiasm; he was determined to hand Barry three articles by his deadline.

He smiled at the thought of having to ask the girls for permission to use them as his principal subjects for the article. Concentrating on the fun aspect and the family bond climbing generated would be the focus of the first in the series. The sport suited children of all ages; the only restriction he could see was height, as they needed to reach the hand holds to tackle a wall. Both girls loved climbing, so he didn't think they'd refuse. Amy needed to give her blessing. If he got them on board first, then she'd find it hard to object. Was that being devious? Maybe, but better than risking her being negative.

The second would be from an adult perspective. He had to complete these two articles for publication. He could then follow up these pieces with one about the difficulties of tackling overhangs and outdoor climbing. And then there would be the one on the health benefits.

Nathan, a keen climber himself, offered to help Luke with any shots he needed and to check for accuracy in his finished stories. He also promised to put Luke in touch with several more advanced climbers. Luke booked himself several sessions at different times of the day to get a real feel for the people who used the venue. Between his own climbing sessions, he'd sit and watch and learn from the others, and try to dig deeper into what they loved about the activity. Everyone was friendly and helpful. They all shared a passionate desire to scale harder challenges, whether for fitness or for the sheer joy of conquering a climb.

The girls were delighted when he told them his plans for the weekend.

He called Charlotte to arrange for her to mind Buster while they climbed.

Meeting up with Sheena was next. She agreed to meet him for lunch at an Italian restaurant on Queen Street.

"Want me to check if it's dog friendly?"

He laughed, touched by her thoughtfulness.

"Not necessary. Charlotte is minding him."

He'd deliberately picked lunchtime, as Sheena was still stuck at the dreadful hotel, and he hated eating alone himself.

Once they were settled and had ordered their meal, he got on with telling her his plans. It never occurred to him she might be less enthusiastic than she seemed before.

"I don't know. These people are going through such an upheaval. I doubt they'll want to be photographed or have time for interviews."

Her unexpected change of heart was another learning curve to be taken on board.

"I realize the timing is not perfect," he said, "but it may help to make sure they're rehoused somewhere decent in the long term." He wasn't sure anything he wrote would influence action, but hoped it would. The want—the need—to make a difference was driving him.

"Let me interview you first, then you can tell me if my questions are too invasive. Or at least help me draft better ones. I'm prepared to try anything to make sure their story is heard."

"Go on."

"Here's the list of questions I thought might work." He spun his tablet round so she could read his question list.

"Bearing in mind the awful accommodation you landed in, I wanted to focus on the need for a better plan being in place for any similar situations. Obviously none of you know the long-term strategy the authorities will come up with, so I'd like to keep following everyone's progress for a while, if only to keep their story in the news so they don't get brushed aside and forgotten."

"That might appeal." Sheena smiled.

He took that as a sign he might be winning.

"What's the next step for you? Have they found somewhere better? And what about clothes and things?"

"There's talk of a flat. I'll hear later. And I've picked up a few things at one of the charity shops to tide me over. I don't want to accumulate anything in that dump; because I don't know what bugs might lurk there."

"Can I come back and take photos of your accommodation, to show how shoddy the places on offer are?"

"Sure."

"I wanted to take a better view from your window, to pass on to the fire safety officer." As he spoke, he registered he had come up with yet another story idea to work on: dangerous backyards.

Fortified by their meal, Sheena called the family who lived on the same floor as herself and organized for him to meet them. They couldn't believe someone actually saved their parrots. Luke had no intention of owning up to the deed but was interested in finding out how the parrots were doing.

They had been slightly luckier with their temporary accommodation. Their hotel was one of a chain, away from the centre of town and better than the dingy hole Sheena had landed in.

Sheena, having made the introduction, left him to organize his interview.

The family and their three children were all crowded into one large room. Luke asked if he could take photos. They agreed, and he took a few shots which showed how cramped the conditions were for a family of five, which had a mattress on the floor for one child. Then he suggested they head to the nearby playground to allow the children to play on the swings while they talked. The parents, who had up to now been too shocked to think beyond clothing, eating, and sleeping arrangements, were happy to escape the confines of the room. It seemed they hadn't thought about what facilities might be available in the area for the children, who desperately needed to burn off some energy. The kids wasted no time in abandoning the adults to enjoy the playground equipment.

Luke took it slowly. He wanted to bond with these people and not scare them off by appearing too nosy about their circumstances.

"Great kids." He liked that they helped each other on and off various structures.

"Yes, thanks for bringing us here. We had no idea there was anything like this so near."

"What happened to the parrots?" he asked.

"Who told you about that?"

"Sheena."

"The parrots are as much members of the family as the kids. I couldn't believe it when a firefighter came out carrying the cage. The family would have been heartbroken if we'd lost them along with everything else."

"Where are they now? Not in the hotel with you?" Luke asked, careful not to let on he was the rescuer. They were talking to him as a journalist, not as a firefighter, and he didn't want to blur the boundaries.

"A friend is taking care of them."

He asked about how they were coping with possessions and was reassured to hear clothing was not an issue, as friends had provided them with enough for the moment. Though replacing school uniforms was going to be expensive.

The distance from the children's nursery and school was a problem which they hadn't resolved, and the reason the children were not at school. They hadn't managed to organize transport yet and felt the children were still in shock from the entire event.

"I wish we'd moved when they offered us an alternative a few months ago," the wife said to her husband.

Luke's curiosity went on high alert. He wanted to know more, but held back, reminding himself not to rush them. He waited in case they would add more.

"I told you I didn't trust the guy. I doubt anything he offered would be any better than what we had," the man answered, seeming to forget that Luke was present.

"The Bakers liked the place they went to," his wife snapped back.

"Yes, but it was smaller and miles away from where we wanted to be. Remember, we agreed to stick it out, hoping they'd improve their offer."

She pursed her lips, obviously remembering their decision.

Luke decided now was the moment to remind them of his existence.

"What offer?" he asked, trying not to sound too keen. Sheena had mentioned someone had been trying to encourage the tenants to leave.

"Oh, some company kept delivering letters, offering us somewhere more modern, just a few miles away. Apart from the Bakers, I don't think any of the other residents who agreed to move are happy with the swaps they made. The new flats they went to are far from perfect, and some wish they'd stayed where they were," the wife said.

"Right now, I'll bet they are glad they made the move. Otherwise, they would be stuck in a hotel like us. All the flats in the block they moved to are full," her husband fired back.

Luke made a note: an article about expectations of a new building might be worth investigating. "You don't remember the name of the company that sent the letters?"

"No, once we decided we weren't interested, the kids used them to draw on the back of them, before they got chucked," she said.

Luke could imagine the scenario. Excellent use of unwanted mail. Another topic. This was ridiculous. He was creating topics out of anything and everything. But it was what he'd need to do to make a living from photography and writing.

"You've been so kind to talk to me," he said, thinking he had heard enough for now, and not wanting to overstay his welcome.

"What made me really cross was while the fire raged, I saw that creepy bastard in the crowd. I thought he'd come to help, but when he realized I'd clocked him, he vanished," the wife said.

Luke's curiosity was now on full alert. "Can you remember his name?"

"No, he wasn't the sort to bother with introductions."

Luke pulled out the photos he'd printed from the video taken on Sheena's phone. Was he mad? What were the chances? Still, he had nothing to lose by trying.

She scanned the pictures and pointed at one. "That's the guy."

There was no hesitation. Her husband took a moment longer and confirmed her choice.

He thanked them for their help. Best to quit while he was ahead. But he couldn't resist asking if they had the Bakers' contact address.

"Of course," she said, and rattled off the details.

He promised he would keep in touch and left them in the playground, fully intending to follow their progress.

Their recognition of the man seen in the crowd after the fire was a bonus he never expected.

He called Sheena to thank her, and she gave him details of another couple who were prepared to talk to him. Then she passed on her good news.

"They found me a tiny flat and I can move in tomorrow. The location makes up for its deficiencies. And I am only tied to a three-month lease, which will give me time to check out for other options if I find it too claustrophobic."

Luke reminded her he wanted to take photographs of her temporary accommodation. "I'll come over in the morning before you check out and take the photos while I'm there."

He made a call to the other tenants she had lined up for him. These were people who had moved before the fire, and they were more than happy to tell him how disappointed they were with their new flat. The alternative accommodation had so many flaws. None of which had been put right. They couldn't even find out who owned the building. The outpouring of anger meant Luke was glad he had recorded their conversation. Was he really ready or in a position to fight their cause for them? He made no promise, but was happy to let them forward copies of correspondence between them and their landlord, along with a copy of the letter they had been sent encouraging them to move. They begged him to investigate, as no one was listening to their complaints.

He emailed the photo of the man identified at the fire and got further confirmation he had been the one who persuaded them to move.

They thought his name was Joe.

Chapter 15

Interviews and getting deeply involved with the crowd at the climbing centre filled Luke's week, along with writing the first drafts of his articles.

The girls were coming for the weekend, which meant he could tackle the fun part, spending time with them, and getting all the photos he needed to complete the first of his climbing series.

He figured that he'd start by showing the enjoyment climbing offered.

Duncan's story was fascinating, but he would cover the fun part of climbing first to get readers on board, before tackling the article devoted to mastering overhangs, and getting out onto actual rocks. After that, he guessed he could write about different places one could go to. The therapeutic benefits might need to be targeted to a different magazine.

The time off work had been a bonus, giving him a chance to prove he could turn his hand to journalism. It hadn't been easy, but he was pleased with what he had done so far.

He had also written an article about being made homeless by fire and selected the photos for that one.

The weekend challenge was to ensure the girls were as enthusiastic as he was, and to get the photos to go with his words.

The girls would be back at five and he checked the fridge was stocked with their favourite treats. He'd even picked up a cake for when they got home.

He still missed the smell of Amy's baking. She used to bake often, though he hardly ever got to taste her cakes because, more often than not, she'd whisk them off to a school or charity event. He couldn't remember when her baking stopped. What else had he failed to notice? No wonder she looked for attention elsewhere.

He looked forward to the house becoming noisy again. The girls loved having music playing, or the TV blaring, and he missed the chaos created by his two energetic preteens when they stayed with Amy. Their coats festooning the banisters; their boots abandoned in the hallway; the crumbs scattered in the kitchen when they raided for snacks brought the house alive.

He preferred a lived-in home feel, quite the opposite of Amy's minimalist style. She constantly tried to make the place match the images portrayed in glossy magazines. It drove him nuts. Much as he loved her, there was no denying Amy was a control freak, and wouldn't settle until everything was in the right place. Nothing relaxing about that. A touch of chaos suited him better, and the girls seemed happy with the relaxation of the rules.

Not that he discouraged them from bringing their plates back to the kitchen and putting them by the dishwasher. A habit he appreciated, as it did away with the need to search the house for dirty dishes.

He didn't rate as a cook, so would often let them choose whether to have pizza, a Chinese take-away, or fish and chips, which of course had to be eaten out of the wrappers. Amy was never keen on any of these options, so it was a treat for the girls, and came with the bonus of more time for sporty things.

Tonight, he'd invited Sheena to join them. It was the first time she'd accepted his frequent invitations to come and meet the girls. He also hoped to quiz her for more information about the company that owned the flats. Some of her contacts had displayed reticence to open up, and he wanted to understand what caused it.

Katie and Janet were more excited than usual, and when he told them about the climbing sessions he'd booked, they flung their arms around him with delight. He told them about his plan to write an article with pictures and asked if they were happy to help.

Katie was quick off the mark with the question, "What should we wear?"

"What you normally wear."

"But you want the photos to look good, don't you?"

He could sense what was coming next.

"We should wear something bright to make us stand out," she said. He wondered when she had become so savvy.

"Yes, but I don't want people to think they have to spend lots on equipment and clothing to make climbing fun."

"Oh," she answered, her frown a sign she didn't like his answer.

"But an excellent call about colour," he said, to soften his response.

She smiled, enjoying that he appreciated her input.

"Tell you what. At the first session, you wear your usual clothes, and I will take some photos of you in them. Then we will get some more cheerful things for your Sunday session, when we have the place to ourselves and I can really focus on you, without other people in the frame."

"You'll take us shopping?" Janet asked. The panic in her voice was a timely reminder of his hatred of entering clothing stores and how badly he had handled a trip earlier in the year, when he dragged them out without giving them a chance to look at, let alone buy anything.

"Should I ask Charlotte to help?" It was the best solution he could think of.

"Yes, please," they answered in unison.

"Fine, I'll ring her later. But we need to decide what to have for supper. My friend Sheena is going to join us. She's offered to collect whatever we choose on her way."

Katie was quick to ask, "What do you think she'd prefer?"

It pleased him she would consider their guests preference rather than her own. "I'm not sure. I'll ask her. Then make sure she gets what she enjoys."

Content with his response, they disappeared into their rooms with their school things, leaving him to make the calls.

Sheena chose Chinese, and he told her which dishes the girls liked best.

Then he called Charlotte. "Hi, I need your help to take the girls' clothes shopping tomorrow for climbing clothes. Last time I took them was a disaster."

"I heard. Don't worry, I can help. I was expecting you'd need me to mind Buster. What time suits you?"

"When do the shops open?" He filled her in on his timetable for the day and asked how it would fit with her, and said he'd sit outside the shop with George and Buster.

With a plan made, he set the kitchen table for dinner. It was something he preferred to do. It meant the TV was not on, and the girls were encouraged to talk to him and each other. He didn't want them to become glued to a screen like many families he had encountered over the years.

Supper was a success. Sheena got on with the girls, and the conversation flowed easily, with lots of laughter.

When they finished eating, he showed Sheena the annex.

"I know it's full of junk at the moment, but once I've cleared it out, I could let it, giving me an income to tide me over if I have to leave the fire service."

"It looks promising, but it needs a lot of work to get it up to scratch."

"I might cajole some lads into helping to move the heavy furniture. Then I can work out what needs to be done."

"Good luck with it." He sensed from her tone that she thought he needed more than a bit of luck.

The next day, they set off early and met up with Charlotte in the shopping precinct.

"Cheeky question," Luke said after greeting her, "but would you be happy to be photographed for my article?"

"I don't see why not? Climbing has been the best post-natal fitness routine ever."

"That never entered my head, but a fantastic angle. I'm hoping the girls will pick out something bright that will be eye-catching in the photos. Please, pick something out for yourself."

"I can't do that."

"Consider it payment for your time. I really need someone who I can ask to stay still while I focus on the shots, and who won't object to being in print."

"Do I get to approve the photo you use?"

"Yes."

"Deal."

George was asleep in his buggy, and Luke was happy to mind both the child and the dog while the girls shopped.

Luke surveyed the riot of colour in the window display of the chosen shop. A mass of giggling teens huddled round the doorway.

Charlotte tapped him on the arm. "I could stay here with George and Buster, and you can go in with the girls." Her smile gave away that she was teasing him and the girls.

Katie and Janet shook their heads and looked pleadingly at him, making it so obvious they didn't want him, let alone need him, in there.

He looked at the girls. "If it's okay with you, I'd rather you took my place. Just remember you're looking for eye-catching climbing clothes, nothing else."

"We can swap places when it's time to pay," Charlotte said with a cheeky grin.

"Enjoy yourselves." He took hold of the buggy handle and pointed to a bench nearby, where he would wait. Charlotte nodded and followed the two excited girls into the shop.

At times like this, he appreciated a woman's touch. Charlotte would make sure they got something suitable, something practical, and not outrageously expensive. The number of times Amy went shopping and came home with things they would never wear, or need, had driven him mad.

Even the girls knew when something was not right for them. They would shake their heads and Amy would look cross and put the things back in the bag to exchange them. He wondered if she did it on purpose to give herself an excuse to go shopping again on the pretext of returning goods, because she never came back empty-handed.

He thought about their conversation, and her new business venture, made possible through Rupert's generosity. Was she motivated by the desire to have her own income, or looking to relieve boredom? It would be interesting to discover what drove her to make the dream reality. She had an eye for detail, which she had used to great effect in their home. But would her clients be happy? He hoped so; Amy would thrive on success.

He had lost track of time when Charlotte returned, looking very pleased.

"Mission accomplished. I think you'll approve of their dazzling and cheerful, and practical choices. They should brighten up your article."

"Thanks." He handed her Buster's lead and let her take his place on the bench. The girls waited by the cash desk, hugging the things they wanted him to pay for. Katie pushed Janet ahead.

Had she expected him to complain about her choice? A brilliant green top was first, and some black and green zigzag patterned leggings were next, topped by a pair of trainers and some socks, and a pair of fingerless gloves. He wondered what else might have been thrown in. A lovely, zingy adult-sized orange top followed. Charlotte would certainly be eye-catching in that. He took a sneaky peek at the total so far. Less than he expected. Charlotte's restraining influence, for sure. He said nothing.

Katie took her place and pulled out her selection. She had gone for a similar set to Janet, but her items were a dazzling turquoise instead of green. The two colours looked fantastic together. He could picture them up there on the wall, and the photos he would take.

Nathan had agreed to open an hour earlier on Sunday morning for them, to give him a chance to get them to pose, without the risk of other children appearing in the shot; a mistake that could end his journalism career in a nanosecond.

The girls couldn't wait to try on their new outfits and get climbing, but he convinced them to save them for the proper shoot the following day. Today was going to be practice only, with them trying out different walls and figuring out the best angles for him to take their pictures. They seemed content with his plan, and persuaded Charlotte to come to watch. She could take Buster home, and then come back and meet them there to see their progress.

When they got to the clip and climb venue, the girls put on their harnesses, and Luke donned a helper's jacket, prepared to assist the children to attach the safety ropes to their harnesses. He attached the neck strap to his smallest camera, so he could take shots of the girls while they climbed to work out what angles would be both flattering and informative.

All his research had added benefits. Apart from getting dozens of photos, he picked up some valuable tips for himself about how to tackle some of the trickier stretches, which might help him master one of the smaller overhangs that had defeated him in the past.

Charlotte came back to watch and get an idea of what to expect when it was her turn to be photographed.

The girls were also going to try climbing on the main wall, so he booked an extra session with an instructor, especially for them. He briefly thought about teaching them himself, but decided it was a bad idea. If they didn't get on with it, he didn't want to be the one to blame. He'd watched the instructor teaching another pair of kids the week before and been impressed with his patience and gentle coaxing techniques that built a child's confidence; just what he wanted for his girls. If they did well, they might try a proper rock face together.

He sat with Charlotte and watched them from a distance.

"I hope you've picked a hunky rope guy for my photo shoot," Charlotte said with a cheeky grin. "I don't think many of this crowd fit the profile that the magazine you're writing for will want." Her gaze fixed on a rather wiry looking man with uncombed grey hair sticking out at all angles.

Luke scanned the room and laughed. She was quite right; none of the climbers there would enhance the article.

"I might ask James," he said.

"James? Do I know him?"

"No, but I'm sure you'll get on. He's coming over to the house later to help clear the annex. Come back with us for lunch. You can meet him then, and if you approve, I'll ask him."

Luke had never really thought about Charlotte's single status, and now wondered if introducing her to James would seem like a setup to her. He remembered being told George's father took off when she announced she was pregnant, and she'd never mentioned a significant other in her private life.

The girls buzzed with excitement when they finished their session, each vying to get his attention about whether he'd seen them do some amazing stretch or their fastest descents.

"Enough," he said. "Get your things, and we'll get an ice cream to eat on the way home."

That was enough to spur them into action to grab their coats and race to the door, while still trying to get arms into their coat sleeves. He loved their excitement; he had worried that facing the big wall could set them up for failure.

They crossed the road by the quayside. Charlotte stopped by a seat near the old tram turntable while the girls debated what flavour they preferred. George, content as usual, watched the pigeons fluttering about them.

Charlotte produced a bag of homemade flapjacks. "Need something to restore your energy while you decide?"

The girls nodded enthusiastically and quickly dug into the bag for a treat. Charlotte smiled and offered the bag to Luke.

"You too."

"Thanks," he said. "You know how to make this lot happy."

As he said it, he remembered Amy's veiled hints that Charlotte was more than just a dog minder and babysitter to the family and realized the truth. She had become a close friend, a reliable one at that. And he was glad to have her in their lives. But no way was he ready for anything more. Though he could see how an onlooker could jump to the wrong conclusion.

The girls had barely brushed the crumbs off their lips when they pulled him over to the ice cream vendor. He dug into his pocket for cash and, as he handed it over, he spotted the mystery man who had been in the photos.

The man strode along the quayside with an uneven gait.

With the purchase complete, Luke hurried the girls back to Charlotte.

He pulled out his phone and showed her the picture.

"Do you think that's the man in this photo?"

"Yes. Why?"

"I've been trying to locate him all week. I need to go after him to see where he goes."

"Don't worry, I can take Katie and Janet home."

Chapter 16

Luke ran to the corner of the building to catch up with the man he now thought of as Joe, though he had no proof it was his name.

He was so glad Charlotte had taken charge of the girls, as he wouldn't have been able to follow with them in tow. Especially if the man took the bridge over the river towards the city centre. He caught sight of him just as he reached the bridge, but he didn't go over it. Instead, he headed on down the road, towards St Thomas' shopping mall. Luke slowed down, not wishing to spook the man.

They went ahead at a steady pace. As they approached the traffic junction, Luke sped up. He couldn't afford to lose him if the lights changed before he crossed the road.

The man reached the crossing and pressed the button for the traffic lights. Luke held back, pretending to tie his shoelaces. The lights changed and Luke rushed to cross before the lights reverted to red. Joe never looked back, so Luke felt safe following at a closer distance to avoid losing him amongst the shoppers.

They passed all the chain store branches in the shopping complex and out onto Cowick Street. Luke eased back and kept sight of his quarry.

Cowick Street was one of those areas with the feel of a small village, which he supposed it had once been, before being swallowed by Exeter itself.

There was an older, rather dated shopping centre, with an odd mix of shops. But Joe didn't cross the road to it. He carried on, passing the numerous charity shops that lined the street. A true recycling haven, the perfect location for some of the stuff he had to get rid of from the annex.

How far was he going to have to go to learn anything about this man? He was determined not to give up. His only commitment was with James, who was due round for lunch, but Charlotte and the girls would entertain James if he didn't get back in time.

Joe crossed the road near the Tesco store. Luke slowed down, trying to work out where to wait if Joe went into the shop. He didn't, instead he kept on, crossed the side street, and went into the pub on the corner. Luke ducked into the store and grabbed a newspaper, paid with a swipe of his card at the self-service till, and strolled over the road into the pub. His stop had given Joe time to get himself a pint and settle at a table overlooking the main road. Luke ordered a coffee and found a seat towards the back of the pub, making sure he could still watch Joe. He scanned the paper, glad to have something to occupy him while he waited. A few minutes later, Frank Patterson entered the pub, waved at Joe, ordered a drink, and joined him.

Luke took out his phone, set the video going, and lifted it to look as if he was taking a call. He wanted to capture them together, without them being aware of his actions. How he wished he could hear their conversation. But he didn't dare move closer. Frank was the sort who would be good at remembering faces and would recognize him if he drew attention to himself. Not a risk he wanted to take.

He checked the footage. Both men were clearly in the frame. As soon as he finished his coffee, he got up and left by the back door. He made his way back towards the river and called home. Charlotte answered.

"Sorry, tell the girls I'm on my way now."

There was a taxi rank by the shops; he was glad to see one was waiting for passengers and took it.

Charlotte and James and the girls were in the garden playing with a Frisbee. George was on a rug in the middle of the lawn giggling with excitement at the activity going on around him.

As soon as Charlotte spotted him watching them all, she pulled out of the game and came to stand beside him.

"Hi. Sorry, I think I dropped a clanger. Amy called in with Katie's swimming kit, which she needs for school on Monday. She asked where you were. She seemed annoyed that you weren't home, so I told her you were following a man you had seen behaving suspiciously at a recent fire."

"And..."

"She totally lost it, started ranting on about you being paranoid about arsonists. James overheard the conversation. I could tell he wanted to say something, but he didn't. I don't think she would have been interested in his opinion. In fact, his presence spun her off in a different direction as she demanded to know what he was doing at the house."

"What did he say?"

"He told her he'd come to help clear the annex."

"How did she react?"

"Something along the lines of you being crazy, to think you can make the place habitable. Rupert was waiting outside. He honked the car horn, so she left."

"I'll bet you were glad to see her go."

"Yes, but after she left, James, shocked by her comments, filled me in on things Owen had said about you being paranoid. He thought Owen's response was rather odd and wondered why. He suspects several recent fires resulted from arson, but having seen Owen's reaction to you, hasn't dared voice his concerns."

"You and James have confided in each other rather freely, considering you only just met."

She smiled. "I'd be happy to have him at the other end of a rope."

"Did you ask him?"

"No, but I hope you will," she said. "Perhaps after lunch, when I take Buster for his walk, you can talk to James while you sort out the annex."

Her tact amazed him. So refreshing from someone so young.

"Sounds like a good plan," he answered. Yes, a very good plan indeed.

He checked with James that he could stick around and asked if he'd help with his climbing article and be in the photos.

The enthusiastic reaction to the prospect of climbing with Charlotte resulted in a string of questions about her.

"Stay and eat with us this evening. I'll ask Charlotte to stay too." That was the easy way out of answering the questions. Let James ask her himself.

He agreed. Charlotte accepted his invitation to join them with a huge smile. A quick discussion and a vote for what sort of take away they would order followed, and Charlotte rounded up the children and set off to walk the dog.

James got to work, shifting the heavy wardrobes and boxes that would have tested Luke's strength. He did it all without even breaking into a sweat. Faster than expected, they rearranged the furniture and a clearer vision emerged of what needed to be done to get the place habitable again. They put an enormous pile of boxes and bags to one side for recycling. The charity shops in St. Thomas were the perfect place to distribute them. James loaded Luke's car with a selection to be delivered later.

While they worked, they talked about his climbing articles. Luke was nearly ready to broach the subject of arsonists over a hard-earned cup of tea when Sheena appeared.

He introduced her to James and showed her the improvement made so far in the annex. Her enthusiasm was encouraging, and she had a few helpful suggestions for tweaks to the furniture arrangement that made a difference to the feeling of spaciousness to make it a desirable property to rent.

They all moved to the kitchen, and Luke put the kettle on. Charlotte and the girls burst back into the house, wrecking the opportunity to bring up the subject of arson. He'd wait until after they'd eaten.

"Sheena, can you stay for supper? We're having curry. I can easily order an extra dish. I'd really like you to stay, as there is something I want to talk to you, James, and Charlotte about after dinner."

"Sounds too intriguing to refuse," she answered. "And you know I'm a sucker for curry."

Luke phoned and added a dish to his order. The girls roped Sheena and James into playing a game of Monopoly.

Charlotte stood by Luke in the kitchen while she warmed up some milk for George and asked, "Are you okay? Did you talk to James about what I told you earlier?"

"Not yet. I want to talk to you all when the girls are not around, Sheena, too. She's as much a part of this as anyone. Can you stay for a while?"

"Of course, I can. Once I've fed George, he'll go to sleep. He doesn't care where he is when he drops off. Has this got to do with the man you followed today?"

"Yes. I'll explain later."

The microwave pinged, and Luke went to check if the girls were beating his guests at Monopoly.

The food arrived and as they sat round the table eating, Luke remembered the dinner at this table when he had found out about Amy's affair. He decided not to let the memory stop him from enjoying having company in the house again.

Chapter 17

The girls, though tired, were excited about the next climbing session, and as soon as they'd finished eating, excused themselves and went off upstairs to get ready for bed. He was lucky they had established such a good routine early on, and they rarely fought against it. Other families he knew never cracked the going to bed routine, and never enjoyed an evening without children about.

Luke made coffee and braced himself to share his information with his guests. He decided to be up front and hoped James would add to it without being pushed to do so.

"James, I gather when my wife came around earlier, she got angry about me following a man I'd seen at a fire. She's convinced I'm suffering from paranoia, and to be honest, for a time, I almost believed it."

James nodded but said nothing. Sheena frowned, puzzled as to where the conversation was going. Charlotte busied herself pouring the coffee.

"You warned me a while back that Owen suggested this to you," Luke continued. "I'll always be grateful that you told me. And for saying he might blame himself for my injuries. You were close to the truth. He does. But that wasn't what wrecked our friendship. He knew my wife was having an affair and that complicated things. Or at least, that's what I believed. Now, I'm not so sure."

Luke stopped, took a sip of his coffee.

"I'm convinced there's an arsonist at work. Sheena thinks so too. I've been following up a few leads, and with her help, I've made a connection to a property developer who I think is involved with the burnt-out properties. Today, I followed a suspicious character seen at two recent fires, including the one at Sheena's block of flats. He met up with this developer."

"Who?" Sheena asked.

"I'll tell you in a minute." He turned to James. "Charlotte says you're worried about an arsonist. Is this true?"

James nodded. He pulled his phone out of his pocket.

"You came into the pub while you were off sick and asked Owen about what started the fire at that warehouse. His reaction was a bit off. You'd been injured. It was only natural for you to be curious. After you left, one of the older crew members asked him why he didn't tell you arson was suspected. He said your doctors were concerned that you had become paranoid about the fire."

"He kept changing the subject every time I asked about the fires. I couldn't figure out why. Then you told me about the paranoia rumour."

"Yes, but why not tell you the truth rather than deny it? His shutting you down made me curious. I discovered he did the fire inspection for that property. That made me wonder if he was afraid that if you made a fuss, an investigation might highlight failings in his report."

"Interesting."

"Anyway, as you were recovering and due back at work, I kept quiet. But on the next shout we went to, I was on alert about how the fire started. I was pretty sure it was arson again, but the report came up with an electrical fault as the cause. Owen signed it off. I checked and discovered he'd done the building inspection a few months before. That's when I started taking photos at every shout I went to. Like you, I wanted to make sure the fires stopped. The trouble is, I'm still considered to be a new recruit, so I didn't know who to take the information to. Now I fear it's getting out of control. The last three fires have me worried. If we continue ignoring the problem, there will be deaths."

"Can I see your photos?" Luke asked. Additional photographic evidence was an unexpected turn of events, and one which might resolve some of his concerns.

"I'll email them to you, then you can view them on a bigger screen." He tapped on the dial of his phone, and moments later Luke's computer pinged to tell him he had mail, followed by three more pings.

Charlotte got up. "I'll check on the girls."

"I'll come up in a moment," Luke said as he opened his laptop and clicked on the first file James had sent.

He watched the brief video clips saying nothing. He wondered what James was thinking and wanted to hear his thoughts before he shared his own.

"I need to go up and give the girls a kiss goodnight, then I want you to talk me through your observations. Is that okay with you?"

James was quick to say, "Yes."

"Do you mind if Sheena looks?"

"No."

Luke spun the laptop round and slid it across the table to face Sheena. "Tell me what you see after hearing James' thoughts," he said.

Sheena nodded and tapped the screen to activate the first of the videos.

Charlotte reached the end of the chapter of the book she was reading to the girls, and they snuggled down to sleep after he kissed them goodnight.

He hurried back downstairs, Charlotte with him.

Luke asked her if she had seen the videos. She nodded.

"Good. So, James, please tell us what you observed."

They moved their chairs so they could all see the computer screen. James set the first video going. He paused the screen and pointed out a man in a dark coat, standing by a tree. "This chap seems to appear at most fires. I know fires attract crowds. And the same people regularly pitch up, but this one never stands at the best vantage point. He's always tucked away in the shadows." James tapped the play button again and further on froze the picture. "And this guy I've seen him talking to Owen at two fires. Sorry, it's not the best image of him. I have a better one on one of the other videos."

Luke recognized the men: the man in the shadows was Frank Patterson; the second was the character reportedly called Joe.

James set the video off again and once more froze it. "Lastly, there's this character. He's less shy. He's a regular onlooker. Having picked these three out, I look out for them. And sure enough, they're always there. But more interesting is that I've seen Owen talking to each individual at different times."

Luke said nothing and let him play all his videos. When he finished, Luke selected the video he had taken on Sheena's phone and played it for James to watch. The same characters appeared and now James saw the well-dressed man and Frank Patterson in the same frame. They knew each other. What was their connection? That was something he needed to dig into.

Sheena must have read his mind because she said quietly, "He's a planning officer."

Luke let the information sink in. Of course, Frank would know the local planning officer. He'd be bothering the planning department regularly.

"What about the other two?" James asked.

Luke pulled up a picture of the first character on his phone. "Meet Joe, first identified as a man who delivered letters to flat residents, encouraging them to move to new housing. I followed him today, and he met up with Frank Patterson." He tapped his phone and showed the photo of the two men having a drink together.

"Who's Frank Patterson?" James asked.

"The father of my wife's lover."

He couldn't believe he had described him like that.

"A property developer with an interest in all the properties," he continued. "A pretty obnoxious man, if my single encounter with him is anything to go by. At the moment, I can only guess Joe handles the fires, though whether he actually sets them is unclear. Frank probably orchestrates it all, and maybe the planning officer gets a hefty cut to grant permits to redevelop. As far as Owen is concerned, I didn't know he'd done the fire inspections. That's something to check, but without proof of his involvement, we can do nothing."

"Agreed," Sheena said. "James, you've given us some valuable information. But as Luke says, we can do nothing without absolute proof."

"I understand," James answered.

"I don't know about you, but I'm ready to head home." Sheena stood and picked up her bag. "We have an early start tomorrow. I need some sleep if I am to mind George. I'll be back here at eight o'clock, as planned."

"You're right," Charlotte said, as she picked up her cup to take it to the kitchen.

"Can I drive you and George home?" Luke offered.

"No, it's not far, and you can't leave the girls alone."

"Don't worry," James said, "I'll walk with Charlotte and make sure she gets there safely."

Luke didn't argue, but stopped her from trying to clear up. "Go now. I want you at your best tomorrow."

Luke waved them all off, and then cleaned the kitchen, bagged up the empty take away cartons and filled the dishwasher. The day had not gone as he expected, but he had no complaints.

The people responsible for these fires were clever. James had made a list of the supposed causes of fires in the last few years. A bonfire out of control, a carelessly stored barbeque, a rough sleeper's cigarette, a broken glass creating a magnifying prism, an electrical fault; the list was endless and without duplication. All were virtually impossible to prove, but sufficiently different that the insurance companies hadn't flagged similarities.

Chapter 18

Luke was thrilled at the way the girls behaved while he photographed them. They were brilliant models, which made it easy to capture some amazing shots.

The time came for the adults to climb. Charlotte and James worked as a team as if they had been paired for years. The chemistry between them came out in the photos. Luke never expected that his introduction would be such a resounding success. So successful that after the photo session was over and they set off for home, James came with them. Sheena came too.

When they reached the house, James still seemed reluctant to leave, and offered to move more stuff for Luke. They filled Luke's car with bags and boxes for him to take to the charity shops, and Luke didn't argue when Sheena volunteered to go with him to help unload. As they reversed out of the driveway, she opened up.

"James is lovely. I've never seen Charlotte look so happy in all the time I've known her," she said. "I think we might be in for some babysitting duties."

"He's a nice guy, and I'm thrilled they've clicked. Long may it last. And yes, I'm more than happy to help them spend time together."

With the charity shop delivery done, Luke stopped off to pick up lunch for everyone. On the way home, he checked with Sheena if she'd like to rent the annex. "Surely it would be perfect for you, and you'd be my first choice as a tenant."

"I love it, but not for me."

"Please, can you help find someone who'd like it? I know you'll pick someone who will fit in."

"You met Mabel last week. She's the one who offered to mind Buster while you helped me stack those shelves. Her hip operation keeps getting postponed, and she really needs a ground-floor flat. I think with her mobility scooter, she'll be close enough to the shops and her friends. Shall I tell her about the property?"

"She sounds perfect."

"I'll take some pictures to give her an idea of how big it is, and if she's interested, I'll bring her over."

"Good plan. Someone who loves Buster would be ideal."

"I'll see if she can come over tomorrow." Sheena said. She looked across at Charlotte and James in deep conversation in the garden and smiled.

"Do you think they need time alone?" he asked.

"Too early for that. I don't think Charlotte will jump into a relationship without being sure it is right. She has George to think of, and being surrounded by dogs and children is a great way to get to know him without it getting too personal."

"If you say so, I'll go along with whatever you suggest."

Once lunch was over, Sheena asked Charlotte what she had planned for the afternoon.

"Nothing. I expect Luke will want to sort out his climbing article. I'm happy to mind the children and take them to the park."

"Can I tag along?" James said.

Charlotte smiled. "Sure."

Sheena gave Luke a knowing smile.

"That would be a great help," Luke said. "I need to meet my deadline."

"I'll head off and talk to Mabel and sound her out."

With everyone's afternoon organized, Luke cleared the plates and watched them head off on their chosen pursuits. Then he picked out the best photos, resized them to fit the page and wrote the text to go with them.

Halfway through the first batch, the doorbell rang.

Owen stood on the doorstep, looking awkward. Luke forced a smile, resenting the interruption to his work. He invited him in intending to inquire after Tamsin's aunt. Not that he really cared. Owen's absence had suited Luke, as he didn't think he'd be able to keep quiet about the connection he and James had made between him, and the suspicious characters photographed at the fires. Or that Owen had done the fire inspection for the burnt-out properties.

"What a pleasant surprise," he said, wishing he meant it. "Coffee?"

Owen nodded and followed him to the kitchen. They exchanged chat about the trip to sort out the aunt. Luke told him he had made some progress with clearing the annex and how helpful James had been.

"He's met my dog sitter, Charlotte. I think he might be round here a lot more," Luke said, glad that there was a perfect excuse for James calling round so much.

"I hear you're still chasing your phantom arsonist," Owen said.

Luke grabbed a packet of biscuits and offered them to him while he worked out how to reply. He wanted to ask who told Owen, but guessed Amy had said something. He'd be foolish to deny the truth, since Charlotte had let the information slip the day before.

"Oh, I thought I saw someone I'd seen in the crowd." Luke went to his coat and dug into the inside pocket and pulled out the picture of Joe and handed it to Owen. "This guy? Do you know him?"

Owen studied the photo, shook his head, and put it down on the counter.

"What makes you suspect him?" he asked.

"I keep seeing him in the crowd at almost every fire we've been to lately. Are you sure you've never noticed him?"

Owen studied the picture again. "Sorry, when I'm at a fire, the last thing I focus on is the onlookers. I'm surprised that you do. You can't start believing that everyone in the crowd is an arsonist. Chasing shadows is not healthy."

Luke resisted the urge to show Owen the photo of the two of them talking. Owen denying knowing the man was very worrying. "Why does my looking out for an arsonist bother you so much?"

Owen looked taken aback by this direct approach. He shrugged. "It doesn't. Why don't you show me the annex? I've never seen it properly."

Luke noted that once again Owen was dodging the subject by switching to another topic. Better not to push things at this stage.

"It's been a major dumping ground for years. Thankfully, James helped shift some of the heavy stuff around; I couldn't have done it on my own."

Owen followed him. He expressed surprise at the size, then made the excuse he had to rush off to meet someone.

Luke waved him off and went back to his articles, but the nagging question about Owen's refusal to consider there might be an arsonist at large wouldn't go away. It would be more realistic for him to join forces to prove he was wrong.

When the girls returned, he took James to one side and asked if he'd said anything to Owen.

"I haven't seen him for weeks. Why?"

Luke told him about the visit and the conversation they'd had. "It was probably Amy, but I just wanted to make sure it wasn't you."

"No, not to blame."

"I showed him a picture of Joe. He denied knowing him. I didn't mention I had photos of them together and assume you won't either. Not until we're sure of the significance."

"What photos?" James said with a wide smile.

Chapter 19

Luke couldn't get Owen's visit out of his mind. It niggled as he got the kids off to school. While he tried to decide what to do next, Amy called.

"Hi. Did you send your article off yet?"

"No, I'm about to."

"I'd love to see it before you submit it?" She sounded hesitant. "I'm just down the road. Can I drop in and look?"

This was a first, Amy inviting herself round. Did she really want to read his article, or was there something else on her mind?

"Certainly," he answered. "See you in a while."

He read through the article again, and printed out a copy, pulled up the photo page and studied them again. Had he picked the best ones? He was glad to have someone else to look them over. Amy would ensure he picked the best.

Amy arrived sooner than expected; she hadn't been kidding about being nearby. She asked how he was and looked him up and down, giving him a thorough once over.

"Fine," he answered, wondering if she would believe him. No need to tell her how much pain he still had to cope with. The changed medication didn't work as well as the ones he had been on before. She nodded and seemed content with his answer.

"Coffee?"

"That would be lovely," she said. "Let me get it." A kind but unacceptable offer.

"No, you read the article. I wanted to ask if you thought this was a better picture of Katie than the one I chose." He put the alternative photo on his screen and handed her the print-out. She sat down at his desk and started reading.

He took his time making the coffee. He knew Amy hated having someone hovering over her while she read.

He searched the cupboard for biscuits. The girls had depleted the selection over the weekend, but he found a packet of plain ones, which he added to the tray with the coffee.

"Brilliant article, and yes, those are the best pictures. Can I have a printout of a few of the others?"

"Of course, select the ones you want, and I'll do prints. Have your coffee first," he said, holding out her mug.

"Thanks."

He let her browse, then asked, "Did you say something to Tamsin or Owen about me?"

"Fat chance. I haven't seen either of them for weeks."

"So, you didn't tell Owen I was chasing phantom arsonists?"

"No, what makes you think that?"

"Did you tell anyone I was still looking?"

She stared at him, puzzled expression in place. "I might have said something to Rupert, but why would that bother you?"

"It shouldn't, but yesterday Owen came round, quizzing me about my obsession."

"Well, he was the one who warned me about your paranoia. Said it was quite an issue with firefighters. That's why I worried about your insistence that arson caused the fire when you got injured. Perhaps the young chap who was here with the children told him?"

"No, he didn't, so I need to know who did. Could Rupert have said something?"

"Unlikely—Owen and Rupert never got on."

"What about his father?"

"Why on earth would he?" She looked puzzled. "Don't tell me you think Frank's got something to do with the fires?"

Luke shrugged, not wanting to confirm or deny the fears he had.

She stared at him, a frown forming. "They were on the phone for a long time. Maybe he did. But what's his father got to do with your search?"

"Does his father know Owen?"

"Yes, but why the sudden interest?"

Luke took a deep breath as he tried to figure out how much to tell her. He'd hate for her to think he was trying to wreck her relationship with Rupert, though he'd take it as a bonus. So far, there was nothing to show Rupert had any involvement with whatever was going on. He hoped not, for Amy's sake. The man's father was a different matter.

"Well, I spotted a man I had seen at several fires and who I'm suspicious about." He shuffled through some photos on his desk and pulled out the one of Joe. "This man?"

She peered at the photo. "You think he's responsible?"

"Maybe. Have you ever seen him?"

"No, should I have?"

"I saw him yesterday with Rupert's father."

"So what?"

"Rupert's father has bought a building that recently burnt down. And as you know, Rupert's latest project is on a site levelled by fire. Convenient or what?"

"Are you accusing him of arson?"

"No, but you must admit, they are interesting coincidences."

"Why tell me all this?" she asked.

"I know you don't like Rupert's father; I saw your reaction to his over-friendly touch. Even Rupert reacted and didn't appear to like it either."

"Seriously?"

"Yes, but what worries me is that his father might be the one who alerted Owen."

"None of this makes sense. What's Owen's connection?"

Interesting, she hadn't dismissed the possibility of Frank being involved. Her dislike of the man must be stronger than he had given her credit for.

"Owen did the most recent fire inspection of the property."

"More than one?"

"Possibly. I've only focused on one."

She took a sip of coffee, put the cup down, and wrapped her hands around it in her deep thinking pose.

"You know Owen gambles?"

"What?" If true, that would leave Owen vulnerable to manipulation.

"Tamsin let it slip one day, then went all defensive, so I didn't dig any deeper."

Luke offered her a fresh coffee. He loved being with her and wanted to drag out the visit as long as possible.

While he was waiting for the kettle to boil, Amy scrolled through his photos of the girls. When he returned with the refilled cups, he saw she had gone far back enough in his gallery to find the fire pictures.

He hadn't wanted to show them to her, but it was too late to worry now. He said nothing as she studied the images. She spent a long time staring at one in particular.

"I'm guessing you identified this man?" She pointed to a figure standing a foot away from Frank, slightly in the shadows.

"No, should I?"

"He works for Frank. He's called Mike. I've seen him helping Moira, the manager who oversees the cleaners and maintenance team on the estate."

"So that's her official role. I had her down as Rupert's personal housekeeper."

"No need to be snarky," Amy said. "I took on board that the girls weren't too happy being left with her, and have done what you asked, and had them come here instead of getting someone in."

"I'm grateful for that. And they seem happier about it. They haven't been playing up since then."

Luke enlarged the picture on the screen, wondering how they had all missed noticing this man. He needed to check the other photos and videos to see if he appeared in them.

"Amy, there's no proof of anything, and I certainly had no intention of telling you my suspicions, but I'm not sure where we go from here."

"I don't either." She stared into his eyes. "I don't think you're paranoid, if that helps."

"Thanks. I appreciate that." He broke eye contact to rummage through the pile of photos on the table, pulled out the one of Joe on his own, and placed it in front of her. "If I give you this photo, could you hand it to Rupert and ask if he recognizes him? I believe his name is Joe. But please don't tell him I've made a connection between this man and his father."

"What if he recognizes him?"

"We will know who he is. His connection to the family might be legitimate, in which case, I can cross him off my suspect list."

"Do you want me to ask his father?"

"No, let's wait to find out if Rupert gives him the photo."

"You don't like him?"

"Frank? No, I only met him once, but he struck me as being the worst kind of bully."

"I meant Rupert?"

"Not particularly. Why would I? He ripped my family apart."

Amy reached across and put her hand on his. "Sorry."

Luke felt her sincerity. He felt closer to her now than ever. The temptation to lean over and kiss her was almost overwhelming, but he held back. He put his other hand over hers and squeezed gently.

This was her first apology for leaving. He mustn't let it mess with his head.

"I'm sorry my search has put you in a difficult position, but this is serious. Arson puts people's lives at risk, and I can't ignore the facts. If Rupert's father is involved, things could get tricky."

"Do you think Rupert is involved?"

"I hope for your sake he isn't, but he isn't a fool. He can't be blind as to how his father works. It could lead to his being pulled into any investigation.

And regretfully that would put you in a difficult position."

"It's okay, I understand. Does this change how you feel about the girls spending time with me?"

"I can't say I love the idea, but as long as you're comfortable there, I'm happy to leave things as they are. If you have any concerns, I trust you to bring them back here full time. You too, if things get messy."

She pulled her hand away from his and reached for her bag.

Luke wondered if extending his offer to include her had made things awkward, but he had no regrets. There was one other suggestion to make.

"Listen, I know it's crazy, but can we have a code word to use if either of us finds out anything that potentially creates an uncomfortable situation?"

With no hesitation, she nodded. "I'm happy with that. How about one of us agreeing to arrange judo classes for the girls?"

"Perfect," he answered.

Judo classes had been a bone of contention. Amy always resisted the idea. The topic could be included in a conversation easily.

"If I mention judo in a text or during a call. Find an excuse to get the girls and yourself out of the house as soon as you can. And if you bring up the subject, I'll be there for you in a flash."

"I will, promise. What about our plans to go to Centre Parcs with Rupert?"

"The girls are so excited; of course, you must go."

"I'd better leave now so you don't miss your deadline?"

"Yes, I should get on with it. I promised Barry he'd have it by teatime," he answered, wondering if his offer for her to come home had rushed her departure. On reflection, he was glad he had made it. Now she knew returning was an option.

He thought about trying to get her to stay longer while he printed off the photos she wanted, but resisted. They provided an excuse for her to come back.

As soon as Amy left, Luke sent the first two articles to Barry.

Within half an hour, Barry called him. His enthusiasm raised Luke's hopes that journalism was a realistic possibility.

"I might syndicate these to a Sunday paper for their supplement. Are you okay with that? If they take them, they'll want the rest of the series you've outlined. I'm going to start with the colourful, fun one, then on to the fitness post-baby. The one I'm really excited about is the one you hope to do on outdoor climbing. I'll be able to tie it in with a promo for venues in the area."

"All sounds amazing to me," Luke answered, pleased to have such a swift and positive reaction.

"I can probably book some advertising for clothing to tie in as well. The later ones about climbing for recovery from stroke and injuries might need more thought for placement. But I have to admit they fit well with the follow-up on the challenge of overcoming fear."

He mentioned the figure he'd pay, and the potential that syndicating the articles would likely bring.

"Wow, much more than I expected."

"Well, keep at it. How's the homeless story developing?"

"Nearly there," Luke answered, though he still had to sort the photos.

"Any chance of it by the end of the week? I've got an empty slot."

"I'll do my best."

"Can't wait. You've an excellent eye for detail. I can use more, the sooner the better."

Could he speed up turning his ideas into actual features and create a steady flow of articles? The climbing pieces were fun because he enjoyed the activity. Replicating that for subjects that he didn't enjoy in order to earn a reliable income would be much harder.

He didn't mention the arson story. It was too soon; he needed more facts and didn't want anyone to jump the gun. And he still hadn't worked out if submitting such a story while still working for the fire brigade would be a conflict of interest and create problems.

He finished the story about the quality of new-build properties. Outlining how families he'd interviewed were unhappy with their new accommodation, which had given him an excellent starting point and had promised a follow-up article. He hoped that something would have improved for the families so he would have good news to report. The time spent with the families he could far be more productive than he first imagined.

His only disappointment was a call from Amy begging to change the dates for their trip away with the girls.

"I know the girls were supposed to be back in time for your birthday, but Rupert booked for the entire week, not just a few days. Do you mind terribly? I know you planned to take them rock climbing, but can you put off taking them until the following week? It will give you a chance to test out your skills first without having to look out for the children."

It surprised him at how well thought out her argument was and didn't want to make a fuss. "Are the girls happy about this?"

"I didn't tell them yet. I didn't want to spoil it for them if you weren't happy about the delay."

"So, you want me to suggest it to them?" He was guessing this was her plan, and a very smart move on her part. She was always careful not to make them think she was stopping them from being with him.

"If you don't mind, that would be great."

"Okay, I'll talk to them." He wasn't happy about it, but keeping the relationship with Amy sweet was important, and a few days' delay in celebrating his birthday would not make a difference.

"Hi, girls. Listen, your mum says you can stay on at Centre Parcs for a few extra days, but it means we'll have to postpone my birthday celebrations. I'm happy about it if you are. Especially because I can have two parties instead of one," he added to help them make the decision Amy wanted.

"Are you sure?" Katie asked.

"Absolutely certain."

His assurance worked, because what followed was a garbled account of all the fun things they could do while they were there.

"Well, enjoy yourselves. I will too." He felt bamboozled into accepting the changed dates, but if they were happy, it was okay.

Chapter 20

The following day, Sheena called before he had begun the next article. "Can I bring Mabel round to see the annex? She likes the sound of the place and is desperate to get something on the ground floor, because her knee operation has been postponed again."

"Can we make it this afternoon? I have to drop some things off at the charity shop on my way to pick the girls up from school. I'll be back by four o'clock."

Mabel's visit turned into a tea party in the garden with the girls, Sheena, and Buster. She loved the annex and asked if she could take it. Sheena offered to be her guarantor and produced a formal lease, ready for everyone to sign to complete the deal. Now all that remained was to move her things in on the following day. Luke called James to ask if he could help and to bring his mate, who had a van, which would make it much easier to move the heavier furniture. Charlotte also volunteered to help.

Luke slept well. For the first time in ages, he could visualize a future if he had to quit the fire service.

In the morning, after a team effort, moving furniture, they left Mabel to unpack her belongings. Sheena and Charlotte stayed on to help. Luke and James worked together clearing space in the garage for the mobility scooter, making sure Mabel had easy access to a charging point.

By late afternoon, Mabel had settled in and was ready to host a housewarming party for everyone involved.

The girls adored her. Luke suspected Buster would spend more time with Mabel than at home. Not that he minded. Having Mabel living there felt right; the annex needed to be used, and she was the perfect candidate.

He caught up with Sheena in the kitchen. She had been avoiding talking to him about how she was coping since the fire. The stress of being made homeless had changed her.

"How are things going? Come on, be truthful. I know you don't like to talk about your personal stuff, but I expected to see you at the last support group meeting. Your skipping one bothered me because you basically run that group."

"Sorry, I should have been there for you."

"That's not the point. You've been through a lot, and I'm sure the urge to drink must have hit at some point."

He owed it to her to encourage her to talk, so said, "I've struggled to avoid the temptation."

"Surprisingly, drinking isn't an issue. Making sure everyone else was okay gave me no time to dwell on it."

"That's good, but now everyone's settled, I sense something else is bothering you. I'm guessing you hate your new flat."

"What makes you say that?"

"The speed with which you got Mabel out of that building made it fairly obvious."

"Very clever." She settled herself on the kitchen stool. "Mabel showed me a letter she'd

162

received, suggesting she move. It's the same as the ones we had at the last block of flats."

"Why the hell didn't you tell me earlier?"

"I didn't want to scare Mabel. She would never have moved into the annex if she thought I might want to move."

"Were you going to tell me about the letter?"

"Yes. It's in my bag." She grabbed her bag, rummaged in the depths, and pulled out the letter. "Here." She shoved the crumpled envelope into his hand.

Luke read it. "No wonder you want to get out."

"I've started looking. I only took it to get out of that hotel. I'll be leaving before the lease is up. The rest of the tenants are a bunch of shouting, swearing, litter-dropping louts, probably all drug users too."

"Whoa, you definitely need to get out of there."

"Don't worry, I know. I think finding one pissing in the lift was the deciding factor."

"Let me guess, you were the person responsible for fumigating it with eye-watering disinfectant?"

Sheena grinned. "Yes, I hoped it would be so powerful no one would want to go in there."

"It worked. Why do you think James and I used the stairs to bring Mabel's stuff down? It wasn't to replace a workout at the gym."

She smiled. "Sorry, I did wonder."

"Have you shown Mabel the photos of Joe, and the others we think might be involved with your flat fire?"

"No, I didn't want to alarm her."

"Do you mind if I ask her?"

"No, but I'd rather you didn't explain your interest just yet."

"Fair enough."

Luke took his coffee and went to sit by Mabel. Sheena stayed in the kitchen. He fondled Buster's ear. The dog had staked a place by Mabel's chair, looking as if he belonged to her.

"Mabel, I wonder if you know this man?" He handed her the photo of Mike; the man Amy had identified as being employed by Frank Patterson.

"Yes, he's been around a lot lately." She smiled. "He rents the garage next to the one I used for my mobility scooter. He's always very polite, and even carried my bags up for me one day."

"What about this chap?" He gave her the picture of Joe.

"Yes, he helped Mike unload some heavy boxes the other day. Are they in trouble?"

"No, a friend wants to catch up with them and I offered to help find them."

He needed to change the subject, so asked, "Did Sheena ever say anything about the things she lost in the fire?"

"The thing that upset her was the loss of old photos and original documents to do with family history. She said she could replace everything else."

Sheena approached with two plates, each with a slice of a delicious-looking chocolate cake. "What plans are you two hatching?"

Mabel answered, "Nothing, just discussing the photos and papers you lost."

"Oh, that. I can find them again. When I do, I'll save it on-line to be safe."

Luke sensed the conversation was closed, so took the plate of cake and stood to offer his seat to Sheena, then retreated to join Katie and Janet.

But the discussion still worried him. He'd organize for the fire safety people to check the flats out. He'd ask James to instigate it, better coming from him than reviving the paranoia theory.

While they played, he made a plan. If he could set up a camera to focus on the garage, he might capture the proof he needed. He had to discover what was being stored. Without that information, he couldn't make a move.

Mabel's lease didn't run out until the end of the month. One window overlooked the garages. The perfect place to rig up a camera and he could add a second one in her garage.

The sun was getting low, and the warmth of the afternoon vanishing. Mabel got Sheena to help her back into her new home.

Sheena came to pick up her bag, which was still in his kitchen where Charlotte and James were tidying up. It gave him the chance to voice his concerns.

He pulled out the picture of Mike.

"We all need to look out for this guy," he said. "Amy saw the photos and picked him out. She says he works for Frank Patterson and assured me she didn't tell Owen that I was still looking for an arsonist. So, my guess is that Rupert or his father did. And I think they told him to quiz me to find out why I was looking for Joe, or, as he called it, chasing phantom arsonists. And Mabel has seen both of them unloading stuff into a garage near her flat."

They moved to his computer to check all the photos again and spotted Mike in a couple more. The reason they hadn't noticed him earlier was that he kept himself behind a row of onlookers. Unlike the other suspects who stood brazenly at the front, he skulked towards the back of the crowd and wore a dark knitted hat pulled down low.

Luke shut the computer down. "I'm back at work tomorrow, on training. This gives me a perfect excuse to trawl the archives for case studies to discuss with the new recruits. I'll check out what properties Owen has inspected to see if there's a pattern."

"Good luck with that," James said.

"Sheena, can you borrow the key to Mabel's garage? Tell her someone has offered you a table that is too big for your flat, and you need storage space. She still has the property in her name until the end of the month."

Sheena nodded.

"James, I'd like you to suggest a fresh fire inspection is needed. Say you noticed some issues while moving Mabel out?"

James smiled. "Good plan."

After they left, he went on-line and ordered a remote camera that would connect to his phone. The package was due for delivery the next day. He would leave a note on the door, directing them round to Mabel's entrance and get her to accept delivery.

When he asked Mabel, she said, "Why don't you set up the doorbell system that I had for the flat?" She dug into a box beside her. "Here, it's already connected to my phone. It has a camera, so I can see who's there without having to move. All you have to do is fix it on the door or wall. It has a speaker so I can tell them to bring it round to the side, to my door."

"Great. I'll set it up now."

166

Chapter 21

Luke found it strange being back at work and not on active duty. He set tasks for his new recruits; after a fitness session, he handed round reading material, which he would quiz them on later. This gave him the perfect opportunity to check the fire inspection records while searching for more real scenarios to use for training.

No one questioned his presence as he delved into historic cases. The first file he sought was the one for the old factory site Rupert was currently developing, followed by the more recent fire at Sheena's block of flats.

For both buildings, the fire safety check bore Owen's signature. He made a note and grabbed a file that did not have any connection to Owen.

The new recruits were a keen bunch, so he kept going back to find more examples for them, each time noting another place Owen had inspected. Deeply concerned, he turned his attention to recent fire inspections.

He'd have to confront him. Owen inspecting so many properties which later burnt down could not be a coincidence. He jotted the locations of all recent fires, determined to check them out. Then he did the same with blocks of flats where the crew had no chance of preventing total destruction.

What had Owen omitted from all these reports? And why was he doing them? It was not part of his job; he must have volunteered to do extra shifts. Strange, he had never mentioned doing this. On the surface, there was no similarity with the causes of fire, so perhaps he was wrong to think there was something amiss. If not, whoever lit the fires was extremely clever.

He couldn't help thinking that if Owen had overlooked something on one inspection, he would've been more thorough with the next

Amy's remark about Owen being a gambler troubled him. Was he in debt? Had he been coerced into doing the reports? Or taken on extra duties to pay debts. Confronting Owen could damage their friendship.

There was too much at stake not to take the risk.

"Hi, Owen," he said during his lunch break. "Can I have a word in private?"

Owen frowned and with a shrug of his shoulders followed Luke out towards the station gate. They sat together on the low wall by the entrance.

"Who told you I was still looking for an arsonist?" Luke studied his friend.

Owen's face went red. His mouth opened, but he seemed to have lost the power of speech.

Luke hit him with a direct prompt. "Was it Frank Patterson?"

Owen spluttered. "How do you know?"

"I didn't. But I'm curious. Why is he interested? Is he afraid I might find out there's an arsonist at large?"

Owen gulped, but didn't reply.

Luke stared at him, watching how his friend fidgeted uncomfortably at the way the conversation was going. He waited for a while, but Owen stayed silent. "Are you in debt to him? Gambling, maybe?"

Owen's shoulders dropped as if relieved to be found out. "Yes," he whispered. "I don't know what to do."

"Come to my place tonight so we can talk properly."

"Okay. I'll come after my shift."

"I need to get back to my newbies. See you later."

About an hour later, the station bell went off. Luke was at a computer, so he checked the details of the call. It was another warehouse fire. He tapped the address into the computer and opened the file to see if there had been a recent fire inspection. Owen's signature was on the document.

Luke didn't bother to read the details. He had to speak to Owen before the crew left the station. He tore down the stairs and cornered him by his locker.

"You did the inspection report for this address."

"Did I?" Owen said faintly.

"Yes, and I'm only going to ask you once. What didn't you put in the report?"

"Nothing."

"That's a lie. What did you leave out? Come on, lives are at stake here," Luke said with as much menace as he could muster.

"There were chemicals which they promised they'd remove."

"But you never checked to see if they had?"

"No... I..." Owen looked at him pleadingly. "I'm an idiot."

"Never mind. Can you remember what sort of chemicals?"

Owen nodded and rattled off a list of names. All were highly flammable, especially if combined. A nightmare to deal with.

"You have to tell the boss. You can't let your colleagues go out unprepared." He grabbed Owen's elbow and pushed him towards their boss, Andrew Clarke.

"There's a problem," he said, and stepped back to let Owen explain. Owen, thankfully, repeated what he had told Luke without further prompting.

"They promised they would move the stuff, but I didn't go back to check."

"Thanks for the heads up. We'll tackle it as if the chemicals are still in situ."

"Luke, I want you to come along. Not to go in, but to act as a liaison officer. Take one of the small vehicles and bring your recruits along; they can watch and help with the evacuation of nearby buildings. There'll be plenty of useful things for them to do."

As Luke was getting his new recruits prepared, he got a text from Sheena.

"Martin's been in touch. His homeless friend got a warning to stay away from a warehouse down near the water. It came from the same guys that warned them to get out of the place where you rescued him."

Luke showed the text to his boss. Knowing the fire was most likely deliberate might help them contain the spread.

"The chemical experts are on the way," he told Luke, then muttered something under his breath about bloody developers trying to flatten buildings on the cheap.

The narrow streets made for awkward access. Extension hoses to reach the building would be necessary. Luke set his recruits to work carrying extra reels down the hill to speed things up.

The wind gusted and fanned the blaze at an alarming rate, sending showers of sparks skyward. With the hoses in place, Luke received orders to take his team and check the surrounding buildings were all evacuated.

"Those chemicals could create a gigantic explosion. Speed is the key. Owen, stay with me, so you can relay exactly what you saw to the chemical experts," Andrew said.

Luke rallied his group, dispatched them to check the nearby buildings, and explained the danger.

"There's the possibility that they stored volatile chemicals at this end of the building. No one is certain if they were removed. The plan is to blanket the area with foam as some react to being mixed with water. With luck, this will prevent the flames from reaching them. We have spotted several smaller fires in other areas. The hope is they can safely use water on those, but everyone needs to keep their distance. I'm telling you this so you can explain the urgent need to evacuate the area."

Once his team set off, Andrew gave Luke instructions to convey to the back-up crew coming to help. He pointed to a map. "They've had instructions to approach from the far side. I need to be certain they understand what we are dealing with."

Luke set off to deliver the message. Having relayed the information about the chemicals being stored inside, he made his way back to check how his new recruits were doing. They were working well as a team.

On the way, he spotted a policewoman struggling to hold back onlookers. He pulled his phone out and panned the scene, taking a short video, unsure if there was enough light to capture their faces. The usual suspects: Joe, then Mike hiding in the background, Frank Patterson looking rather smug and finally the fourth candidate of interest, the planning officer, were all present. He stopped filming and moved closer to help the policewoman convince the crowd to move back. As he got nearer, all four suspects retreated. Had they recognized him, or was it a coincidence?

His helmet should have obscured his identity. But he didn't care; he had a shot with all of them present. Maybe it would help convict them, if ever anyone put a case together.

At worst, he could use the photo for an article about the support the police provided to the fire service during a shout.

With his phone in his pocket, he went back to arrange for his recruits to man a hose and let some of his colleagues take a break.

The fire appeared to be slowly coming under control. Now the challenge was to keep it from flaring up.

Luke made his way back to Owen, who was still with their boss, sticking close to the tender and away from the crowd.

Luke pulled Owen aside and said, "I've just seen Frank Patterson and the others in the crowd. Is that a problem?"

Owen shrugged. "I'd rather not find out."

"Probably best to avoid contact. No need for him to suspect you warned us about the chemicals.

Or that your information prevented this fire from turning into a disaster."

"What shall I say if he asks?"

"Blame a spot check on fire inspections. Some paper pusher noticed a spate of fires in the area and double checked. This one is definitely being clocked as an arson attack. The police are going to cordon off the site while the forensic team gets to work. Be prepared for an interview."

"I'll lose my job. What a bloody mess. I should go to the police and own up."

"Before you do, you're coming over to my place. I have things you need to see. Meanwhile, stick close to the boss. Avoid contact with anyone else."

Luke's new recruits were bonding well as a team. And happy to be given a chance to tackle an actual fire and continue the damping down process. The flames were much reduced, and they were close to putting the fire out, preventing the spread to the end containing the chemicals.

While supervising them, he caught a moment with James. "Did you take any photos of the crowd?"

"Yes, the usual suspects gathered. Got them all."

"When this shift is over, I need you to go to Sheena's block of flats. I bought cameras to set up to monitor the garage there. Could you install them for me?"

"Is Owen involved with this one?"

"Yes, and I'm playing for time, so don't say anything."

"Sure."

With their shift over, the crew headed back to the station. It was too late for a trip to the pub. Luke took his boss to one side.

"Please come to my place. There are things we need to discuss regarding Owen and his fire report. I have things to show you. And Owen will be with me to explain his part in this. Trust me, this is important."

"I have things to do here first."

"Fine, as long as you promise to come."

He frog-marched Owen over to his car. "You're coming to my place, no arguments."

Owen seemed resigned to whatever fate was about to fall on him.

Back at the house, Luke spread the photos he'd gathered on the table. He pointed out to Owen the ones of him talking to all the suspects bar the planning officer. No need to ram home the significance of these images.

"Tell me about the inspections. How did you get involved?"

"I got into debt. Frank bailed me out. Later, he put pressure on me to help him. He would tell me when a property was due for inspection and insist that I find a way to do it."

"How did you orchestrate that?"

"I'd offer to work overtime. The inspection team is always behind schedule, so an offer of help was readily accepted."

"Did he tell you what to leave out?"

"No. I had to show him the report before I filed it. He'd promise to sort out the issues I highlighted, saying there was no need to put them in the report. I should have realized I was being used."

"It doesn't look good for your long-term prospects, but I'm going to ask Andrew not to fire you." Luke said.

"It's not the boss I'm worried about. Frank's lot will kill me if they think I grassed on them."

"You think you could be in danger?"

"Yes, I bloody well do."

"Have they tried to contact you?"

"I don't know. I left my phone in my locker at the station."

"Good move. If I can persuade Andrew not to fire you so everything seems normal, do you think you'll be safe?"

"It might help."

"Fine, let's see if he'll agree."

"I doubt he will. I'm prepared to resign to save him the hassle of having to fire me."

"It may not be necessary."

"You're kidding. My actions caused one man's death and your injuries."

"Maybe, but until they are caught, it will be better if you are still one of the team. And there's no harm in trying."

James arrived, and Luke handed over the cameras without inviting him in. "Can you set them to record on your phone for now?"

"No problem."

"The boss is coming over. I'll be handing over all the information I've gathered so far. Are you okay with me giving him the copies of your footage?"

"Absolutely. Let me know the outcome."

When Andrew Clarke arrived, Luke knew him well enough to spot he wasn't in the best of moods.

"Coffee or something stronger?" he offered.

"I presume I won't enjoy whatever it is you dragged me here to listen to." He looked across to see what Owen and Luke were drinking. "A stiff drink sounds appealing, but under the circumstances, coffee might be sensible."

"Look at these while I get it, then I'll fill you in on their significance," Luke said and passed him a folder holding all the evidence he had gathered so far.

When he came back and put the coffee on the table in front of his boss, he sensed a change in his attitude.

"I'm sorry, Luke. I should have taken your fears about an arsonist more seriously."

"Don't worry about that. What we need to do now is to make the people responsible pay for their greed. They are clever and we need to expose them."

He explained the significance of the photos, and the role Owen played, and how the arsonist had evaded suspicion.

"The best thing you can do would be to keep Owen on as a firefighter. He's prepared to resign, but for his safety, it needs to appear that no one suspects his involvement. Doing so will give the police time to examine the evidence in the folder before these crooks can cover their tracks."

Andrew frowned. "If I agree and take this to the police, will you abide by whatever the police want you to do?"

Both nodded.

"Who else knows about all this?"

"James," Luke answered, wondering if he should also mention Sheena and Charlotte, but decided it was unnecessary. But, to make sure that this didn't get swept under the carpet, he added, "And I've shared everything with Barry Quick, a journalist colleague. I trust him not to print anything without police clearance."

"Is there anything else I should know?"

"My friend who lived in that block of flats that burnt down last week moved into a new block and is unsurprisingly nervous about another fire. She discovered the residents have received letters inviting them to move. It is the same as the one circulating at her previous address. Owen has done a recent fire inspection. This place is likely to be their next target."

"And the address?"

"It's in the folder. Right now, James is setting up cameras to focus on the garage because we need to catch these guys at work. We think they are storing stuff in one of them. Maybe health and safety could do a spot check. That way, Owen won't be seen as the source of information."

"Thanks for the warning, and don't worry, I'll arrange for that to happen," Andrew answered. "I heard you requested a check on some other properties, something about the back gardens. Is that connected with this?"

Luke told him it had nothing to do with this issue. But having seen the rubbish accumulated in the backyards, he thought he should put in a request for a random inspection.

"Excellent spot. I'll pass on everything you've told me to the investigating officers. And I understand the logic behind keeping Owen's offer of resignation quiet for now. I'm not sure how long I can do that for. The police might think differently. Under the circumstances, it would be easier if you went on leave. If I remember rightly, you just had time off to visit a sick aunt," he said, looking directly at Owen. "Best to say you have to go back to her bedside."

Luke gave him a second file. "This is a copy of everything we have shared with you, which you can pass on to the police."

"I'll speak to DI Roland Hughes. He's worked with me before and we've become friends. He will no doubt want to speak to you both, so make sure you take his calls."

Owen explained about his reluctance to use his phone.

"Fine, but get another one, and let me have the number."

After he left, Luke asked Owen how much Tamsin knew about his debt problem.

"Nothing."

"Be completely honest with her. She needs the truth. And do what Andrew suggested and get yourselves out of town."

Chapter 22

After Owen left, Luke regretted not asking him if Rupert was involved. He couldn't call him to ask, because Owen had told him he left his phone at the station to avoid taking any calls from the men involved with the warehouse fire.

He considered leaving a message with Tamsin, but decided against it. No. Better if he called round and asked before they left town.

The more he thought about Owen's involvement, the more he realized it was guilt that made Owen sit by his hospital bedside. The fool might have guessed they would torch the place, but assumed they would make sure no one was in the building before doing so; and probably deluded enough to think a fatality might end their hold over him instead of tightening the grip they had. But it didn't ease his worries about Rupert's role in the entire scheme of things.

Luke had to believe Rupert wasn't involved. On the plus side, Rupert hadn't appeared on camera at any of the fires. And he was out of town right now, and been away in Cornwall with Amy and the girls, on the day Sheena's flat fire occurred.

Luke set about transferring his frustration into a rough draft of an article on arson and property developers. If he could prove all he suspected, he would have the basic outline in place, and with a tweak or two would be ready to go to press. If nothing else, Barry would get a major scoop, and maybe syndicate the story. He would, of course, need to double if not triple check the information to avoid legal issues, or printing something that might prevent the police from getting a conviction.

The fire department would have to approve it too, though they couldn't really complain. Their failure to spot the arson clues on more than one occasion would be an embarrassment, and something he could use to his advantage if they proved difficult.

He was about to leave when James called.

"I've put the camera in place. How did the chat with the boss go?"

"Fine, I passed on everything we have so far, and he's agreed to keep Owens' role quiet as long as he takes time off. Can you spread the word that Owen had to visit Tamsin's sick aunt? I am just heading over to his place. I want to ask him something before he leaves town."

"Sure. I can do that. Have you spoken to Amy?"

Luke thought for a minute. Part of him wanted to drive straight to Center Parcs and pick her up. But what would that achieve other than to alert the Pattersons they were under suspicion?

"I've been thinking about that. Amy knows what I've been working on, but the police need time to gather evidence, so meanwhile everyone has to carry on as normal."

"Does that mean climbing is still on tomorrow?"

"Yes, my birthday treat. Shame the girls will be missing, but I've agreed to have a second celebration when they come back, probably next week."

"Well, it should be fun. Charlotte and I will pick you up at nine. Sheena is coming to your place to help Mabel and has generously offered to have George for the day. So, it will be a day out for the grown-ups."

Luke laughed. "Great, see you then."

After James hung up, Luke went back to his computer, compiled his proposed article and all the documents used to prove his theory into one folder and saved them to his drop box. And sent a link to Sheena with an explanation of the latest developments. He asked her to make sure he'd covered everything. He didn't tell her he'd lied to his boss that Barry had all the information already. For a moment, he wondered what made him say it. A sense of self-preservation or because he didn't know who else was involved with Frank Patterson's dodgy dealings? One thing was for sure: Barry would get all the information as soon as he could safely do so without compromising a police case.

And then he considered what he should do about Amy and the girls. He wanted them away from Rupert. But until he was sure Rupert was in on the arson, it would look as if he was making a fuss out of spite. No, he had to talk to Owen first, before he sent any message containing the code word.

He decided it would be as easy to cycle over to Owen's house as he knew that parking in that area was always a problem in the evening, and it wasn't very far to go. He grabbed his helmet, slung on a jacket, and set off. The traffic was light, and he made good time. The streetlights cast an orange glow on everything. Just as he turned into Owen's street, his bike chain jammed. He was cross with himself, as he had forgotten to tighten the nuts the day before, when he noticed it was slack and hadn't clipped on his tool kit. He'd leave fixing it until after he'd spoken to Owen. After he chained the bike to a convenient rail, he continued up the street on foot.

There was a car with its lights on, engine running further up the narrow road, and he assumed they were waiting for a space to become available. It was a quiet location, most curtains were closed, and apart from a cat slinking down the road, the street was deserted. A door higher up the street opened, letting out a stream of light which Owen stepped into. He was carrying a bag.

Luke was glad he was still there. He had wondered if he should have come earlier. He quickened his pace. A movement caught his eye. A figure emerged from the shadow of a tree in Owen's front garden. He had what looked like a raised baseball bat aimed at Owen. Luke shouted. The bat bore down. Cracking Owen's head. Owen stumbled. let out a moan and fell towards his car, doing his best to stay upright. The man swung the bat low and knocked his feet out from under him. Owen tumbled to the ground, and the man kicked his head.

Luke didn't have time to consider the danger he might put himself in by intervening. He had to do something. The only thing to hand was a black wheely bin parked outside the neighbour's house. Luke grabbed the handle and charged, shouting at the man to back off. The man turned and raised his bat again, this time aiming at Owen's head. Luke saw it coming and ducked, but the momentum of the bin knocked his assailant sideways with tremendous force. The bat flew out of his hands and rolled under the car.

For a second, Luke locked eyes with the unarmed man. The car that had been waiting up the road roared down the street, stopping for a second for the attacker to jump in before it sped off. Caked mud obscured the registration number. But Luke noted a faulty taillight on the driver's side.

His yells had brought Tamsin running out. And the neighbour's lights came on. Luke shouted for someone to call for an ambulance and the police as he knelt down to check on Owen.

"Can you hear me? Don't move. Help is on the way," he said. Owen tried to speak, but all that came out was a moan. Tamsin was on her knees. She reached out and begged Owen to say something.

Luke put a hand out to stop her. "Don't move him."

She looked up, and he could see the fear in her eyes. She nodded, and just held Owen's hand, and said, "You'll be okay."

The neighbour emerged and handed Luke a blanket. "The police and ambulance are on the way. Is there anything else I do to help?"

Luke thanked the man and shook his head. "Did you see anything?"

"Only the man jumping in the car, as it drove off. I can't believe this has happened here. This is usually such a quiet, safe place."

Much as he wanted to reassure the man, he didn't dare suggest this was a targeted attack. Which he was certain it had been.

The pair of them stayed where they were on their knees, only vaguely aware of a crowd gathering nearby. At last, the ambulance arrived, and the paramedics took over. They listened as Luke described what he had seen of the attack. The blow to the head, the fall, the kicking. They put on a neck brace, and then slid Owen onto a stretcher board, and Luke and the neighbour helped to lift it onto the trolley. Once Owen was inside the ambulance, Luke put his arm round Tamsin to comfort her.

"Get your bag, and coat and keys. I am sure they'll let you go to the hospital with him. Take some cash. Enough for a taxi home."

He helped carry the bag Owen had dropped and placed it inside the front door.

"Thanks. Can you make sure they don't leave without me?"

"Don't worry, it will be ages before they can move." He had seen the paramedics at work often enough to know they would not be rushing off before they had done everything they could to make sure Owen was stable.

Tamsin hurried back, clutching a large bag, and was quickly ushered into the ambulance. They wanted to get Owen to the hospital without delay. A sign that his injuries could be more serious than Luke had thought.

"I'll come to the hospital in a while," he said to Tamsin as she nervously climbed aboard.

As he watched the vehicle drive away, he noticed the policeman standing beside him.

"Can you tell me what happened?"

Luke described seeing Owen come out of his house. And explained the sequence of events. "When I knocked him off balance with the bin. He dropped the bat, which rolled under that car." He pointed to the car behind Owen's.

A second policeman bent down to look. "I can see it." He dug in his pocket and pulled out a glove, and reached in and pulled it out for everyone to see. "I'll get this bagged up," he said and walked over to the police car.

"Did you recognize the attacker?"

Luke shook his head. He didn't think so. He described him as tall, dark-haired, well built, and added details of the car that the man had been driven off in, and the damaged taillight.

Doubts crept in. Had he met the man somewhere before? There was something familiar about him. But he couldn't place him. Had he been at the fires? Once that possibility crossed his mind, all he wanted to do was check the videos and photos to see if he could identify the man.

Luke chose not to mention the situation Owen was in, and that it was likely he was being targeted. He'd talk to his boss first and get him to tell his friend, who was looking into the fires, about the attack. He gave his details and made his way back to his bike, hoping he could fix the chain easily.

He approached his own home carefully, keeping a watchful eye out for any strangers lurking or an unusual car parked on his street. Nothing there. This whole thing was making him paranoid. He stopped long enough to call Andrew and tell him about the attack on Owen, and that he hadn't mentioned the arson connection to the attending policeman.

Before he left for the hospital, he had to send a message to Amy. This was getting serious. Now, being unable to question Owen about Rupert's role, he had to assume that Rupert could be involved. So, getting Amy as far away from the Pattersons quickly was important.

He didn't want her to come here. If they had attacked Owen, he could be a target, too. No. He had to think of a way to tell her not to come home, and do it so she'd get it was urgent. He didn't dare call, in case Rupert was with her. He had to think how he could word a message that would convey all he wanted without actually saying she could be in danger.

Where she would be safe? And how could he tell her without naming the place? Then he remembered the surprise break they had been planning for the girls before his accident and before Rupert disrupted their lives.

He pulled out his phone, checked a website, made a booking. Then tapped in the text to Amy.

'Decided that you're right. Getting the girls to learn to paddle board is much more urgent than Judo classes. That place we had looked at is perfect. Just turn up. All booked. Speak to you after the weekend. Love to the girls. Luke.'

That done, he made his way to the hospital to find Tamsin. To his relief, she had called her sister, who together with her husband had arrived to support her. It seemed Owen required brain surgery to deal with a serious blood clot. And after surgery, they would keep him sedated until the swelling went down. So, there was no point in his hanging around the hospital.

Before he left, he asked Tamsin how much Owen had told her. It seemed she knew enough to understand that she should not go back home. She promised to stay with her sister for the time being. Satisfied he had done all he could, he went home to look for a picture of the attacker on his computer.

Chapter 23

Luke's phone buzzed early in the morning. The girls had sent him birthday wishes by text. He was glad they hadn't called; he didn't want to have to pretend everything was fine. Sometimes when they sent a text, he would call back. Today he didn't. And hoped they would think he was driving or had his phone on silent. He convinced himself he had reassured them that missing seeing him on the day was good, as it meant a second day of celebration when they came home. The bonus being that he'd be able to try more challenging climbs than he could if they were with him. Which was true, and he might even get to finish the magazine article he had started.

James, Charlotte, and Sheena all arrived on time. Luke got them inside quickly, and told them about the attack on Owen, and described as best he could the man who had been responsible.

"Sheena, please tell Mabel not to answer the door to anyone. If Owen's attack is related to what we think it is, then I might be in line for trouble.

"Don't worry about Mabel. I had planned to spend the day here with her with George."

Charlotte looked worried. "Are you sure we should go?"

"Of course, you should." Sheena replied, "I'm more than capable of keeping George safe, if that's what you are worried about?"

Charlotte blushed, shook her head, and answered. "Sorry, I'm just not used to leaving him with anyone."

"Go on, have a great day." Sheena picked up George and pushed them towards the door. "I have your phone number and will ring you if there's a problem. With two of us to dote over him all day, and Buster to play with, he'll be fine. Get on out of here."

They were taking Luke's car, and he offered to let Charlotte drive, as she needed to get more confidence on the road. She had passed her test but hadn't yet taken the car out on her own. She shook her head; He wondered if having James as a passenger would be too much of a distraction. He didn't pressure her as he loved the drive to Dartmoor.

It was a perfect day for tackling the outdoor climb. The sun was shining, and the scenery on the drive up across the moor to the place where they'd arranged to meet Nathan was a feast for their senses. And best of all, they had the place to themselves, as there were only three other vehicles in the parking area. One of which was Nathan's. The other belonged to a couple with a large black dog, which seemed intent on dragging the owners up the path faster than they wanted to go. He wondered if they would let him loose when they got further away from people. It looked like the kind of animal that would be hard to control.

With their rucksacks on their backs, they followed Nathan to the climb he thought would suit Luke best for his first attempt at a rock face. In what seemed like no time at all, they were at the base of the climb and able to study the formation of the rocks.

Charlotte produced a flask of coffee, and as they drank it, Nathan told them he'd already been up to the top and attached safety ropes. He pointed to them. "Tell me what obstacles you see and tell me how you think you should deal with them.

Luke studied the two lines of ropes and proceeded to talk through what he expected to find. A couple of times Nathan interrupted to describe what couldn't be seen from the ground, and the way round the problem, sometimes drawing with a stick on the soft soil by their feet. Then he patiently ran through the route again until he was sure they understood the difficult stretches.

"The first part will stretch your legs. In the next section, your arms will be tested. You can take a break on that ledge for a while and rest your muscles. Then you move over to the left and use that fissure in the rock for your first foothold. There are quite a lot of safety pins on the route. If you feel the need to take a rest, clip into one with your safety rope. That way, you can give your arms a rest for a moment or two while you get your strength back. James, can you go up to keep an eye on the safety line from the top, while I keep the tension right down here?

"I want James to take a shot of me from above. Is it safe for him to do so?"

Nathan nodded. "Probably best if you lie flat on the rock rather than lean over." There is a good flat area a few feet below where the rope is anchored that would do nicely.

After a brief discussion with Charlotte and James, they worked out where the best shots might be taken. Charlotte would take pictures from the bottom, and James would do his best from the top.

"Follow that winding path, and you will find the spot." Nathan pointed to a narrow path. "I left a rope bag up there so it will be easy to find the right place." James took the camera and listened as Luke gave a few final tips about the best grip for a downward shot to help keep the camera steady.

"If you have to take the neck strap off, make sure you have the wrist strap on." Luke said, "I don't fancy getting hit on the head by a falling camera."

James laughed and winked at Charlotte before setting off up the winding path to the top.

Luke emptied the contents of his pocket into his rucksack that Charlotte would mind while he was climbing. He put on his harness, attached a couple of safety clips to the belt. "Will two be enough?" he queried.

"Because of your previous injury, take eight. If you use one and detaching it is difficult, simply release it from your harness and leave it attached to the ring on the rock-face. I know that's not normal practice, but I'd rather you did that than risk hurting yourself. Don't worry, I'll collect them later. Better to be safe than sorry."

Luke did as instructed and attached himself to the rope Nathan had set up earlier. Nathan then checked that everything was as it should be and handed Luke a helmet.

"This has a two-way speaker and a camera on top. Just let me know if you need to stop or want me to direct you."

His nerves tingled. A moment of guilt hit him because he was glad the girls were not here. This was his first big climb, and he wanted to savour the fact that he could do this. After all the pain he'd gone through, this was the most strenuous activity he'd participated in so far. The perfect birthday treat.

Nathan took up the slack on the rope. "All set," he said.

Charlotte nodded. "James is in place. Enjoy yourself."

Luke faced the rock, picked his first foothold and the corresponding handhold, and took the first step up the rock, feeling the gentle tension as Nathan tightened the slack on his safety line.

He loved climbing on the indoor wall, but the fresh air, with the sun on his back, made this a whole new experience, and he was loving it. Without too much trouble, he made it past the first obstacle Nathan had pointed out. Next would be the section that would test his arm's strength. Long stretches were required, and he soon understood Nathan's concerns.

"Nathan, I'm not sure I can reach the crack above me," he said. "Any alternatives you can suggest?"

"Try to reach directly above your head rather than to the left. There is a small crack there that should help."

Luke reached up and groped the wall until he found the crack. He pushed his fingers into the narrow slit in the rock and managed to get a grip, which enabled him to move his left foot up to a higher foothold. From there, he was able to push upward and reach a better spot with his right hand.

"Thanks. That worked," he said.

"Good. Once you get to the next ledge, tie yourself in. Take time to soak up the view." Luke did as instructed, then shuffled round on the ledge to take in the vista.

The moorland, bathed in sunshine, was dotted with sheep and a dozen wild ponies grazed on the slope to his right. He wished he had a camera on him to take a photo to remind him of this moment. He looked down. Nathan had stepped away from the base of the rocks, far enough away that he could look up to see Luke, but still keeping the safety rope tight.

He looked for Charlotte and spotted her crouched behind a rock, behaving oddly. She seemed to be trying to catch his attention and was gesticulating towards the parking area.

Luke followed the direction she was pointing and saw a man moving towards Nathan. His face was hidden by a cap, but his uneven gait was recognizable. Joe. What the hell was he doing up here? No wonder Charlotte was cowering behind a rock.

Joe kept going until he reached Nathan.

He peered up at Luke on the face of the rocks, and without bothering with any greeting, he asked, "How long will it take for that guy to get to the top?"

His question was loud and clear on the two-way system.

An innocent enough question, under normal circumstances, but with all that had been going on, Luke wasn't sure his curiosity was just that.

"Once he gets going again, probably half an hour," Nathan answered.

The man grunted and retreated, stopping briefly to focus on Luke before heading toward the path that led to the top.

As soon as he was out of sight, Luke waved to Charlotte and pointed upwards. He needed her to warn James that Joe was on his way.

Charlotte gave him the thumbs up sign, and he returned the signal before she too disappeared.

It had wiped the pleasure of the climbing experience out in seconds. Joe could not be trusted.

He said quietly to Nathan over the radio connection, "I think that guy is looking to make trouble."

"The man with the limp?"

"Yes, take care. I don't trust him."

"Noted. Stay where you are for a moment."

Nathan fiddled with his phone, and Luke could hear him talking to a friend. "Can you get over here quickly? We may have a spot of bother for you to deal with."

Nathan asked how worried he was.

"Very. I can't decide if I should go on up or try to climb down."

"Neither. You are safer where you are. Follow my instructions. I promise you will be fine. Release your safety line and move about three feet to your right to that deep crack in the rock. Tuck yourself into it. You'll be able to stand firm. Use the anchor points that are there. Clip into at least one, preferably two, if you can. There's an overhanging rock that will protect you if he does anything silly."

"What about James?"

"I'm pretty sure Charlotte has alerted him. Don't panic. My climbing mates are on their way. Whatever happens, I'll make sure you're okay."

His heart pounded as he fumbled with the clip with sweating hands. In all his years in the fire service, he'd never experienced fear like this. What was it about Joe that made him feel so vulnerable?

"Are you tied in?" Nathan asked.

"Yes."

"Trust me and don't move. I'm going to see what's going on."

Isolated in the cleft in the rock, Luke puzzled over how quick Charlotte had been to hide from the man they called Joe. True, she'd seen his picture, and seen him that day when Luke had spotted him down by the quay. Had his strange limp been memorable enough to make her cautious?

He took a deep breath, wondering how long he'd be stuck on this ledge. Then he worried about Amy and the girls. He wished he could speak to her to explain why he had triggered the code word. Now he was worried she might not have been able to get away, or worse, didn't understand his message. What if she thought he was making something out of nothing?

Chapter 24

Luke couldn't help but wonder about Nathan's decision to leave him stuck in the middle of the rock face.

Surely he'd be better off on the ground, and it wouldn't take Nathan long to help him descend. He began to work out the route back down and realized descending would not be easy. Even with Nathan on his safety line directing him, it would be a slow process.

He wanted to question the logic of staying put, when the safety rope Nathan had anchored to clips at the top of the climb came slithering down the rock like a manic snake. The length that was still attached to him fell away. A moment later, the second line that Nathan had put in place for James to use flashed by.

Now he understood Nathan's instructions. Making him clip himself to the wall had been a clever call.

Self-preservation instincts made him haul the remains of the rope attached to his harness up. It not reaching the ground was a major concern, but he pulled it up anyway, hoping he could attach it to something to make his position more secure.

A flurry of pebbles rattled down the slope, barely a foot away from where he sheltered. The size of the stones increased rapidly. And soon rocks as big as his head were raining down. He hoped and assumed that Nathan had made it to a safe place away from the avalanche of debris.

"Don't even think about moving," Nathan said firmly but quietly over the radio. "The overhang will protect you."

Luke was grateful for the link. The two-way communication made him feel less isolated and relieved that Nathan was safe. But what about James?

"Now I understand why you wanted me to tuck myself in here."

"You're safer in that spot than anywhere else. My mates will be here soon to make sure you come down safely. Trust me, and don't do anything foolish."

More stones came crashing down, bouncing off the protruding rocks and flying in all directions. A large one launched itself towards Luke. It smashed into his arm above the elbow. Luke let go of the rope he'd been hanging onto and fell backwards against the uneven wall. The only thing that saved him was the combination of the confined space and the safety ties that held him upright and stopped him from falling sideways into the narrow gap.

The pain intensified; all he could do was take deep breaths to ease it. He reassessed the situation: his safety ropes were still secure. Could he inch his way deeper into the crack?

"What happened?" Nathan asked.

"A rock hit my arm," he gasped. "I think it's broken."

"Don't worry, help is on the way."

His mind raced through multiple scenarios. None were good. The clatter of rocks ceased. A good sign? Maybe not.

A scream shattered the unnerving silence.

Was it James? The crack in the rocks had muffled the sound, making it indistinct. His position restricted his outlook. The only thing visible was the distant outline of another tor on the moor.

"What's going on?"

From the sound of heavy panting, he guessed Nathan was still racing up the path to the source of the scream.

The pain in his arm was increasing, making him dizzy. The lack of space prevented him from moving to look at the damage. Numbness in his feet made adjusting his position a challenge. With his good hand, he tested the safety lines. Reassured that they were firmly fixed, he slowly edged his body away from the rough wall he had been forced against. He wanted to shift to face towards the opening. He wasn't sure how long he could cope in this claustrophobic space; facing outward might make the experience fractionally better. Looking down, he spotted a growing pool of blood dripping from his elbow.

The injured arm made any attempt to get out impossible. And his position in the crevice made staunching the flow of blood too hard. He had to trust Nathan and believe that help was on the way.

Trying to distract himself from his predicament, he focused on the events that made him a target. Which led to fresh concerns. Charlotte, where had she gone? He couldn't bear the thought that being associated with him and his investigation into fires might have put her in danger. And his family. Amy and the girls, would they become targets?

"Nathan, speak to me," he pleaded. "What the hell is going on?"

"Give me a second," was the gasped response. "I'll tell you when I reach the top."

At least the line of communication was still working. That was a comfort of sorts. He listened to Nathan's panting, then heard him say, "James, are you okay?"

"I'll live, but he's not doing so well," James answered. Luke had to concentrate to hear his response.

"What happened?"

"Charlotte was trying to signal something. I turned to look, and this guy was about to brain me with a rock. He caught me a glancing blow on the side of my head. I passed out for a moment. When I came round, he was hurling rocks over the edge. I kicked out at his legs. He spun round with a huge rock in his hands. I think he intended dropping it on me, but lost his balance, and while trying to steady himself, got his foot wedged between two rocks. He dropped the stone. It landed on his trapped ankle. I heard the bone snap. That's when he screamed. He begged me to move the rock before he passed out. But I didn't dare. Moving it could cause him to bleed out unless there's someone capable of dealing with his injury."

"You did the right thing. Sit down while I look at him."

"Is Luke okay?" James asked.

"He's safe. But stuck on a ledge, waiting for help to come. Luke Did you get all that?" Nathan added, almost as an afterthought.

"Yes," Luke answered, relieved he hadn't been forgotten, and that James was at least talking and sounded all right. He heard Nathan instruct James to look at him, to follow his finger, and asked if he had a headache or nausea. It seemed James had passed the basic tests.

"Does anyone know where Charlotte is?" Luke asked, feeling out of the loop.

"No. James, if you feel okay, take this helmet and look for her. Go down slowly. The last thing we need is for you to fall. Keep talking to Luke and don't let him attempt to come down without help."

"Fat chance, my arm is smashed above the elbow," Luke answered.

"All the more reason to stay where you are."

"What about this guy?" he heard James ask.

"Needs more than two of us to deal with this. Go and make sure the other two are safe, and direct anyone who comes to head up here first. Here, take my phone. Call the ambulance service. Tell them this guy will need a helicopter ride for a speedy evacuation if they want to save his leg."

"Do you have a first aid kit? If so, shall I bring it up?" James asked.

"Not much point. Like you said, best not to meddle. He needs the professionals. Find Charlotte. Give us all one less thing to worry about."

A lot of strange noises followed as the helmet changed hands. And then James' voice became loud and clear. "Luke, can you hear me?"

"Yes, don't fret about me. Make sure Charlotte is okay."

Now he had to listen to James breathing hard as he descended the slope. Finally, he came into view and Luke said, "I can see you." James looked up and located him. He waved.

"Charlotte probably headed towards the car. Be back in a moment."

Luke closed his eyes. His arm was throbbing; the slightest movement made the pain intensify. He concentrated on the deep breathing techniques he'd been taught to conquer pain while being weaned off the painkillers after his skin grafts.

"I've found her. She's safe," James shouted.

"Great, now figure out how to get me down."

"Relax. The experts are here, and an ambulance crew, though they are going to deal with Joe first."

"How's your head?"

"I'll be fine. Got a thick skull."

"Liar, make sure you get it checked out properly."

"I will."

"Ask Charlotte to check my phone. I need to know if Amy replied to my text."

After a moment, he heard Charlotte say, "It looks as if she did. There's a reply, just a thumb up emoji."

Luke felt a bit of relief. Odd that it was just an emoji. She'd never used one before. Not Amy's style, but maybe Rupert had been there, and it was a quick way to respond. He hoped so. But wished she'd showed more clearly that she'd understood his message. All he wanted to do was speak to her; she needed to know what was going on.

"Ask Charlotte to call her on her own phone, not mine. Don't tell her what's going on. If Amy answers, just say she wanted to know how the kids were enjoying themselves."

"I get it. You're worried about them," James said. "Leave it with us," Luke heard him talking to Charlotte. Then he said, "The rescue team has arrived. I'm going to hand over the helmet so they can talk to you about your position."

Once again, there were strange noises as he passed over the helmet and Luke listened to a man who introduced himself as Steve.

"Don't worry, we'll soon have someone up alongside you." Another shower of debris drowned the rest of the conversation.

Chapter 25

The wait for help dragged on. A shaft of sunlight reached into the crack he was stuck in, raising the temperature to an uncomfortable level. His throat was dry. His water bottle attached to his belt on his freshly injured side was tucked so far behind him he'd never grasp it, let alone detach it. The blood drips were slowing down. The heat, the pain, and dehydration were causing increasing disorientation.

Steve's reassuring voice kept repeating help was on its way.

"One of my team has gone to the top to set up a rope for you, which will take a while, so you need to be patient. They'll have to put in new anchors at the top, and clear loose stones out of the way. So, stay tucked into that crack until someone can assist you to abseil down."

"I can't straighten my arm or grip anything with it. And I doubt I'll be able to release myself from the safety ties in place."

"Don't worry, we'll find a way. That crevice is the safest place for you to wait."

To distract himself from the pain and the nightmare of being trapped, he went over what had put him in this situation. Without a doubt, Joe intended to kill him. Had the same people intended to kill Owen?

Where did it leave his family? They could be in danger. Now he wished he'd spoken to Amy and could be sure she understood the urgency of his text.

He wasn't prone to constantly checking his phone for messages. But being trapped without a means of communication was tough. All he wanted to hear was that Amy had got herself and the children away from Rupert.

He spoke into the microphone. "Where are James and Charlotte?"

"The ambulance crew are checking him over. His girlfriend is with him."

"Can someone find out if she's spoken to my wife?"

He heard Steve relay the message.

The list of those aware of his plans to go climbing kept going round and round in his head. Amy, James, Charlotte, Sheena, Mabel, Nathan, and a couple of people at the climbing centre, all of whom he trusted. He was sure Rupert knew as well, because of the confusion of the dates with their Centre Parc booking, overlapping his birthday. Which left the big question; was Rupert involved, or had he unwittingly shared this information with his father? Luke, much as he hated Rupert for his part in splitting up the family, having been forced to spend time getting to know him, had seen how different he was to his father. Which Luke based on the single encounter he'd had with the man.

If so, Frank Patterson was the person most likely to have sent Joe to kill him. He couldn't think of anyone else who would benefit from his being out of the picture.

The evidence pointing to arson attacks was incriminating, but surely not enough to resort to murder. Had he missed something? Was there more at stake than dodgy property deals? What about the death of Martin's friend? That might be incentive enough.

He had been fortunate that both James and Charlotte had come to Dartmoor to keep him company.

Joe probably expected him to be alone, an easy target. James' car had been playing up, so they had come together in one vehicle.

Charlotte had voiced concern about leaving George. But had been persuaded to come along. Would his house be a target? He'd never forgive himself if anything happened to George, Sheena, or Mabel. How could he warn them? He was about to ask Steve to contact them when Steve cut in with fresh instructions.

"Prepare yourself for another shower of stones. Keep well tucked in."

Soon more muck descended. Steve gave a second warning, and another dustier cloud of debris came down, making breathing difficult.

"I think that's the lot. Stay where you are just in case the climbers dislodge more." Steve said, "Someone will be with you soon."

The cramp in his legs had set rigid. Would he be able to move when the time came for him to wriggle out of this crack in the rocks? He longed to quench his thirst, but knew he would have to wait.

Further flurries of stones and dust descended. Then Steve said, "Nathan is nearly there with you. Follow his instructions and we will bring you down."

"Okay."

A little later, a shadow blocked out the sunlight. Nathan had arrived.

"Can you inch your way back out of the crack?" he asked. "Then I can sort out your ropes."

"I can try." The stiffness in his legs made it almost impossible to move. He shifted his weight and attempted to shuffle sideways out towards the moving shadow. It was reassuring to have Nathan suspended alongside him, inching sideways into the crack Luke was stuck in.

"My legs have cramped, and I can't move."

"Don't worry, we can figure it out."

He and Nathan had discussed daring rescues during his research, and Luke was confident that if anyone could get him down without incident, this man could.

Nathan clipped himself to one of the rings on the wall and assessed the situation. Without being asked, he offered Luke a water bottle and held it while he took a swig. He dug into a pocket and pulled out a sling. He knotted one end, slid the fabric over Luke's head, then carefully took hold of the injured hand, slowly lifted it, and slid it into the sling, then pulled the fabric back to the elbow. Luke had to bite his lip to prevent himself from yelling out loud.

"I'm not bothered about the bleeding," he said. "This will help support your arm while we descend." Luke had to admire his skill and the calm way he took control.

"Okay, now for the fun bit, I'm going to clip a new safety rope onto you, and then I can attach your harness to mine. I'll take you down on my back. Let me do all the work. The guys will manage your weight below. All you need to do is hang on to me with your good arm. The three sturdy lads below will keep our ropes tight and allow us to descend slowly as I navigate round the tricky rocks."

"I can't undo the ties I have in place."

"Don't worry, I'll cut them free once you're secure."

Nathan reached in and severed one tie, which allowed Luke to get closer to him. Nathan tightened some ropes, then cut the other tie. Finally, he gave a few more instructions. "Do you understand what to expect? And do you feel secure?"

"Yes."

"Good. Let's go. Keep it steady. When they tighten the rope, try to slide your feet a bit at a time. Great, that's working."

Luke inched his way to the mouth of the crack, and following Nathan's instructions, attached himself to an extra shoulder strap Nathan had added to his harness, then put his good arm round Nathan's torso. This left both Nathan's hands free to ease them away from the rock face.

"Ready?" he asked.

Luke answered "Yes."

Satisfied Luke was secure and comfortable, Nathan spoke to the team below. "Take up the slack now."

Luke felt the tension bite on his new safety rope. Nathan's also became tight. The strange sensation of being slowly edged off the ledge followed. He chose not to look down. His trust in Nathan and the team was absolute. His role was to avoid making any movement that might disrupt Nathan's concentration as he made his way across the rock face before going down.

"You okay?" Nathan asked after a while.

"Fine, what about you?"

"Good. Not too much further."

"Nathan, make sure they know I don't want any pain relief." Luke needed to say it now, as he felt faint, and couldn't take the risk of someone administering something that might trigger his addiction. Nathan was aware of his earlier dependency on drugs after his operation, so would understand the importance of the request.

He closed his eyes and concentrated on steady breathing.

The experience of being suspended, with no control of his destiny and having to trust others to this degree, was alien to him. Tensing up would make the job harder for Nathan.

When his feet touched the ground, his legs refused to support him, and folded under him so he ended up on his knees. Hands gripped him on either side and more hands reached out to release the clips that attached him to Nathan. They gently lowered him to the ground, and he was surrounded by strangers, among them a man in a high visibility jacket.

Nathan said quietly to the man, "Be careful. He's had issues with dependency in the past and says he doesn't want pain relief medication."

Then Nathan encouraged the others to step back to let the paramedic do his job.

A long string of questions left Luke feeling like a fraud. No, he didn't think he'd hurt his legs, and couldn't explain the weakness. The man put a dressing on the bleeding arm and adjusted his sling. He explained his colleagues were dealing with the other injured man.

Luke resisted the temptation to respond that he had got what he deserved.

"Where's James?"

"In the ambulance, being checked over by a colleague," the paramedic answered.

With help, Luke sat up and then slowly got to his feet to make his way toward the waiting ambulance. He had to find out if Charlotte had spoken to Amy. But was disappointed to discover she had already left to go home to George.

The whirling sound of a helicopter drowned out any chance of conversation with James.

Chapter 26

As soon as they were moving, Luke inspected James. There was a big gash on his forehead, and his clothes were streaked with blood, but his grin was reassuring.

"Hope you feel better than you look?" Luke said.

"Not too bad, but you should have warned me someone wanted you dead." James grinned at him. "By the way, I got some interesting shots of your climb before his attempt to kill you."

"Really?" Luke had almost forgotten James had climbed to the top to take photos of him ascending before the attempt on his life.

"Did Charlotte speak to Amy?"

"No. Her phone is switched off."

"Where did Charlotte go?"

"She's taken your car. She wanted to warn Sheena and be with George. We thought they should know what happened. Especially after the attack on Owen. I've also spoken to Andrew Clarke to make sure this gets connected to the fires."

"Good."

"Charlotte promised to let me know when she gets there. She was nervous about finding her way, but I made sure someone helped set up the Sat Nav to make sure she didn't get lost."

Later, there was a buzz from his phone. James looked at the message and handed Luke the phone.

It read, 'All well here. Heading to the hospital to wait for you. Tell Luke I still haven't spoken to Amy.'

"Thanks." Luke handed the phone back, trying to hide his disappointment.

"You're still worried?" James said as he took hold of his phone.

Luke nodded. He would be until he'd seen for himself that Amy and the kids were safe.

The ambulance ride seemed to take forever. The crew were all people they had worked with on shouts, true professionals, who refrained from asking for more details about the incident than necessary.

Charlotte was waiting for them at the entrance to the hospital. George was with her, which meant she couldn't stay. She had only come to check on them and to give Luke his phone and charger, and to say she'd come back later, after they'd seen the doctors and knew if they would be discharged.

"It hasn't stopped ringing," she said as she handed over the phone. "I didn't dare answer, as I didn't know who was calling. I hope that was the right thing to do."

"Perfect."

Duty done; Charlotte turned her attention to James. For a couple so recently met, they had become very close.

Luke scanned the list of missed calls. None from Amy. But five from a number he didn't recognize. If it was urgent, they would no doubt call again.

He hated to interrupt the pair, but he needed an answer to the question that had bothered him during the last few hours.

"Charlotte, what alerted you to trouble?"

"I was talking to Sheena when I spotted Joe and told her he was there. She told me to hide and to warn you."

"Thanks. Your warning saved my life."

A nurse interrupted their conversation to call Luke for his x-ray and James for a scan for his head injury.

"If it's okay with you Luke, I'll keep your car so I can pick you up if they think you're okay to go." Luke nodded, and Charlotte turned to James, "And if they insist you need someone around because of the bang to your head, then I'm happy for you to stay at my place."

"Thanks."

She turned back to Luke. "Sorry, our plans to celebrate your birthday were such a disaster. So lucky the kids weren't with us."

"Yes, very lucky."

The next few hours dragged as they waited for x-rays to be examined, and for the doctors to decide what needed to be done. Luke called Tamsin to check on Owen's progress. Nothing had changed. He was still being sedated.

"Sorry, I can't come and sit with you. I'm stuck in A&E with an injured arm," he said, "A climbing accident," he added, to avoid telling her what happened. She had enough to contend with without alarming her further. But he promised he'd be there as soon as he could.

His phone buzzed again. The same caller as before. This time, he answered.

"Luke, glad I've got hold of you. Do you know where Amy is?" Rupert sounded anxious compared to his normally cool tone.

The fact he didn't know Amy's whereabouts was something to celebrate. But was it too soon?

"No. I thought you were staying on for a few extra days. Perhaps she's gone to do some activity with the kids and forgotten to tell you." Luke said.

"That's what I thought at first, but she's taken the car, as well as my phone and my laptop. I had to get a new phone to call you."

Luke wanted to cheer. The judo warning worked. Rupert calling from a number he didn't recognize now made sense. He was tempted to ask if she'd packed all her clothes, but decided it might hint that he had been expecting her to take off.

"She hasn't contacted me," Luke said. "She's probably remembered some meeting she didn't want to miss and has gone back to your place."

"Maybe. But she should have left a note for me."

Luke really wanted to end the call. "I'll let you know if she gets in touch."

"Because she took my phone. I can't track her." Rupert said.

Track her. Luke bit back, asking what he meant. If she knew Rupert could track her, it would explain why she took the phone and laptop.

"Don't worry. I'll contact you on this number if I hear from her." Luke hit the disconnect button before he added something he'd regret.

Knowing Amy wasn't with Rupert made him feel he could risk calling her.

No response, so he sent a text, 'Rupert called. Worried, and wondering where you went with his phone and laptop. Let me know you're okay.'

"She's not with him." James said. He had obviously overheard one side of the conversation.

"No."

"That's good, isn't it?"

"It is, if he's telling the truth. For all I know, he could be holding her somewhere, and just trying to make out she has gone off with the kids."

James stared at him wide eyed. "You don't really think that?"

"With someone trying to kill me. It's hard not to have crazy thoughts. I won't rest easy until I speak to her face to face."

"I understand. And I don't blame you."

A nurse came and brought them a cup of tea each and a sandwich." Sorry they aren't very exciting, but it's the best I can offer. You'll be here for a while. The department is very busy today."

About half an hour later, he got a text from Amy, 'Love the bell tent. Girls paddle boarding'.

He understood her cryptic text. This was where he hoped they would go. It was the place they would have gone during the Easter break if he hadn't been injured. This should be a safe place for them. Now all he had to do was to join them.

He lay back down and closed his eyes, releasing some of the tension he had been holding in. As he lay there, he planned his next move. First, he had to convince the doctor that he was fit to leave the hospital. Charlotte would be busy taking care of James. He'd have to find someone to drive him up to be with Amy. He thought about Sheena, but she needed to keep an eye on Mabel. Which left Barry. And with such a headline breaking story going, there was no way Barry would turn him down.

He opened his eyes and looked at James. "What happened to my camera?"

"Charlotte took it back to your place. I got a couple of good ones of you at the bottom of the climb. And, gruesome or not, I took a picture of Joe, while he lay there with his leg trapped. I doubt you can use it, but the police might want them."

"What did the boss say when you spoke to him? Have you kept him up to date on Owen's progress?"

"I did, and he's told D I Hughes. Who agrees the attacks are connected."

"Great."

"I've told Sheena everything. I'm surprised she hasn't turned up yet."

At that point, the medical team came back to discuss their injuries.

"The x-ray shows you've broken the bone above the elbow, a clean break and not out of line. The break is too high for a cast, which means you will need a sling to keep it immobile while the bone repairs itself. Your open wound needs to be thoroughly cleaned and dressed. I can prescribe painkillers and antibiotics, but there is not much else we can do."

Luke was quick to demand non-addictive pain medication.

"I can't risk going down that route again." The doctor understood and chose an alternative to the pills he would normally prescribe.

When the doctor left, the nurse said, "Your friend Sheena is waiting. Are you up for a visitor?"

"Yes, please."

"She has a policeman with her, who also wants a word. Shall I let them in once your dressings are done?"

"Yes, the sooner, the better."

Chapter 27

The police officer with Sheena introduced himself as D I Roland Hughes. He was a dark-haired, stocky man, younger than Luke had imagined, with a warm smile. He thanked Luke for all the material he'd passed on. "Your investigation seems to have triggered panic. They must have a lot at stake to try to kill you."

"Yes, and not just me. I'm worried Owen is still in danger."

"I agree. Don't worry, we have put security in place. But you need to take care. I won't bother you with questions about today's events. I have enough from your instructor, Nathan, and the rescue team to make an arrest. When the suspect comes out of surgery, he'll be charged with attempted murder."

Luke winced; the pain kicked in again. He took a deep breath, closed his eyes, and exhaled, counting slowly as he breathed out.

Thankfully, Sheena picked up on the signs and suggested that they leave him in peace. "I'll see you back at your place. Mabel has a spare bed, so I will stay with her and be around to help if they let you out."

Soon after Sheena left with DI Hughes, James was given clearance to leave the hospital, and Charlotte picked him up.

"I feel bad leaving you here on your own," Charlotte said. But Luke shooed them off the ward, reassuring them that Barry was on his way.

They had only been gone a few minutes when Tamsin came rushing over to his bed.

His first thought was that Owen had died. But she soon reassured him he was still the same, and that they were going to reduce the sedation gradually. His most recent scan looked encouraging.

"What happened to you?" she asked.

Luke told her the truth. "Someone tried to kill me. I think Frank Patterson was behind it, and it ties in with the arson, and with the attack on Owen."

"It's all my fault," she rambled on for a while, blaming herself for introducing Owen to Frank, and then Amy to Rupert. Eventually, she dug into her handbag and found a fresh tissue and blew her nose.

"Sorry, I should never have gone on like that. But I feel so bad, because Amy left you, and I'm to blame."

"Don't blame yourself. You just concentrate on Owen and his recovery."

She blinked back her tears and blew her nose. "You're right, that's what matters now. But I struggled with the fact that you called to check on him after all he did, covering up the arson evidence. Then accusing you of being paranoid. Failing as your friend."

"He told the truth when it mattered, and that's enough for me."

"I'm sorry I didn't do more to put Amy off Rupert. I knew it wouldn't end well. After you were injured in that fire, I thought she'd come to her senses, but I was wrong, and I know it has put you in a tricky position with his father's dodgy dealings."

"It isn't your fault."

"Maybe not, but I hate it destroyed your marriage."

"Yes, me too."

Tamsin's phone chimed. She gave Luke an apologetic look and answered the call.

He was close enough to hear both sides of the conversation and realize that Rupert was the caller.

"No Rupert, I have no idea where Amy is." Tamsin answered sharply. She turned to Luke and gave him a puzzled look. Luke shrugged, and pointed to himself, and then put a finger up to his lips, hoping she would get the message not to tell Rupert he was there.

"Good luck finding her," she said, then added, "Sorry, I can't chat now. If I hear from her, I'll let you know. Bye." And with that, she disconnected.

"Do you know where Amy is?"

Luke avoided answering, and said, "Rupert called me earlier, said she took off with his phone and computer."

"Good for her. I hope she took them all. And I hope she's done with him for good. Frank Patterson and his lads are a dangerous bunch. Owen was terrified of them. Luckily the spot where they attacked him was covered by CCTV, so the police will have more chance of picking them up. One thing you can be sure of is that Frank won't have got his hands dirty."

"That's probably true."

Tamsin stood up. "I need to get back to the ward now."

"Thanks for coming. I'll be back to sit with him when I can."

The nurse came with a packet of non-addictive painkillers, a prescription for more antibiotics and his discharge papers. "You're free to leave."

He thanked everyone and made his way to the coffee shop. Barry had arranged to meet him there.

"What the hell happened to you?" he asked when he saw Luke.

"Someone tried to kill me."

"You're kidding." He laughed, but soon his jovial expression changed. "For real?"

Luke nodded. "A long story. I could do with a coffee, while I enlighten you. Then I need you to drive me somewhere."

"Sit down. I'll get it for you. Your usual?" Luke nodded and settled himself at the table. Barry went to the counter and placed the order. While Luke waited, he sent a text to Sheena, asking her to send all the information they had gathered to Barry. He needed to get clear of this mess, because digging deeper could be dangerous for his family.

Barry returned to the table with the coffee, along with a handful of sugar sachets. "I thought you looked as if you needed extra."

"I think you might need some yourself when you hear all I have to tell you."

"Go on. You have me intrigued."

"The only promise I want from you is that you liaise with DI Roland Hughes and my boss, Andrew Clarke, before you print a word. I don't want to give the culprits any reason to escape justice."

"Deal. I've worked with Hughes before. He's fair, and we get on."

"Good."

At that point, Barry's phone pinged. Emails were coming in.

He looked at the screen, frowned, was about to reach out to inspect, when Luke stopped him.

"I asked Sheena to forward you a stack of photos, and information and some part-written articles. They will need to be fact checked before they can go to press. You can publish them when you get permission to do so. This has become too personal, which is why I want to hand it over to you."

"Sorry, you can't quit. Let me guess, the Pattersons are involved."

Luke nodded. "Anything yet on squeaky clean, Rupert?"

"No." Barry answered. "He's too clever to let any of his father's muck stick. And there's plenty of that. I'm sure he has a weak spot. I'll keep digging. Is Amy still with him?"

"There's been a development." Luke had to be honest with Barry. "She knew I was investigating Frank, and we had an arrangement that I would send her a message if things got tricky."

"You sent the message?"

"Yes, and she took off. I haven't spoken to her yet. She doesn't know what happened on Dartmoor, and I want to explain it to her in person. That's where you come in. Can you take me to where she is? But we have to stop at my house on the way."

"What? Using me as a cheap taxi now?"

"Quit complaining. This is a huge scoop."

It didn't take long to get from the hospital to the house. Someone had parked across his driveway, so Barry pulled into a space on the other side of the street.

Luke stepped onto the curb. The wind had picked up, so he adjusted his jacket back onto the shoulder of his injured side. Barry was sitting in the driver's seat, his phone pressed to his ear. Luke decided not to wait for him. He set off across the road. He broke into a run when he heard an ear-piercing scream coming from his house. What the hell was going on? He reached the gate and saw a man with a petrol can in one hand. There was a pool of liquid at his feet. He held something in his other hand. Sheena was standing by the garage door, clutching a fire extinguisher, screaming at the top of her voice. The man dropped the can and threw what was in his hand down.

The pool of liquid burst into flames. Luke tried to go faster, but the pain in his arm shot through his body, slowing him down.

Sheena was racing towards the flames. The man turned to run and was heading straight at Luke. But he couldn't escape. His hands and sleeves were alight. So were his trousers. His movement was making matters worse, fanning the flames.

Luke had to stop him. He yelled to Barry to shut the gate. The man, realizing he was trapped and that his clothes were alight, froze for a second. Luke shouted. "Lie on the grass."

The man was cornered, but his instincts made him keep running towards the gate.

Luke charged and kicked his legs out from under him, then practically fell on top of him. He had to smother the flames before more damage was done. Pulling his jacket off his shoulder, using one hand, Luke did his best to cover the man's burning hands. Barry, seeing what he was doing, removed his jacket and threw it over his legs to starve the fire of oxygen.

With the flames extinguished. There was nothing else they could do for the man who writhed in agony on the tarmac. The smell of burnt flesh hit Luke, making him want to retch. It brought back the vivid memories of his own injuries.

"Try to keep still." Luke said, "you'll make things worse if you move." The man stared at him, a look of recognition in his eyes. Then Luke placed him. This was the man who attacked Owen. And he'd been cleaning the pool at Rupert's house. Antonio. So, there was a link.

The distant sirens sound got closer. Soon they were surrounded by police, ambulance crews, and firemen. Who had called them? Having emergency services on the scene so fast was rare.

A paramedic approached him and asked if he was okay. Luke knew that there was only one answer he could give. He straightened himself up and said, "I'm fine. Concentrate on him."

Sheena suggested he went into Mabel's annex while the fire crew assessed the damage and made sure everything was safe. He wanted to resist, but he hadn't the strength to argue, not that Sheena would have listened.

"Can I come too?" Barry asked and introduced himself to Sheena. "I'd love to hear about your part in this drama."

"Of course," she said, and led the way round to the entrance to the annex. Mabel took one look and told Luke and Barry to sit down and presented them with mugs of tea.

Luke knew that shock was setting in. The movement needed to get the man on the ground and to cover the flames had jolted his broken arm, and while adrenalin had been in full flow, he had done what was necessary. Now he felt utterly drained. He drank the tea and did some deep breathing exercises. He needed to be calm. He had to find Amy and fill her in on the drama unfolding around him. Sheena joined them.

"You don't have to do anything or talk if you don't want to," Sheena said softly. "Everything is under control."

"Who called the police?"

"Mabel. It was because of the doorbell camera that you set up. After Charlotte came for George and told us what happened on Dartmoor, we were naturally nervous. We knew about Owen, so we didn't want to take any risks."

Luke nodded. He was listening.

"So, when your doorbell went off," Sheena continued, "Mabel showed me the screen on her phone. It was the man that Amy had identified as Mike. He had a large carrier bag with him, which he put down on the step. We decided not to respond. He tried the bell again, and we watched as he signalled to a big guy lurking by the gate, pointing for him to go round to the back. I went to the kitchen window that looks out the back and saw him break the glass of your kitchen door and let himself in. Mabel called the police. Then she saw Mike take a can of petrol out of the box and remove the cap. So she told the police to alert the fire brigade."

"You did the right thing." Luke shook his head. "But you didn't have to come charging out to tackle the blaze yourself."

"Why not? When you rearranged things in the garage for Mabel's mobility scooter, I helped move the fire extinguisher. So, I knew exactly where to find it. And I was hardly going to sit indoors and let your house burn down."

"Anyway, Mike put the can down and seemed to argue with someone on the phone. Then, the front door opened, and the big guy came out. He had your computer. Mike grabbed it. He pointed to the can of petrol, giving him instructions, and handed him something. Then Mike hurried away with the computer and went out the gate. I saw him get into a car on the other side of the road. That's when the other guy picked up the can, and recklessly splashed petrol inside the front door and the porch, getting it all over himself. The man seemed angry. I don't think he realized how much had splashed on his hands and clothing. It was only when he triggered the lighter that he realized what he had done. His hands caught fire, and he dropped the lighter. That's when his trousers burst into flames."

"You must have been terrified, especially for Mabel. It's awful that she moved to be safe only to have danger follow her."

"I only had the extinguisher because I thought I could scare them off. Because the fire was between me and him, I couldn't reach him to stop him from getting so badly burnt." She stopped talking for a moment. "All I could do was try to minimize the damage to your home. So that's what I did."

It felt surreal listening to her calmly telling of a traumatic event while sipping tea surrounded by Mabel's antique furniture and ornaments.

"Next thing I knew, you were there, with the man on the ground, yelling at him to lie still as you threw your coat over him to put the flames out. You don't know how glad I was to see you. You too, Barry, and the rest of the crew who turned up." She got to her feet. "Stay with him Barry, Mabel has been making tea for everyone. I'm going to take it out for them," she said, as she left them alone.

"Brave lady," Barry said, "How are you holding up? I hope your arm is okay."

"I'll live, but I still need to see Amy."

"I know, but you should find out what the damage is before you rush off. And another cup of tea wouldn't go amiss. I think I'm in more shock than you. Dealing with fires is not normally on my agenda."

Sheena came back and sat with them. "I've talked to that DI who your boss was dealing with. He wants a word with you. I told him to come over when he's ready. From what I can see, you'll need two new doors, both front and back. And there's smoke damage, but I am not sure how bad that is as they wouldn't let me inside yet. Seems the fire didn't spread further than the hall."

"What happened to Mike?"

"When things looked to be going wrong, he tried to drive off, but the incoming fire engine blocked his way. He abandoned his car and ran. When they chased after him, he threw the computer over a wall. They gave up, but you'll be pleased to know they've retrieved your computer."

"Will Mabel be okay? It's not been the best introduction to her new home."

Sheena laughed. "She's having a great time. Hasn't felt so useful in years."

"Feeling useful has its merits." Luke turned to Barry. "Is your car blocked in? If not, I need to get out of here."

Barry went to find out.

"Sheena, I need a favour." Luke said. "Can you persuade them to let you into the house? I need a few things. The big bottle of cream beside my bed, some easy to pull on clothes, enough for a couple of days."

He didn't want to waste any more time talking. Amy and the girls were his priority.

When Sheena returned with the bag, he told her he'd be heading off.

"But you need to talk to DI Hughes first."

"I know. There are things I didn't share with him that will add clarity to his investigation. Perhaps you could fill him in."

"What in particular?"

"I don't think I told him how Rupert and his father fit in. And that Amy moving out was an added complication. I'm worried about her. She knew my concerns about Rupert's father, but I had no proof. We agreed that I'd send her a message if I thought it was time for her to leave."

"And you sent the message?" Sheena asked.

"Yes, and I got a reply that she understood. She's gone somewhere safe, but I am not prepared to share that information with anyone until I have spoken to her myself. Rupert's looking for her, and I don't intend for him to find her."

Chapter 28

The drive to the lake campsite, where he expected to find Amy and the children, would take at least an hour. Time he would use to give Barry a rundown of events from the fire that caused his initial injury, leading to his first suspicion that arson was the cause and right up to his rescue from the rock face.

"I hope you understand now why I need to step away from this story." Luke said after he related the chain of events.

Barry glanced towards him and said, "I understand your reasoning for wanting to get shot of the whole affair. And I'm grateful for your trust in me, but you are involved, and stepping aside isn't the answer."

He was surprised at this reaction. He'd expected Barry to be keen to take over.

"I even lied to my boss last week. I told him I had shared all my information with you, and that you're the only reporter they should talk to, and promised them you wouldn't blow things out of proportion for the sake of a sensational headline."

"Thanks for your confidence. I'm flattered, but why would you think I'd avoid a sensational headline?"

"It's not your style. Which is why I want to hand the story on to you. I swore you would not use a single photo or name a victim or a suspect without clearance. Please don't let me down."

"I'll do whatever I can to help. But you are still part of this."

Luke knew better than to argue with Barry, so said, "Sheena has already sent you the files, and as soon as I know Amy is safe, you can set to work."

Barry kept his eye on the road. "You mentioned Frank Patterson when we met up ages ago. I did some digging. Interesting man, I'll let you have a copy of my findings. What makes you think his son is involved?"

"That's it. So far, I've found nothing that connects him. But I'm pretty sure he told his father I was investigating, and he knew I would be on Dartmoor climbing."

"Interesting."

Barry hit a pothole in the road. The jolt ran through Luke, making him groan.

Barry pulled into the next gateway and stopped.

"Sorry, I didn't see it. I forgot about your injury."

"Give me a minute." Luke closed his eyes and concentrated on his breathing. He could do this. He could manage without pills. He had to. Gradually, the pain triggered by the jolt eased, and he opened his eyes again.

Barry's look of concern made him smile.

"I'll be okay. Thanks for stopping." Barry passed him an open bottle of water. Luke took it and drank a little.

They sat for a while in silence, mulling over the situation.

"When we get there," Luke said, "would you mind if I go to find her on my own? There's a café. You can check out all the files Sheena has sent to you while I talk to Amy."

"Are you sure that's the best plan?"

"What do you mean?"

"Amy's going to want to know what happened to you, and I'm guessing you'll pretend you fell over rather than tell the kids the real story."

"True."

"Let me come with you. And while you let the girls wish you a happy birthday and all that, I can quietly fill Amy in on what you told me."

Luke accepted that this was a better plan. He had been wondering how she was going to react when he arrived.

"Does she know you're coming?" Barry asked.

"No. Her phone is switched off. And to be honest, I'm not even sure she would have understood my message."

Barry's phone buzzed.

He pulled it out and scrolled down the screen. Luke expected him to respond to his messages, but he looked at Luke. "Sheena's sent me a load more stuff. I will look later. First, let's see if we can find Amy and your girls. But do everyone a favour; take the painkillers they gave you at the hospital. I know you don't want to get hooked on pills again, but you're in no fit state to see the girls the way you are now, all hunched up in pain. You won't fool anyone, especially your two rascals."

Barry was right, he had been close to admitting defeat himself. He dug into his pocket and pulled out the box of pills, and handed it over to Barry and watched as he read the instructions. He popped the blister pack and passed Luke two pills, followed by the opened water bottle.

"Thanks," he said after he'd swallowed the medication. He would have preferred to take one pill, but Barry had a point. He needed a clear head to deal with the girls.

"Are you going to give me the exact location, so I can set my Sat Nav, or are you going to sit there trying to remember the way?"

Luke sighed and told him to head for the campsite at Wimbleball Reservoir. Barry fiddled with the buttons on the car's navigation system, shoved a disk into the CD player, and said, "Let's go. I'll avoid potholes. Just relax."

The disk he had chosen was soothing choral music. Luke studied the car's dials and noticed Barry had the heater on full blast, even though it was a warm autumn day. He wanted to ask him to turn it down, but didn't have the energy. Barry, true to his word, was taking the route slowly. The thick hedges that embraced the lanes hid the stunning views, which could be glimpsed through the gateways they passed on the way. Luke closed his eyes to rest while he could.

When he woke up, he was alone. Barry had parked in a shady spot near to the café. Luke guessed he had gone off to find Amy. He was tempted to go looking for them himself. But was feeling weak and decided it was probably better for Barry to alert Amy to his condition. The pills had eased the pain a bit. He hoped the effect would last long enough to fool the girls.

Barry had left the water bottle with the cap off within reach for him. Adjusting to using his right hand for everything, after months of having to train himself to use his left, was another hurdle he would have to overcome.

His hope of getting back to normal was further away than ever before. He was putting his trust in Barry to make the most of the information he'd been given. It wasn't quite how he hoped to get his journalism career on track, but it was the best he could do for now.

He scanned the path up from the water's edge. Barry was on his way up the path. He wanted to get out of the car to greet him, but couldn't reach the door handle without putting pressure on his broken arm. Barry pulled open the door and leaned in and said, "I can't find them." He was out of breath. "Nor can I find the manager to ask if they arrived. What sort of car is she driving?"

Luke shook his head. "I don't know. She has his car. Did you check the bell tent area?"

"No, is that where you think she will be?"

"That's what I booked. Help me out of here, and we can go together."

They hurried over to the bell tents. The area was almost deserted, but one man was sitting near a tent reading a book.

Luke approached him. "Excuse me, you don't happen to know if my wife and two girls are staying in one of these tents?"

The man looked warily at Luke and Barry and said, "What's your name?"

Luke was surprised to be asked, but then maybe Amy had said something about avoiding someone. "Luke. My wife is Amy, and the girls are called Katie and Janet. I made the booking, but I am not sure if they've arrived."

"What do you do for a living?"

"Fireman."

The man smiled. "They've gone off with my wife and kids to the yacht club. They should be back soon, as the girls have a paddleboard lesson booked. Grab a seat while you wait. You don't look too good. Your wife said you'd been injured, but I thought she said you were okay."

Luke, too exhausted to explain that this was a recent injury, sank into the chair on offer.

"I'll head that way and see if I can catch up with them." Barry didn't wait for an argument, as he set off.

"You look like you could do with a drink. I can do tea or coffee. By the way, my name is Dave."

"Tea would be great."

Dave nodded. "Won't be long."

Luke shifted in the chair, trying to position his arm more comfortably, then closed his eyes and tried to relax. The next he knew was that Amy was leaning over him shaking his leg.

"I've been so worried since I got your text. Barry said what happened wasn't an accident."

"No, but I'll mend. It's a clean break and should heal without complications." He took her hand in his. "I'll fill you in later. Are the girls okay?"

"Yes, Barry took them to the café. They'll be here in a moment."

"Sorry, I didn't phone to explain what was going on. I thought sending a text would be safer than calling. I wasn't sure if you'd be able to speak freely."

"When I read your message, I realized it was urgent. I convinced Rupert that the girls and I were going to watch Frozen for the umpteenth time, and I suggested he go to the gym to avoid it and asked him to pick up burgers on his way back to the lodge. He didn't hesitate; a week with the girls was stretching his patience."

"No surprise." Luke muttered.

"Don't go there," Amy said.

"Sorry."

"Anyway, I watched him go, and grabbed some of the girl's clothes and some of mine. I heard his computer ping. It was unusual for him to leave it open when I was around, so I took a peek. There was a message from his father. He said something had gone wrong, and he'd be on their boat and keeping a low profile, and suggested Rupert did the same."

"Interesting."

"Yes. I was careful not to close the computer lid, as I was sure he had a password lock on it. I took it as it was, grabbed his phone too, and left. I headed to the nearest town to find a computer repair shop. I said it was making funny noises and asked them to make a backup before it died on me. The guys there were ever so helpful, did the backup, and offered to check out the machine. I said I couldn't come back to that area but asked them to see if it had any tracking programs loaded, because I had an ex-stalking me. They found a couple and disabled them."

"That's why you switched your phone off?"

"Yes."

"Well done. I thought I'd tell the girls that I fell over after my climb and landed badly against a rock."

"Fine. But later, I want the full story."

"Is that an invitation to stay?"

Chapter 29

When the girls spotted him, they squealed with delight and bounded towards him. The sling registered, and they ground to a halt. Their widespread arms primed to give him a hug, dropped to their sides.

The reaction coloured by his previous injury spared him from a painful reunion. They took turns to lean in to give him a birthday kiss. "Mummy didn't say you were coming."

"She wanted to surprise you."

"We missed you." Janet said.

"I missed you too." Normally he tried not to say that, as he never wanted them to carry guilt over being with their mother rather than with him. But today, it felt right.

"What happened to your arm?" Katie asked.

Luke launched into a tale about how he had seen a giant rabbit coming over the hill and had been so distracted by the creature he hadn't looked at where he was going. "I tripped over a rock, fell sideways and banged my arm so hard; it broke."

"Will you have a scar like on the other side?" Janet asked.

"No, but I will need lots of help to do things."

"We can help you."

He kissed their foreheads, grateful to have such thoughtful children.

"Why don't you both take me and show me your tent? I'm rather tired and could do with a rest for a while. Mum can stay here and chat with Barry. He has lots of boring stuff on his computer he wants to share with her. I'd much rather hear about your paddleboard lessons than listen to all that again." Luke looked towards Amy and Barry. "You okay with that?"

They nodded.

"Good. Don't leave without speaking to me."

Barry smiled. "Of course not."

The girls' apparent joy at having him to themselves, and the chance to boast about their newly gained skills, made the walk to the bell tent seem short.

It was bigger inside than expected. He sat on the edge of the bed and listened to their excited chatter. Then Janet picked up her book and brought it over to him.

"Are you going to read to me today?" he asked, hoping that it might save him from the task. He took off his shoes and swung his feet up onto the bed. "I'll lie down and listen."

She looked a bit surprised at the change of roles but ran round to the other side of the bed, adjusted the pillows to make herself comfy, leaving a gap between them. His previous injury had taught them to be wary of snuggling in tight. She waited while Katie climbed onto the bed beside her and settled herself down to read.

When Luke woke up, it took a moment to work out where he was. Amy was outside, talking quietly to Barry. The girls had gone; the book abandoned on the bed beside him. He sat up, slipped on his shoes, and went to join them.

"Good to see you awake. Barry was wondering how long to leave you sleeping. He wants to go, but has a few things to clear with you first."

"Fire away." Luke said.

"We've read all the files that Sheena posted, and there are a couple of people mentioned, and I'm not sure how to contact them if I need to. Martin, the homeless man, is one."

"Sheena has his contact details. She can also give you names of the others who were living in the flats that moved before the fire and those who lost their homes."

"And the climbing contacts?"

"Nathan at the climbing centre will put you in touch with them, and the chaps who came to the rescue. I told him I was handing the articles over. He's happy to help. As far as the arson story goes, you'll have to run that past my boss, Andrew Clarke. James can introduce you to him."

"I will, I won't let you down," Barry said. "The major problem we have right now is Rupert's computer and phone. There are serious legal implications to avoid. Amy copied all the files from them onto a backup disk because his computer wasn't locked. But that doesn't give us the right to delve into those files, tempting as it might be."

Luke understood Barry's concerns. Much as he wanted to prove that Rupert was untrustworthy, doing the wrong thing could destroy the fragile relationship he had with Amy. And he wasn't prepared to do that.

He turned to her. "What do you want to do?"

She shrugged. "I was so frightened when I got that message. I reacted rashly and fled with the computer. I don't know what made me get the copies done, or if I want to know what they contain."

"So far, I haven't unearthed any proof Rupert is involved with Frank's schemes," Luke said, "But Frank telling him to lie low implies Rupert knew what he was up to. Have you passed that information on?" Luke asked, wondering what else he had missed while sleeping.

"Yes," Barry said, "I spoke to Roland Hughes, the copper that your boss was in touch with. With luck, they'll pick Frank up before he gets too far away."

"Did you tell him about Amy having the computer and phones?"

"Yes, but I didn't mention that she had copied his files." Barry said, "To be honest, I'd keep hold of them even if you don't know what's on them. Having them might be enough to keep the family safe."

They sat silently, letting the information sink in. And then Luke remembered something odd that Tamsin had said after Rupert called her.

"Amy, I think you should talk to Tamsin. When I saw her at the hospital, she muttered something about dodgy dealings. When I told her you had taken his computer and phone, she said she hoped you got them all. But I was still in shock, so didn't take it in. Find out what she meant and persuade her to talk to Barry. She may know things that will help."

"Good call," Barry said, "and until we know what to look for, I think we should return his computer and phone via the police. Let them decide if their interest in his father merits them checking his devices for information."

"And the copies I made?" Amy asked.

"Do as Barry suggested. Hang onto them for insurance. They may come in handy one day," Luke answered. "Where are the girls?"

Amy smiled. "Playing Monopoly with their newfound friends in the tent over there."

"Good," he said. "Make that call to Tamsin. She could do with a friend right now. But don't tell her where we are. Find out how Owen is."

While Amy called Tamsin, Barry asked what Luke planned to do.

"I'll stay here with Amy and the kids. I don't like the idea of them being alone, not that I would be much use in a crisis. As far as I know, you're the only person who knows where we are. Which is good. According to Sheena, the house stinks of smoke and petrol, so probably best to stay away for several days. Maybe longer."

"I have a weekend cottage you could use."

"Thanks. I might need to take you up on the offer. I'll talk to Amy about it. But everything depends on Rupert's role in all this? I can't push her decisions."

"No. I get your dilemma. Do you think you can make a go of it again? From what I can see, she still cares for you."

"I can't think that far ahead."

Amy had walked away to make the call, and now she was almost breaking into a run to get back to them.

"Tamsin says Rupert always had a couple of phones on the go. I don't remember ever seeing any others, but she's sure he kept one in his golf bag. On the few occasions when she caught him using it, he was speaking French."

"Interesting. That fits with something I dug up about him, which I had intended to follow up," Barry said.

"His golf bag is in the car." Amy pulled the keys out of her bag. "Shall we check if she's right?"

"If you don't mind, I'll stay here." Luke said, "Any chance of a glass of water, or something to take my pills with?"

"Good to see you're being sensible." Barry said, as Amy passed over a bottle of water. "He seemed to think he could cope without them earlier."

She shook her head. "That's no surprise."

Luke watched them go up the path. A second phone might be very revealing. Rupert was looking more suspicious.

Amy came back clutching a small black leather zipped bag. She plonked it on the table in front of Luke. "Not one phone, but three, and a memory stick. What the hell is he hiding?"

"I'll ask the police what to do with them." Barry moved away to make the call, leaving Luke alone with Amy. It wasn't long before he came back with a plan. "I'll take the phones and computer to the police. They'll inform Rupert that you've contacted them and will return his car soon. Which stops him reporting it as stolen. They'll say you were concerned he might report you as missing. They agree it would be good for you to stay on here until they've had time to talk to his father, who is in custody."

Luke looked at Amy for her approval.

"Sounds sensible to me. There's plenty of room in the tent, as long as you're prepared to share the double bed with me."

He stared at her for a moment. He hadn't considered the sleeping arrangements. But with his arm in a sling, it would be the same as it had been when he came out of hospital all those months ago. Intimacy not included, though she was still holding his hand.

"I can cope, if you don't mind."

"The girls will be thrilled."

"I won't be much fun," he pointed to his sling.

"They're used to you being out of action."

"I guess they are."

"Good. I've had an idea." Barry said. "To stop Rupert making a fuss about his car, why don't I leave mine here with you and drive his back to the police station?"

"No." Amy said firmly. "Rupert was very protective of his car. I don't think he'd be happy if you took it."

"Barry, can you get us a new phone? And ask the police to check if Owen and Tamsin's phones are being tracked."

"Good call." Barry said. "I'll head off now and see you in the morning."

Chapter 30

After Barry left, Amy suggested taking a stroll round the reservoir to the outflow dam. Luke wanted to spend time with the girls so agreed, though he wasn't sure how he'd keep up. The children ran backwards and forwards, adding twice the distance that the adults took. But never far enough away from them for a serious conversation to take place.

Luke was relieved, as there were too many uncertainties about their relationship that could turn sour if he said the wrong thing. They made it past the sailing club, but the uneven path made it tough going. His trussed-up arm was throbbing unbearably.

"Sorry, Amy, I am going to stop. Probably best if I head back, but you go on with the girls." He hoped she wouldn't try to persuade him to keep going.

"We can come back with you."

"No, please carry on."

When the girls came running back to them, she said gently, "Daddy's tired. He's heading back for a rest, but we can go on."

"Okay," they responded in unison, and darted off down the path.

Luke was grateful. He needed time on his own. He still hadn't got over the shock that his investigation had become so dangerous. He reached the tent, found his unfinished coffee sitting on the table, which he used to swill down a couple of tablets. Today was not the day to suffer. The bed offered the comfiest place to rest his arm. He grabbed one of the children's fleeces, rolled it in a ball to help prop his arm up when he lay down. The campsite noises were a distraction, but not unpleasant, distant chatter, laughter, footsteps running down the path. The smell of wood-smoke and sizzling sausages wafted in the air.

Waking up was strange. He was on the wrong side of the bed. He didn't want to move because even the slightest adjustment to his position hurt. The barely perceptible sound of the breathing of the other three in the tent was soothing, so he focused on that.

Slowly, his thoughts turned to the obstacles his latest injury would create. How the hell was he going to plaster cream on his scars? The friction of the sling on his neck was something he was going to have to sort out soon. He didn't feel he could ask Amy for that sort of help. But he was going to have to figure out a solution.

Leaves falling on the tent roof were an added distraction. Amy turned beside him. Her proximity triggered unrealistic desires, desires that had lain dormant since his first accident. Why now when he could not act? The only solution was to get up.

He pushed aside the cover that someone had spread over him and eased himself to a sitting position, slid his feet into his shoes. Now all he needed to do was to see if he could open the tent flap without waking the family.

The morning air had a chill in it. He made his way to the shower block and returned to sit in a camp chair outside the tent to watch the sunrise.

Gradually more and more people emerged from their tents and the rattle of cups, kettles, and murmured conversations filled the air. Dave from the neighbouring tent came, and in hushed tones, offered to get his fire going. Luke accepted, knowing that lighting a match was beyond his capabilities. The kindness of strangers continued, as the man's wife came over with a blanket to put round his shoulder, and a warming cup of coffee.

Luke wished he could repay their kindness. Now all he could do was enjoy the moment and wait for his family to emerge. The longer he sat there, the more pleasure he got from the pace of camp life.

Barry arrived earlier than Luke expected. He had come bearing fresh pastries, muffins, and a flask of strong coffee, along with a sense of excitement. "Hi, you're looking better today. Manage to get some sleep?"

"Yes, I did. Perhaps more than you. You look as if you've been up all night."

"Close to the truth. There were so many things to check up on. By the way, James is doing well. Charlotte's taking good care of him. Owen's the same, but that's what we expected."

"Shame, I hoped that he'd have woken up by now."

"They might try today." Barry poured himself coffee and continued. "Sheena packed a load of stuff for you. Blame her if anything is missing. She and Mabel are fine. Seems the damage is not as bad as they led you to believe. The lads from the station came over to clean up."

Luke was surprised that they would do that. Perhaps Andrew Clarke felt it was recompense for failing to spot the arson links.

Barry kept turning and looking around anxiously. Luke wondered if he was afraid that he'd been followed.

"Where's Amy?" he asked.

"Still asleep. All this fresh air seems to have wiped the family out. I expect they'll wake soon. So, tell me, what did you discover?"

"You'll have to wait for Amy when she's about. I will fill you in. Meanwhile, have some coffee, and one of these." He pushed a box containing a selection of pastries towards Luke. As soon as he had taken one, Barry filled his cup with coffee from his flask. He tried to hand it to Luke and realized that with one arm out of action, and the other holding a pastry, there was no way he could take the cup. "Sorry, I'll put it over here for now."

He set the cup down on the bench that was out of reach. To move to get it would be too painful, so Luke settled for eating the pastry.

Of course, when Amy appeared, so did the girls, so Barry held back from telling his discoveries until all the pastries had been consumed, and the girls were ready to head to the water for a paddleboard session.

Luke could tell Amy was as keen as he was to grill Barry, but nothing was said that would alert the girls to the strange situation unfolding around them.

Before they walked down to the water's edge with the girls, Luke asked Amy to find his pills. He had hung on too long and his arm was hurting too badly to ignore.

The girls ran on ahead, and the three adults followed. As soon as they were afloat, Luke turned to Barry.

"Okay, start talking."

"Amy, I took the liberty of investigating your business ventures."

Amy gave him a questioning look.

"Yes, I'm particularly interested in your import business."

"I've no idea what you're talking about. I only have the business for my design work. Rupert set it up for me."

"And you know nothing about importing furniture and other sundries?"

Amy stared at him wide eyed and shook her head.

"With the interior design business, you are the sole trader, and only contact."

Amy nodded and waited for him to go on.

"The second import business has a named associate, Moira Sullivan. So far, I haven't found out anything about her."

"The only Moira I know is Rupert's housekeeper. But her surname isn't Sullivan. It's Walker. I remember thinking it didn't fit, as she didn't look the type who ever walked further than crossing the street." Amy looked over at Luke. "She's the woman the girls made a fuss about and didn't want to have babysitting. To be honest, I don't blame them. She's a sour faced individual."

Luke remembered the incident well. Both girls had been sulky all day when they had been with him. It was so unlike them that he had to find out what was wrong. He bribed them with the promise of a treat; all they had to do was tell him what was upsetting them. Janet cracked first. Tears trickled down her cheek as she told him that they didn't want to go home, because the scary lady was going to be looking after them.

"Why were they so against her?" Barry asked.

"She would send them to bed long before bedtime. And once, when Maria was in charge, they were locked in their room." Luke answered.

Amy looked shocked. "Why didn't you tell me?"

"It didn't seem necessary," Luke now wished he'd let her know before. "When I said I didn't want them left with strangers, and that if you were going out, they had to come back to my place. You agreed to my request."

"Amy opened her mouth to say something, but Barry butted in.

"I'll check that name out when I get back. Maybe that will clear things up."

"Let's hope so." Luke said.

"I did as you asked and spent time with Tamsin. Poor woman is distraught. She blames herself for everything. I got her talking about Rupert. And once she started, I thought she would never stop, but some interesting snippets came out. She asked if you were picking up Rupert's messages."

"No, I stopped checking."

"Mind if I take a look?"

Amy dug into her pocket and pulled out her phone and handed it to Barry.

He turned it on, and it started to ping as a string of messages loaded.

"Ten missed messages. Looks as if they were all from Rupert. Mind if I read them?"

"Be my guest." Amy answered.

"He's rattled. Seems he doesn't care about the computer and phone. All he wants is his car."

"Did he say phone, or phones," Luke said.

Barry looked back at the screen. "Phone."

"Did the police tell him they had the other phones?"

"I'm not sure. I'll check."

The group of paddleboarders were back from their excursion round the reservoir with their instructor. They had a bit of a splash about in the water before they finally hauled their boards ashore. Luke went down to meet them.

The girls waved to him and carried on, helping to stack the boards before running to join him.

"Hungry?" he asked, certain that the answer would be yes. Enthusiastic nodding showed he was right. "Good, let's go back, you can get those wet suits off, and then we'll head to the café for something to eat."

He found Amy on her own. Barry was wandering in the distance, in deep conversation on his phone.

She reached out to touch his hand as he sat down. "Are you all right? Barry's over there, talking to DI Hughes."

"Good. I wonder what suggestions he'll have to get Rupert off your back."

The girls interrupted the flow of conversation and happily devoured a flapjack, each followed by a bag of crisps, all washed down with a carton of juice. Once they were fully charged, they begged permission to go and play with their newfound friends. Permission was granted, and they ran off laughing.

As soon as they were out of earshot, Barry filled them in on his conversation with the Detective.

"Rupert doesn't seem bothered about collecting his computer or phone. He's demanding that you return his car immediately. I said that he kept calling and sending texts, but that you hadn't replied. You're afraid and you're not ready to face him. I even told him about his latest offer to send a hire car and get the driver to pick up his."

"What did he say about that?"

"You're doing the right thing, ignoring the calls. The only thing that is even slightly incriminating on his computer and phone is that message from his father, which is why they were willing to hand them back. Rupert probably thinks the others are still hidden in his golf bag, which is why he's so keen to get his car back."

"Makes sense," Luke said.

"With the added information about the extra business in your name, he wants you to stay on here until he's had time to dig deeper and work out what they are up to. The extra phones and memory stick are still being examined."

"So, with nothing on his computer or phone, so far Rupert is managing to keep his squeaky-clean image intact." Luke said.

Amy shot him a puzzled look. He explained. "You were moving my family in with him, so naturally I did a thorough background check."

She sighed and turned back to Barry. "What next?"

"Are you two prepared to stay here for another day at least?"

"I can live with that. What about you, Amy?"

"Yes, but Barry, I've been thinking about my business set up. Rupert was the one that was keen to get it rolling. I was wary, but unlike Tamsin, I didn't back off. She told me that he'd offered to set her up in business, but she turned him down. I remember her telling me that Owen was very pleased with her decision. He told her he never trusted the guy, but neither did he tell her about his gambling debt or about how they dragged him into their dodgy dealings."

"I think you've got the right idea," Barry said.

"So, he was using me?" she asked.

Luke shrugged. Most likely, but he wasn't going to say so. This was something Amy must figure out for herself.

"The business set up. Did he do it, or did you?" Barry asked.

"He did."

"And the bank account? Did he set that up too?"

"He took care of everything. Gave me papers to sign, which I did, and hey presto. I had a business up and running."

"That may be the answer. He had all the information required to set up an extra business to launder money."

Amy stared at him, letting the information sink in.

"Will I find myself in trouble if he has?"

Barry shrugged.

"Maybe there's evidence in my office. Here," she fumbled in her bag and dug out a bunch of keys, wound one off the key ring, and handed it to him. "This is the key to my office. They're welcome to search the place. There's a filing cabinet in the corner with a pot plant on it, which was there when Rupert offered me the space. I have no idea what's in it. I never had a key to it. I didn't need to use it; I had my own filing cabinet. Maybe there's something there that will help figure out what's going on."

Barry decided to run it past the detective before accepting the key. Her office might give answers. "Are you sure you don't want to be there when they go in?"

"No, and I don't care if they have to tear the place apart, if it gets to the truth."

"If you're talking to DI Hughes, ask if they found out why Rupert's father needed to lie low." Luke said.

Barry walked away to make the phone call, saying the signal was better further up the campsite track.

As they watched him, Luke took the opportunity to check with Amy if she was sure she was happy about him staying.

"Yes, I am. I had my first decent night's sleep, because I knew you were here." She touched his hand. "Believe me. We want you here with us."

Luke accepted his role stopped at father and family support. It was enough for now; at least they were all together.

Barry returned with a concerned look on his face. When asked what was up, he quickly smiled and pretended there was nothing to worry about.

"Yes, they'd like to search your office. He asked me to check if you pay rent on the place."

"Yes, not much. Rupert told me it was a tax-deductible expense."

"Very true, but the police will need your permission in writing, then they won't need a search warrant."

"Have you got paper or will an email do?"

"Here, this should be good enough." Barry shoved one of his reporters notepads across the table, along with a pen.

While she was busy doing that, Luke asked, "What happened to Frank?"

"He's still in custody. They'll keep him there while they investigate the attack on you. They're also trying to link him to the incident at your house, and to the beating that Owen took. And still working through the information you supplied."

"What about Joe?"

"Luckily, he's been filling the police in with his part in it all. Trouble is that his confession might not be admissible evidence because of the pain relief he's on. The medication could explain his eagerness to implicate Frank and put him firmly in the frame. As for the incompetent pair who were arrested at your house. Neither of them have been charged yet. Antonio is still being treated for his burns, which are not as bad as they would have been if you hadn't floored him and smothered the flames. The police want to make sure that any charges made will stick. By using a lesser charge, they hope to keep Frank in custody while the investigation continues."

"I hope they can keep him locked up." Luke said.

"DI Hughes is surprised by the fact that Rupert has refused to come in to see his father."

Amy said, "That's odd. They always seemed so close."

"Trouble always lets you know who really cares." Barry said. "Make the most of the peace here while you can."

Chapter 31

The day together was different to days spent as a family in the past. Because they didn't want to take Rupert's car anywhere, they were confined to the campsite. Barry had delivered groceries and a bag of clothes and other items for Luke. The first thing Luke did after Barry left was take stock of the things supplied.

It was fairly evident that Charlotte had given Barry some tips on what the girls would like. And some of his favourite snacks were included.

Amy peered over his shoulder. "Did you tell him what to bring?"

"No, but I'll bet Charlotte steered him in the right direction."

Amy gave him a quizzing look.

"Yes, and when you see her next, you can thank her for my being alive."

"What do you mean?"

"She came to Dartmoor with me and James to watch us climb. She warned us she'd spotted Joe and told Sheena she had seen him. And when I told Nathan that I didn't trust the guy, he made me move to a spot with an overhang. James saw her signals, but didn't understand what the problem was, and that's how he came to get knocked out."

It was the first chance he had of filling Amy in on the climbing disaster. "When I got down, she told me you had replied to my text. I was so relieved that you had taken me seriously."

"I liked that you chose this as a safe place. I wondered what you were up to, and who I could trust, especially when I read the text from Charlotte asking if I'd got your message, rather than a call from you."

Their conversation was interrupted by the girls, who wanted to know if they could go for a walk with their friends. Amy went with them to discuss the plan with the other family. Luke stayed where he was. If he kept his arm still, it didn't hurt. While he fancied a walk, he knew it would only trigger pain, and he'd need more pain killers. Sitting quietly was preferable.

Amy returned to collect snacks for the girls and their friends to take on their trek. "Join them if you want. I'll be fine here on my own," he said, though he hoped that she wouldn't leave him.

"No, I'd rather stay and talk without the girls distracting us."

The girls ran over and gave him a quick kiss and a cheerful wave as they rushed off down towards the path that would take them around the reservoir.

"Amy, mind if we put the chat off for a while. I could do with a shower, but I'm not sure I can manage on my own. Can you help?"

"What sort of help?" she asked.

He shrugged. "Dressing, undressing, trying to make sure I don't unwittingly shock the other campers by appearing naked in their midst."

Amy laughed. "Of course, I'll help protect your modesty."

He started to pull things out of the bag. She nudged him out of the way and took over and laid out a clean set of clothes. Then she grabbed his wash bag and a towel.

"Anything else you need?"

"You don't happen to have any cling film here?"

"What for?"

"To protect the dressing on my arm. It doesn't matter if you don't. I'm sure I can avoid getting it wet."

With everything ready, he suggested, "It might be easier to take the sling and t-shirt off here. I can put a towel over my shoulder to cover up."

Amy nodded and said, "Tell me what to do."

"See if you can slip my elbow out of my t-shirt while the other one is still in the sling."

She did as asked, rolled the shirt up, stretched it to pull it down his arm, then once the arm was free, tried to get his head out, but the sling was in the way.

"Don't untie it," he said. "I'll never be able to get it this comfy again. See if you can slide it towards my hand. I'll hold the arm steady as you do it."

Amy did as requested and lifted it over his head. Then did the same with his t-shirt.

"There are stains on your dressing. Your wound is still weeping."

"Its fine. I'll get it looked at in a day or two." He knew he should have made Barry stop at a chemist to pick up his antibiotic prescription. Another day wouldn't hurt.

She draped a towel over his shoulders, picked up his things and led the way.

With one hand holding the injured arm, he was helpless. Amy, aware of the problem he faced, turned the taps on, and gestured for him to sit down so she could take his socks off. When he stood up, she worked his track suit bottoms off and let him step in under the flow, then put gel on a sponge so she could wash his back and down his legs. He hadn't expected her to go this far, but wasn't able to refuse her help. And it wasn't as if she had never seen him naked before. She moved back a step and suggested he turned so she could soap his front. He side stepped to avoid getting his arm under the spray and faced her.

"I hope the girls are having fun," he said, to take his mind off having her soap his body. There had been no intimacy between them since he got burnt, and he was struggling to handle this.

"I'm sure they are. I'll walk round to meet them once we're done here."

He figured she was finding this as awkward as he was and was keen to put space between them.

"I think that will do."

Amy stepped away, grabbed a towel, and attempted to wrap it round his middle. To avoid any more awkwardness, he sat on the bench provided. She turned the tap off and took a second towel to pat his back and legs dry. Luke was helpless. He could not release his injured arm, so had to let her continue.

She put clean socks on, slipped his feet into fresh underpants, and into the clean joggers, and when he stood, pulled them up.

Back at the tent, Amy grabbed the cream that he had for his scars, and without a word, squeezed some onto her finger, and gently applied it to his bumpy, burnt skin. He watched her face. She neither smiled nor grimaced. Next, she helped get a clean t-shirt on in the reverse order of how she had taken the other one off. Slipped the sling back over his head and guided his elbow into it.

Her next act of kindness was to hand him a glass of water and a couple of his painkillers. He was too stunned to refuse.

"Will you be alright if I head off to catch up with the girls on their way back?"

Luke nodded, grateful to be left alone. The intensity of being touched by Amy so intimately had left him reeling. He had never loved her more, but knew he couldn't tell her.

Luke watched her go, closed his eyes for a while, and waited for the painkillers to kick in. The shower had taken more out of him than expected, both physically and mentally.

After a while, he walked up to the café, got a coffee, and called Barry.

"Any progress?"

"Yes. He has a plan for returning Rupert's car. Do you think Amy will be willing to help?"

"Probably, as long as I can go with her. Maybe Charlotte could come and mind the kids when we do it."

"Good idea. I'll check if she's available."

The prospect of facing Rupert wouldn't be easy for Amy, and the less time she had to stress over it, the better.

When they got back, the girls were tired but buzzing because they had managed to walk so far. They chatted away as they played cards, and Luke lapped up the congenial family atmosphere and wished they could stay on here indefinitely.

All the exercise and fresh air made everyone happy about having an early night.

When the girls settled, he retired to bed. Amy lay down beside him and touched his shoulder in a goodnight gesture.

"Are you all right? You feel hot." she whispered.

"I'm fine, nothing a good night's sleep won't fix." He had wondered if he might be running a temperature but decided not to make anything of it.

Once again, he woke early and crept out of the tent. He was burning up. He sat by the dead fire and watched the sun rise, grateful for the cool air.

Barry appeared before the sun was up, armed with coffee and pastries.

"Don't you ever sleep?" Luke asked.

Barry laughed. "Not when so much is going on. DI Hughes is coming over shortly, and I've asked Charlotte and James to come to mind the kids while you and Amy drop Rupert's car back. I'll follow you there to make sure you get in and out in one piece and take you home."

"That won't be necessary; Amy's car is parked at Rupert's place."

"Oh, I hadn't taken that into consideration. But I'll follow you anyway, just to be on the safe side. I'll stay out of sight. I don't fancy becoming a target."

"What do you know that I don't?" Luke asked.

"Best you don't know before you go there."

"You must be able to tell me something. I won't tell Amy if that's what you're worried about."

"Moira Walker is the woman involved with the company in Amy's name. She appears to be involved in more than we bargained for, but I can't give you details." He paused for a second. "Hi Amy, did you smell the coffee?"

Amy approached, smiling. She gently stroked Luke's shoulder, then found a mug and held it out for Barry to fill. "Goodies to eat too. You must want something…"

Barry laughed. "Busted."

"Only that they want you to take Rupert's car back to him. I'll go with you. He's even fixed for Charlotte and James to keep the kids occupied while we're doing it." Luke said, hoping that Barry wouldn't say they'd discussed the plan the day before.

"Do I have to?" There was fear in her eyes.

Luke realized not telling Amy about Moira's role in whatever was going on was sensible. The less Amy knew, the easier it would be to hand over the keys, collect her things and her car and get out of Rupert's life. The only trouble was that he didn't know for sure if that was what she wanted.

Barry looked concerned. "I think it is what the police want. DI Hughes will explain the plan when he gets here."

The girls emerged from the tent and were soon munching the pastries that Barry had provided.

"What time is your board session?" Barry asked. "Can I come and watch you?" They giggled and ran off to put their wet suits on.

There were shrieks of delight when James and Charlotte arrived with Buster on his lead, and George in his pushchair.

Charlotte gave each of them a hug and said Buster had been missing them.

James greeted Amy and Luke with a warm smile. "Good to see you found a nice place to hang out. Oh no, that mad hound of yours has found a stick. Looks like I'm needed." And he chased off after Buster.

A few minutes later, DI Hughes strolled towards them.

Luke felt as if his life had been hi-jacked by these people. He knew they were doing it because they cared, but it didn't make it easier to accept that he had agreed to whatever they suggested.

Barry offered the detective his chair. "I promised to go down with the kids to see them get on their boards. I'll leave you to fill Amy in on what you need her to do."

"Nice spot," he said. "How are you both holding out?" He looked at Luke for a response. Luke nodded.

Then the detective focused on Amy. "Glad to meet you. Sorry for all the trouble this has put you through. There was nothing on the computer and phone that you took from Mr Patterson. He knows we have them at the station for him to collect. The other phones that were found in his golf bag have opened a whole new investigation. The information is still being processed, but I can't disclose any details."

"Does that mean Rupert's involved in what you're investigating?" Amy said.

"Yes, I'm afraid that it looks as if he could be. Which is why I've come to ask if you would be prepared to return the car for us? We'll put the phones and memory sticks back in his golf bag, where you found them. He'll have no reason to suspect that we have had access to them. Do you think you can do that?"

"Do I have a choice?"

"It would be easier for everyone if you agree," Luke said, even though he was not sure if he should encourage her.

"You've already told us he hates other people handling his car, which is why I'm asking you to do this. It gives you the perfect excuse for not returning it sooner. I've also arranged for a sniffer dog to come out to make sure there are no drugs involved."

"Drugs?" Now she was wide-eyed with shock.

"It is just a remote possibility that we ought to check while we can. We need to make sure there's no other reason for his over-reaction to you having his car. Maybe he just wants his clubs back. Or those phones."

"If I could drive, I'd do it for you." Luke said. "But I can't."

"Fine. I'll do it. When do you want me to go?"

"This morning would be great," the detective said. "Text Rupert and tell him you will be over at around noon."

"And then what?"

"You can come back here, or you can head home to Luke's place."

"I think I'd like to come back here. But can you check my car for tracking devices before I go anywhere?"

"No problem. Can I have the keys of the car so we can get the sniffer dog to work? Then you can show me exactly where in the golf bag you found the phones."

"Barry helped me find them. Perhaps he should come too." She beckoned to Barry, who had found a vantage point between them and the place the girls were having their board session. He hurried back and went with Amy and the detective to the car.

With James and Charlotte keeping an eye on the dog and the children, Luke had a moment to himself. He was feeling rough, but was determined not to let it show. Getting rid of the car was important. He wished Amy had said she'd like to go home, but a little longer here was not a bad alternative.

He took a single pill. He had to cut down before he became reliant on them.

Chapter 32

DI Hughes and his team did their inspection and made sure that everything was back in the car, as it should be.

Amy spoke to the girls, who were excited about spending the day with Charlotte and James.

Luke couldn't help thinking they would be more fun to be with than with him.

As soon as they were on the road, Luke dared to ask, "What excuse are you going to give Rupert for your sudden departure?"

"That you told me you were worried his father was involved in something dodgy, and when I saw his father's message saying things had gone wrong and he was skipping the country, I thought it best to leave."

"Near enough the truth."

"Yes," she said, "but explaining why I took his computer and phone will be harder."

"Say you weren't thinking straight. You were frightened for the girls."

"That might work. I'll tell him I can't possibly stay while his father is under suspicion of trying to harm you. He can't argue against that."

"I agree. Tell me more about Moira Walker. What was her role?"

"To be honest, I was never sure. She manages all the properties on the estate, supervising a team of workers."

"Terrorizing from the little I saw." Luke watched for her reaction. She shrugged.

"They were always super-efficient, and usually worked when we were out. They'd come in to clean, unload the dishwasher, feed the washing machine, and do all the household chores. It took a bit of getting used to, but Rupert insisted they carry on as before. I confess, I wasn't complaining. Keeping that place sparkling was a daunting prospect."

"So, she didn't actually do the work herself?"

"I doubt it. She always wore a black suit, usually with high heels with her hair looking as if she had just stepped out of the hairdressers. Hardly suitable for cleaning toilets or scrubbing floors and she wouldn't have had time, as she looked after a couple of Rupert's other developments."

"Do you know where?"

"I'm not sure. Rupert finished them before I met him. She was going to take on the Topsham one when it was finished. She's very ambitious."

Luke put the radio on, texted this information to DI Hughes, and copied it to Barry.

She drove carefully, dodging the potholes, making it a smoother ride than the one he had with Barry.

The journey took less time than Luke expected. Amy looked over at him as she pulled into the driveway of the gated complex.

"Ready?"

"Yes. How about you?"

"I'll be glad to get it over with."

As she approached the gate, high-tech vehicle recognition made the gates swing open. Luke was impressed. He always had to press the buzzer and wait for security to let him in.

Amy rang the doorbell rather than use her key. Rupert answered the door quickly. It was as if he'd been waiting for them. He looked disappointed when he registered she wasn't alone.

He leaned in to give her a kiss. Amy dodged it and placed his car keys on the table in the hallway. Rupert pretended not to notice and focused his attention on Luke.

"What happened?" He pointed at Luke's arm.

"Someone tried to kill me."

Rupert looked shocked. He probably hadn't expected such a blunt answer and for a moment seemed lost for words and turned his attention to Amy. "Why did you take off like that? I've been worried sick."

"Sorry," Amy repeated what she had said earlier to Luke in the car, and added, "maybe I was hasty taking your computer and phone to the police. They said they would return them to you. Did you get them?"

"Not yet," he replied. "I'm not bothered about that. I just want to know when you're coming home?"

"I'm not," Amy said. "Not while your father is under suspicion of wanting to harm Luke."

Rupert's mouth twitched. Luke waited for him to defend his father.

"I wish I could explain what's going on. But I can't. Not now, maybe never."

"That's just it. Without total honesty, there is no way I can stay."

"I understand. I expected that's what you'd say, so I've had your things packed. I didn't know what else to do." Rupert's shoulders sagged, and he let out a regretful sigh.

"If you can't tell me what's going on, there's no reason for me to stay."

"Your bags are in the cloakroom." He led the way and opened the door to the right of the main entrance. It was larger than Luke's kitchen and had space on the racks for more boots than they had at the fire station, a single pair of boots and a pair of gleaming white trainers were under a long row of hooks, with only three coats hanging up. Not a bag in sight.

"Where the hell did they put them?" Rupert muttered. "Sorry about that. I'll check what they did with them." He pulled out his phone and made a call. Luke listened in but could only hear Rupert's side of the conversation. "In the pool changing rooms... What a stupid idea... Can you get someone over here to help... What, there's no one around... Where is everyone? Oh, never mind, we can manage."

Rupert disconnected, and said, "Sorry, someone thought it would be a good idea to put them in the storeroom off the pool changing area rather than clutter up the cloakroom. Seems all the staff are off sick, so we'll have to carry them ourselves."

Luke wondered if Rupert had any idea that the pool attendant Antonio was in hospital, Joe too. Or if he knew that his father's employee, Mike, was in police custody.

They made their way back across the hallway, through the lounge, and through the sliding glass door into the pool area.

Luke was hot, but convinced himself it was down to the excessive heating in the house. On entering the pool area, the suffocating, chlorinated atmosphere struck him. As they wouldn't be lingering, said nothing, and followed Rupert round to the far side of the pool and into the changing area. There were several closed doors, and they stopped at the last one. As Rupert opened it, Luke heard a bang of a door slamming shut, and what sounded like a key being turned, followed by the click clack of high heels. He guessed that Moira Walker had come to help. He hoped so, because he wouldn't be much use carrying bags. There was one each for the girls and two cases for Amy, and a couple of small rucksacks.

"I'm sorry. I can only manage the small ones." Luke reached for the rucksacks.

"Thats fine," Amy said. "I am sure between us we can sort out the rest. The cases have wheels."

As they trundled their way back to the pool, Luke heard another door slam. This time he was certain he heard a lock click.

He turned to Rupert. "Is there someone in the house?"

"I don't think so, but it could be the pool guy, or the maid."

As they stepped back into the pool area, the smell of chlorine had intensified to an alarming level. They needed to get out of there quickly.

"Hurry, we need to get out of here." They skirted round the pool, back to the door to the house. It wouldn't open. "I thought I heard Mrs Walker. Why would she lock the door?"

"No idea. It's never been locked before. I don't remember it having a key," Rupert said.

"These fumes could kill us." Luke scanned the pool area; a canister lay on its side at the far end of the pool. He held his breath and hurried over to look. The lid was lying on the tiles beside it. He grabbed the handle and pulled it upright. Chlorine, but more alarming was an empty bottle of bleach beside it. A lethal combination. He spun round and tried the door to the pump room. Locked.

Rupert coughed as he struggled to open the sliding glass doors facing the garden. Amy's eyes were streaming.

"I can't open it." Rupert croaked.

"We'll have to break the glass." Luke's years of fighting fires made him aware of how tough patio doors could be to break without the right tools. "We need something heavy and something sharp."

Amy handed Luke a round stone from the planter in the corner. "This any good?"

"Perfect. but I need something sharp too." He scanned the pool's surroundings. There was nothing.

The cloud of chlorine was becoming unbearable. Luke was struggling to concentrate, then spotted that Amy was still wearing her engagement ring. It had a small diamond. All he could afford at the time. Maybe that would help.

"Pass me your ring?" He pointed to her hand.

Amy nodded, slipped the ring off her finger, and handed it over.

"Do you have high heels in your bag?"

"Yes." She unzipped the bag next to her and dug down to the bottom and pulled out a shoe. "Here."

Luke was busy scoring the corner of the window with the ring. He signalled to Amy to hold the shoe with the heel against the scratched patch. Once it was in place, he smashed the rock against the shoe. Nothing happened. He tried again, but the impact of the movement ran through his body and his injured arm, making him moan.

Rupert tapped his shoulder and gasped, "Move over, let me try." Luke was in too much pain to argue and slid away to let Rupert take his place. He copied Luke's actions but had taken the shoe from Amy and had better control as he hit it repeatedly with the rock. There was a deafening bang as the glass crazed. He hit it again. The inner pane cascaded down; millions of pieces of glass showered them. "Find the ring to score the second layer of glass." Luke gasped. Rupert and Amy rummaged in the broken glass until they found the ring, and repeated the process of scoring and hammering, until with another deafening crack, the second pane shattered.

A blast of cool, breathable air hit them. But they were still not out of danger.

"Move." Luke said, helping Amy out to the terrace filled with topiary bushes. Escaping the gasses didn't mean they were safe. They had to wash the toxins off their skin fast.

His throat burned. All he could do was croak, "Is there a tap out here?" Rupert looked puzzled. "We must hose ourselves down before the chemicals burn us."

"It's that idiot Antonio's fault." Rupert gasped.

"Not him," Luke spluttered. "He's in hospital." Luke hadn't the strength to explain. He was more interested in finding a tap.

Amy pointed to the far corner. "Over there," she said, between coughs.

Luke dug his phone out of his pocket. "Call Barry. Chlorine gas poisoning. Hurry." It hurt to speak. In fact, everything hurt. But he had to get the tap to work. He stumbled to where Amy had pointed, found the tap with a reel of hose pipe attached with a spray nozzle on it. He tugged a length of hose free. "Rupert, turn it on."

Luke blasted water over his own head and face first and then aimed the spray at Amy. She gasped as the chilly water hit her, but let the water run over her face and body. When she was soaked, he pointed the jet at Rupert to hose him down. His injured arm was hurting and making him dizzy. He dropped the hose, which snaked and arced at his feet, but he didn't care he had to sit down. He stumbled to a low terrace wall and sank onto it.

"Rupert, the chemical mix was deliberate. I heard Mrs Walker's heels clacking on the tiles. Why would she want to kill you?"

"Kill me?" He shook his head as the question sunk in. "Too complicated…"

That was enough for Luke. He couldn't waste time talking. He had to go after her. "How do we get out of here?"

"There's a gate round the side." Amy pointed towards the corner of the house.

"Come on." The sound of sirens grew louder. "The code for the main gate. Barry will need it..."

He heard her repeating the number as Rupert recited it to her. "We're in the garden," she said before another rasping cough hit.

Thank heaven Barry insisted on following them. At least someone knew where they were.

"Amy, I'm sorry," Rupert's voice cracked as he punched in a code for the gate that closed off their garden. "It's all my fault."

"What do you mean?"

"No time... Amy stay here. Rupert, let's go, we need to find Mrs Walker. She's got some explaining to do."

As he passed Amy, she touched his arm. "Stop. You're burning up, don't go," she said, trying to hold on to him.

"I'm fine." He pulled his arm away and followed Rupert, who was running towards the front of the house opposite his own. The huge double garage doors were partially open, and still rising. Moira Walker was busy loading bags into a Mercedes coupé.

Rupert shouted to her, "Stop. We need to talk."

She reached deep into the boot and spun round to face him, wielding a heavy wrench. "Too late for that. Stay back." She inched her way round to the driver's door and in a flash got into the car and slammed the door, and activated the central locking system.

Rupert darted after her and grabbed the door handle. But too late. She had already locked it.

The garage door was still slowly rising. Luke's only hope was to stop it so she wouldn't be able to leave. He ducked inside and found the manual override switch and set the door to close, but it was very slow moving. And she had started the car. He needed to distract her to give the door time to lower. He moved to the passenger door, tugged at the handle, then banged on the window. She turned to face him, panic in her eyes. She stared for a moment, then looked away and grabbed the gear lever, trying to get the car into reverse. Nerves made her fumble, but eventually selected the right gear. She eased her foot off the clutch. The car reversed slowly.

"You won't get away?" Rupert shouted. "I'm going to tell them everything."

"You won't dare," she screamed back. "Your father won't let you."

"He won't be able to stop me."

"You have no idea what he's done."

"Maybe, but it has to stop now."

Luke checked the position of the garage door; it was coming down. But still not low enough to halt her.

He banged on the window again. She put her foot back down on the clutch. The car stopped moving.

"Why did you want to kill me?" Luke yelled.

She turned to look at him. "You should mind your own business." And then pumped the accelerator and lifted her foot off the clutch.

With the engine revved up, the car shot backwards. The garage door had come down far enough to catch the top of the boot. The force bent the hefty bar that ran along the bottom of the door.

She was jolted forward, bashing her face on the steering wheel. Undaunted, she slammed the car into first gear, shot forward, then back into reverse for a second go at getting out. This time, the boot crumpled, and the rear window popped. The sturdy door bar buckled further, jamming the mechanism. The lifting motor whined under the strain, and then, with a blinding flash, a deafening bang, and a belch of smoke, gave up.

Undefeated. The woman took another lurch forward, and then, revving furiously, tried once more. But the door bar didn't budge. This time, the impact triggered the air bags to go off.

Luke crawled under the gap and rammed a plant pot on the car exhaust, hoping it would kill the engine. It took a few minutes before the engine died.

She was trapped. The electrics of the car had fused, and the door locks were jammed.

Luke leaned against the garage wall. Too exhausted to move. He closed his eyes. A few moments later, he felt Amy touch his hand. He opened his eyes to find her kneeling beside him.

It took great effort, but he managed to speak. "Phone, record." And pointed to the gap under the door. Amy didn't argue. She quickly tapped the buttons on the phone and slid it under the door. She stayed where she was, listening to Rupert firing questions at Moira Walker.

"What made you decide to kill me?"

"You've become a liability. Just like your father."

"Was he next on the list?"

"He will be if you don't get me out of here."

"You're going nowhere." Rupert laughed. "Time you learned about fear."

"Wait until your girlfriend learns the truth about you? Do you think she's going to stick around once she learns what you are?"

"You've already destroyed that relationship. You can't hurt me anymore."

"Don't bet on it. I'll drop you in it big time. If I go down, so do you. You might not know it, but you're implicated in everything I've done. Your father too. I even let you believe you owned your house and let you live here as a precaution against you turning on me."

"I don't care about the house. I'm done with the lies."

"Think again. You have no idea what your father did to protect his precious son. He wanted to give you the world. And now you're going to shop him. That's gratitude for you. I'm glad I never had kids."

"Good thing you didn't, or you'd have pimped them too."

Luke watched Amy's face as she listened to the conversation. There were tears in her eyes. Rupert still had her attention. Would she ever be free of him? He was aware of a flurry of activity and footsteps approaching.

Amy called out. "Over here."

Luke registered police and ambulance men approaching. He touched Amy's arm. "Make sure Barry hears the recording, then pass it on to DI Hughes" The dizziness overwhelmed before they reached him.

Chapter 33

It took a moment for Luke to work out that he was in the hospital. The smell, the clatter of equipment, and the hushed tones were so familiar. How had he got here? He couldn't remember. All that came to mind was Amy's expression as she had listened to the conversation between Rupert and Mrs Walker, and the feeling he'd lost her again. But her scent filled his nostrils. She was here with him, her hands gripping his. He opened his eyes to check. Yes, it was her, and when she realized he was awake, she lifted his hand and kissed it.

"I'll get the nurse," she said, as she removed the oxygen tube that was wrapped around her ears and left him.

He was hooked up to an oxygen supply, and had a drip attached to his arm, and a clip on his finger attached to a machine by the bed. He had so many questions to ask, but the nurse who bustled in was more intent on changing the dressing on his arm than talking. "Do you know where Amy went?"

"Oh, she's with the other man who came in at the same time as yourself. She'll be back as soon as I'm done."

She didn't have to say his name. Luke knew it had to be Rupert. The man still had the power to pull her in.

"Your wound is looking better. The antibiotics are working well. You'll soon be good to go." The nurse said as she tidied up her trolly of dressings.

With his dressings changed, and the antibiotics kicking in, Luke could reassure Amy on her return that he'd survive.

"What's been going on?" he croaked. "How's Rupert?"

"He'll be okay. Asthma made the chlorine hit him harder than it did us." Her voice was raspy. "He keeps asking about Antonio, wondering why you knew it wasn't him."

"He blamed Antonio, not knowing he burgled my house and suffered serious burns when he tried to set it alight. Tell him that."

Amy set aside the oxygen tube again and went to pass on the message, returning quickly to her oxygen supply.

Luke waited a moment. "What did he say?"

"He was shocked, but D I Hughes arrived. So, I left them alone." She squeezed his hand. "We'd never have survived if you hadn't been there."

Self-preservation had a lot to do with his actions, but she didn't need to hear that.

"Where are the girls?"

"Still at the campsite with Charlotte and James. They're having a fabulous time. I told them you were back in hospital having your arm looked at. They seemed to accept that and are happy to stay where they are for now."

"And Owen?" His brain was in overdrive, trying to catch up.

"Tamsin says he's doing well. No memory issues as far as they can tell."

"Are you and she okay?"

"I think so. She's struggling and needs a friend."

DI Hughes interrupted their conversation. After checking how they were, he asked for their help. "Rupert wants to talk, but he says he needs you both to hear what he has to say. Are you willing to come to his room? I've checked with the nurse; she can rig up oxygen masks for you if you need them."

"That's fine with me. What about you Amy?"

She nodded. "Best to let him say what he has to."

Within minutes, Hughes wheeled Luke into Rupert's room with Amy following.

Once they were all there, Rupert began, hesitantly at first, and with a rasping voice.

"Moira Walker has controlled both my life and my father's for years. Most of the time, in such a subtle way, I barely noticed. But since you came on the scene, Amy, she's been more and more demanding."

"What did she have over you?" Amy asked.

Rupert swallowed, and Luke almost felt pity for him. "I was an idiot." He took a deep lungful of air and continued. "I was set up with a date. The girl was a real stunner, who said she was eighteen. We hit it off. The relationship was intense. Unknown to us, photos were taken. Photos that Moira Walker used to manipulate my father. The girl was only fifteen. I had to stop seeing her or risk being labelled as a sex offender."

"What happened to her?" Amy asked.

"She vanished. I had no way of contacting her. To be honest, I was too terrified to try. Her age, and the position it put me in, scared the hell out of me. Six months later, I saw her picture on the front page of the local paper. She had committed suicide. The investigation into her death triggered a tremendous scandal involving wealthy men who had abused her. It transpired she had been forced into multiple relationships and couldn't take any more. I tried to convince myself our relationship was different, and that it had nothing to do with her death."

Amy put her hand up to her mouth, her eyes filled with tears.

"I would have done something for her given the chance," Rupert continued. "I spent months waiting to be arrested."

Luke wondered what Rupert hoped to achieve by sharing this tale.

"My father shared my fears. He drilled into me the need to stay above the law in everything I did. I had to become a model citizen. He promised to help. All I had to do was follow his instructions."

"And what were those?" Luke asked, breaking his intention not to take part in the conversation.

"He got a friend to take me on as an apprentice, to learn about site development. Then he set up a project for me to manage. He guided me from the side-lines, sourced all the materials and labour. He told me not to question him. When that project ended, he let me think I owned the house I live in. But it seems it was never put in my name. Moira Walker says she still owns it. My father only recently told me that his actions many years earlier put her in jail, and she had used me to get revenge. I never got a straight answer out of him about his involvement with her. But he made me promise to do what she asked without question."

"And you were happy to go along with that?" Amy said.

"No, but I didn't think I had a choice. The threat of exposure still hung over me."

"So why tell us now?" she said.

He leaned toward her and said almost in a whisper, "Because I love you."

Amy blinked. She hadn't seen that coming.

Luke sat thinking, what's he got to offer now? His home is gone. He's admitted to having sex with a fifteen-year-old. He's been under his father's influence for so long, and probably can't function without him giving the orders. Could his revelations sway Amy? He prayed not.

"Rupert," Amy reached out to touch his hand. "I'm sorry, but we're over. And it has nothing to do with what you have just told us or what has happened with your father. When we were all together in Centre Parcs, you pretended you enjoyed being with me and the girls, but I could tell you were struggling. I knew then that we would never make a long-term relationship work."

"But I tried."

"That's just the point. You had to try. It wasn't natural. You don't love my children, and we come as a package."

Rupert's shoulders sagged. There was no argument to counteract her reasoning.

Another awkward silence followed. Luke couldn't take his eyes off Amy. There were tears in her eyes, and she was still holding Ruperts hand. She might have stepped away from him, but it was obvious to Luke that her feeling for him remained strong. At last, she slid her hand away from his.

Luke broke the silence to break the intensity of the moment. "You said your father told you not to query his instructions. Didn't you ever wonder what he was up to?"

Rupert looked at him, almost in surprise as if he had forgotten that there were others in the room.

"I did. He said Moira suggested my apprenticeship. She needed someone with an unblemished record in charge. He helped her to achieve that. All the men who came to work were experienced. I assumed they were illegally here. The fact they didn't speak any English was not a problem as there was always an interpreter on hand, so I couldn't complain. The materials always arrived on time, and were up to standard, and I had no need to question where they came from, or the price paid."

Seeing Luke wasn't satisfied, he continued, "It was easier to just go along with doing as he said. Though more recently, he was behaving oddly, and I wondered what he was up to. He kept booking me on holidays abroad or sending me on some random business course. It never occurred to me he was making sure I didn't get caught up with his underhand dealings."

Luke hoped his next question wouldn't upset Amy. "So, Rupert, why haven't you told the police about this before?"

He shook his head. "I never had the guts."

"Shame, it might have removed that woman's hold over you," Luke said gently. It was hard not to pity the man.

Chapter 34

At last, the doctors declared him fit to go home.

Sheena had been on the phone and had promised to sort out lunch for them all. Charlotte was there with the girls and James was going to pick them up from the hospital to bring them home.

When they arrived, Sheena opened the door for them. Amy ushered Luke in ahead of her.

A rousing cheer greeted him. Balloons festooned the hallway, along with a welcome home banner. The girls ran towards them, and Buster jumped up and down, trying to work out what all the fuss was about and who to lick first.

Luke surveyed the gathering. Barry, Charlotte, James, Mabel, a couple of others from his crew, his boss, DI Hughes, and, best of all, Owen, sitting in a wheelchair, with Tamsin by his side. Then he spotted Nathan, and Duncan, and Martin.

Sheena stepped forward. "Apologies for taking over your house. We wanted to welcome you home. And Barry has an announcement to make."

"I certainly do." He took her place, and with a wide grin said, "It's time to celebrate. Luke's work has been syndicated to a national paper." He dug into the shoulder bag that he always had with him and handed out copies of the magazine. "These contain the first of Luke's climbing articles. The rest will follow over the next four weeks."

Everyone cheered and started flapping through the pages to find the article. Barry opened a magazine at the right page and held it out for Luke to see. The girls squealed with delight when they found their picture, which covered most of the page. And Charlotte and James shared a hug when they saw one of them working together.

"But that's not all. One of his articles about homelessness has been accepted, and articles about your accident and the fire here that have also been taken up by multiple papers. I have copies here for you to read."

Amy touched Luke's arm. And mouthed. "Are you okay with all this fuss?" He smiled. She cared. Everything else was a bonus.

"Yes, what about you?"

"Fine. Unexpected but lovely that they care so much." They walked over to Owen.

"Great to see you here. We're a right pair. We'll have to work out together," he said, pointing to his arm.

Luke turned toward Tamsin, who was hugging Amy. Their friendship restored. Owen's grin showed he had seen it, too.

"Something smells delicious. I'm starving."

Sheena and Mabel waved him towards the kitchen. Enormous pots of curry and rice were ready for serving. The aroma was mouth-watering. Sheena handed him a plateful and encouraged him to move on to make way for the others. Most of the guests were happy to eat standing up. But with only one hand in use, Luke put his plate on the dining table and sat down to eat. Andrew Clarke joined him.

"I'm really sorry. I should have taken you seriously from the start, then none of this might have happened."

"I doubt that we could have stopped them sooner. There wasn't enough evidence. I think Hughes will agree with that."

"Take all the time you need to recover," he said.

Luke nodded. Now was not the time to suggest he might like to become a part timer. He needed to talk to Amy about that. He looked around to watch the interaction of the group, enjoying how the girls and Amy made sure to include Mabel in the celebration. James and Owen seemed to have plenty to talk about, and Tamsin was helping Sheena.

Soon the party broke up and as Roland Hughes was leaving, he said to Luke, "That recording you took of the conversation between Rupert and Mrs Walker has been a great help. Rupert's confession has given us lots to work on. Naturally, she's denying everything. And Frank Patterson is still refusing to talk, even though both Joe and Mike have told us how involved he was."

"Has Rupert spoken to his father yet?" Amy asked.

"No. Very adamant he won't."

"Would you like me to persuade him?" Amy offered.

Luke couldn't believe he heard right. She wanted to talk to Rupert again.

"It might work. I'll see what I can arrange. But are you sure you want to do this? Perhaps Luke can bring you up to date on everything we know about his father."

She nodded, and they both watched the man leave. Luke wanted to scream. Rupert was going to keep coming between them. Yes, she was unlikely to go back to him, because he couldn't accept her as a complete package with the girls, but she still had feelings for the man. And Luke wasn't sure how he was supposed to deal with his jealousy and how to stop himself from blurting out the question he didn't dare ask. Did she still want to be with him?

Instead, he made an offer. "I can come with you; unless you'd prefer someone neutral, Tamsin maybe?" Luke hoped it would make her feel he was happy for her to keep seeing Rupert.

"I'll think about it," she answered.

With the guests gone, the dishes in the dishwasher, the children vanished upstairs to rediscover the treasures in their bedrooms. The two of them sat in silence. After a while, Amy asked if she could see the information Luke had collected on Frank Patterson.

They moved to his computer and sat side by side, and he found the relevant files that he thought she should read. "These are the outlines of articles I wrote, which I shared with Barry. Obviously, he can't publish anything without fact checks and permission from the police. We can't afford to mess with their prosecution case."

Amy took a deep breath when she finished reading them.

"I can't believe you knew all that, and still let me live with Rupert."

"I never found anything to show Rupert was involved. And Barry hasn't either."

"But the case against his father. How will that impact him?"

"I'm guessing his development contracts will dry up. Anyone who connects him to Frank will want to steer clear. Your business will suffer too, especially the work that was connected to them."

"So basically, I'm homeless and lost my business."

"Not true, your home is here, and you have proved you can make a success of your business, so I can't see why you can't continue."

The girls reappeared and asked if it could be a pizza night. "Daddy can eat it with one hand, so it would be good for him."

He loved they had worked this out, and that Amy would need convincing.

Amy smiled and shrugged. "What do you think? Pizza, or beans on toast." Making the alternative dish something she knew he wouldn't pick was touching.

"It has to be pizza," he answered.

The girls snuggled up beside him on the sofa, while Amy made the call for a pizza delivery.

It was so good to be home. But he couldn't help wondering what the investigations would uncover, and when they would feel safe again. Nothing had been normal since his accident, and he had almost forgotten what normal felt like.

Chapter 35

The following day, the phone kept ringing.

"You won't believe the interest there has been in your climbing article." Barry said. "A couple of the papers that have weekend lifestyle magazines want to run something similar. Can you tailor the articles to suit their format, and maybe pick different photos to go with it? They want to do the follow up ones too. Just wait till you see your bank balance. I want to pop over later and talk to you. I hope that will be okay."

Then his boss sent a text. 'Very impressed with your climbing article. Everyone sends their wishes for a speedy recovery. Let me know when you're fit for duty.'

Nathan contacted him, full of thanks because bookings were pouring in."

There were calls from people wanting him to promote things for them. Which reminded him of the articles he thought about doing, but hadn't had time to research.

His arm, while still very painful, was nowhere near as bad as it had been those first few days. The dull persistent ache he could live with. Returning to work was unlikely for some time. But he could research those topics. Writing could change lives, and if he quit fighting fires, maybe he could still do useful work with his camera and writing. A very satisfying thought to hang onto.

DI Hughes called round. He was more interested in talking to Amy than giving Luke information on how his investigation was going.

"Amy, about your offer to help. Do you really think you can convince Rupert to talk to his father?"

"I can try, but no guarantee that I'll succeed."

"Do you want me to come along?" Luke asked.

She shook her head. Hughes put his hand out. "Sorry. Probably best for her to talk to him alone. If it's okay with you, we could go now. It shouldn't take long."

"Why the rush?" Luke fired back.

"Frank Patterson won't talk. And if Rupert refuses to see him, we'll have to release Frank while we gather more information about his role."

"What about Moira Walker? Will you have to let her go, too?"

"No. We have enough to keep her locked up on remand while the prosecution service put a case together. The charge of attempted murder will take priority, but her involvement with illegal immigrants will also be high on the list. Antonio, Bogdan, and Maria all arrived illegally, and used as slave labour to pay off their debts. Barry has promised not to release the story while we collect evidence to make a case against her. The big push is on to catch the people traffickers who brought them into the country."

"Good." Luke said.

"Yes, but that's only the tip of the iceberg." Hughes looked over to Amy. "We need to go now. Time is running out. Luke, I'll fill you in on the rest when I bring her back."

Amy nodded and grabbed her bag and moved toward the door with more enthusiasm than Luke expected. He didn't dare comment on her eagerness, knowing it would make him sound petty. He had no right to complain about her actions. All he wanted was for her to give him a chance to rekindle their relationship. And there was still a long way to go.

"Charlotte is collecting the girls from school, but I should be back by then." Amy said as she left.

Luke tried to look relaxed about her going, but hated that she had agreed to see the man. His biggest fear was that sympathy would bring her closer to Rupert again.

The girls came home, and Luke distanced himself from their fun. He couldn't stop worrying about how she was coping with seeing Rupert. Amy had been gone much longer than he had expected. When she finally got home, she was alone and utterly exhausted.

"DI Hughes sends his apologies. But it worked. Rupert persuaded his father to talk."

Luke wanted to ask why it had taken so long. But the girls bounced into the room full of excitement. "Charlotte helped us make chocolate brownies, and she's put the kettle on."

Amy hugged them both. "They smell delicious. I can't wait to taste them." She sank into a chair. The strain of the afternoon was clearly visible, but she put on a smile when the girls came back with a plateful of rather sticky brownies.

Charlotte brought in a tray with tea on it. "We were so busy baking we haven't taken Buster for his walk. Would you like me to take him and the girls to the park for a while?" She said as she set it down on a low table near Amy.

The relief on Amy's face was clear, so Luke answered for her. "Great idea, if you're sure you have the time."

Charlotte smiled and said, "I'm meeting James there, so it fits in perfectly."

Katie piped in, "Can we take him some brownies?"

"Good idea. I am sure he'll enjoy them." Amy said. And with that, the girls hurried off to find Buster's lead and headed to the door.

When the door slammed behind them. Luke looked over at Amy. "Tough afternoon?"

She rubbed her hands over her face. "Yes. Rupert was in a state. I've never seen him like that. It took ages for him to calm down. He's feeling guilty about my business being caught up in his mess. And so angry with his father. I had to get him to see that his father had probably been in too deep to do anything other than obey that woman, and that he needed to hear his side of the story. That if he didn't, it would eat him up. Eventually I got through, but he said that he'd only speak to him if I went with him. I didn't think I had a choice. He knows I have little love for his old man, but I know how important it is regarding getting Moira Walker locked up. So, I agreed."

She reached out and poured a cup of tea. Luke waited for her to continue. Rushing her might put her off.

"We went into an interview room where Frank was waiting. He had been begging to speak to Rupert, and his face lit up when Rupert went in. He was less pleased to see me, but didn't complain. We sat opposite him. And it was soon obvious that neither of them knew where to start. So, I found myself as intermediary. I told Frank that Rupert hadn't wanted to see him, but that he needed to know exactly what hold Moira Walker had over him. Without that information, there was no hope of them ever having any sort of relationship. Rupert needed to know every sordid detail, and that it was the only way that they could be free of the woman and her threats. And that Rupert had told the police about the girl, and everything he knew about her business that might incriminate her."

She drank some tea. "That's when Rupert spoke up. Telling his father, he was likely to go to prison for his part in ordering the arson attacks. Frank looked shocked, but when Rupert said that the only way to salvage their relationship was for him to talk. He no longer had the excuse of protecting Rupert from her blackmail attempts."

Amy paused, shook her head. "I've never seen anyone change so quickly. I had to feel sorry for him. He seemed to shrink in the chair, looked bewildered, then after a moment looked directly at Rupert, and said he'd do it and to get DI Hughes in to take his statement."

"Well done." Luke wanted her to take a break. Retelling the story was hard on her.

But she seemed keen to continue.

"I thought they'd want me to leave. But he insisted I stayed. Maybe he thought I would stick around for Rupert. Who knows? The man is a mystery to me. Even Hughes was surprised when he refused to have a solicitor present."

"I'll bet he was."

"One of the first things he did was apologize to me for his part in creating a second business using my information. Moira had made him do it. She had become so demanding, and the more he did for her, the deeper in he got. He was terrified she would turn on him. She'd ruined so many people during his years under her thumb."

"He told me that my interior design business was completely legit. The import export one was not, but he never found out what she intended to use it for."

"That's good, isn't it?"

"I guess so, but he told them it wasn't her only fake business. She had at least three other bogus companies, one of which she used for importing drugs. Once he started, there was no stopping him. She had broken up his marriage to Rupert's mother, who thought they were having an affair. He was so angry and decided to set her up and as a result, she went to prison on a fraud charge. She figured out he was to blame and used Rupert to get her revenge. And once she started, the manipulation became more and more intense."

"No holding back then?"

"No. He told them all he knew about her employees, and how scared they all were of her. And he'd never discovered what she had over them and chose not to delve too deeply. Sometimes being in the dark was a good thing. He also admitted his part in bribing the planning officer and getting Joe and Mike to set the warehouse fires. He admitted asking them to beat up Owen and rob your place, which would be empty because you were going climbing. But swore he didn't give orders for Joe to kill you. Which ties in with Joe's confession. He already said Walker gave him the order."

Amy let out an enormous sigh. "D I Hughes suggested we leave it there for today. And I think everyone was happy to stop."

"Rupert was told he could carry on using the house. The chlorine problem has been sorted. No one is sure what action they'll take over the underage sex activities. That's in the hands of the prosecution service. Frank is being held while they go through his statement and work out what charges he will face. He didn't seem to mind; I think he's terrified of what she could arrange if they released him."

"Wow, that's a lot to take in. It must have been difficult for you."

"Yes, but I'm glad I could help. With luck, he'll be able to get on with his life now the truth is out. It will be tough for him."

"Yes, but thanks to his father's efforts, very little of the mud will have stuck to him."

The girls returned, putting an end to their conversation. He decided not to press for her to continue. When she was ready, she would talk.

Over the next few days, Luke couldn't pinpoint what was different with Amy. To his surprise, Amy and Mabel and Sheena bonded in a surprising way. Her relationship with Tamsin was back on track and stronger than before, which he was glad about. Tamsin was more caring and devoted to Owen than he ever expected.

The biggest change was perhaps how Amy treated Charlotte. One morning, Amy went with her to walk Buster, and they were laughing on their return. Something he hadn't heard Amy do in a long time.

A week later, he nursed a mug of coffee and watched Amy as she kneaded dough. There was a calming rhythm to her movements as she folded and pushed the dough with the heel of her hand. She had promised to make pizza for the girls for supper, something she hadn't done in a long time. Her decision pleased them all because her homemade pizza beat the take-away options. It seemed she had found joy in spending time in the kitchen baking and being a homemaker again.

Her return had not been too tricky. It seemed natural to head to separate rooms as they had been before. Luke wondered if and when they could put her affair aside. He loved having her back in the house and wished they could erase the previous months and get back to what they'd had. No. On reflection, perhaps not. That relationship failed. Getting back together had to be on a sounder footing. If only he knew how to reach that goal.

"Stop staring at me like that," she said, breaking the thread of his daydreaming.

"Like what?"

"Like you have something on your mind, but don't dare say it."

"That obvious?" She could always tell when he struggled to say what he wanted. But this time, he couldn't avoid the issue. "The truth. I love having you at home. But I don't want to go back to where we were."

"You don't?" She frowned. "Why not?"

"It didn't work… You left."

She gave the dough a few more hard rolls and dipped her hand back into the flour pot. "Good point. I suppose it didn't?"

"You obviously weren't happy, and I didn't see it."

She straightened up, brushed a strand of hair off her face with the back of her hand, leaving a trail of flour on her cheek, and locked eyes with him. Neither of them said anything, but his brain was in overdrive.

Why hadn't it worked? He'd taken his eye off what mattered? They'd stopped communicating as they should. He hadn't given her room to dream.

He'd been too wrapped up in his own career to notice she was unhappy. So many things were wrong, but which one was the one that broke them?

"I guess we stopped communicating," he said, "and I'm sorry about that. I hope from now on, we will be totally honest with each other?"

"I'd like to think we can," she said as she plopped the dough back in a bowl and covered it to let it rise. Then she turned away to wash her hands in the sink, and wiped down surfaces, and put things away in the fridge.

Luke took it as a sign: enough for now. Probably time to take Buster out.

A few days later, Amy surprised him. "You know what we said about needing to communicate better? Well, I thought you should know I've been talking to Rupert." She locked her eyes with his.

Luke took a deep breath. "And." Was all he could think to say. His brain was in overdrive, trying to process the information. Was she telling him to warn him she was about to leave again? Or was she looking for moral support?

"The police are unlikely to take action over the girl. But he's worried you might print the story. Will you?"

"No. Not without a prosecution case. Her death has caused enough grief."

She smiled. "Thank you."

"But I can't promise not to mention his father in any story about the arson cases, or his connection to Moira Walker when her case comes to trial."

"That's fair, and I'm sure he'll understand. He's keen to apologize. He didn't believe you when you suggested Moira had locked us in. You must have thought he was a complete idiot."

Luke shrugged. "I don't blame Rupert. Apart from me, he wouldn't have been expecting anyone wanted him dead." She looked shocked. "No need to look surprised. I hated the man. He'd destroyed my family."

An awkward silence followed as the admission sunk in.

"I'm sorry I hurt you." Amy said and stared at him, waiting for a response.

He stayed silent.

"I'm not looking for excuses. I don't understand why I fell for Rupert. Maybe something was lacking at home, or maybe I was searching for a more exciting life that seemed out of my grasp. He was attentive, boosted my self-esteem, and allowed me to act out my dreams." She paused for a moment.

Luke was ashamed that she had needed someone else to see her needs. If she had more to say, he daren't stop the flow.

"Now it feels so shallow. A crazy infatuation. I admit I loved being in the limelight, the glamorous dinners, being recognized for my talent rather than just being a wife and a mother. But since coming home, I've realized how unimportant that was."

Where was this leading? It still didn't answer the question about how she felt about them as a couple.

"Which leaves me wondering what, if anything, in that relationship was real. Rupert is a charmer, and I was charmed. Is it enough? I don't think so. Seeing the way his father manipulated him was scary. Going along with his father's demands made him almost as bad as his father, and a fool for not questioning him. All of which made him either dishonest or incredibly stupid."

She stared into her cup. Luke couldn't decide if she had finished. Should he intervene? Probably not.

"I'm embarrassed that I succumbed to his charms. And that I never gave you a chance to know what was going on in my head. I'll always be grateful for his help in boosting my confidence with my business, but that is the only legacy of the affair. I know now it's over." She leaned back in her chair and sighed.

Luke let her admission sink in, then said, "It was as much my fault. I should have seen that you needed more than I was offering. I was too wrapped up in my career to even notice that you were crying out for something of your own other than being a wife and mother. I will try to be more supportive in the future."

"Do we have a future?" she said.

"I'd like to think we do, but no need to rush," he answered, not sure if that was the right response. Living separate lives in the same house was hard, and he wasn't sure how long he could survive. But she had to be the one to make the next move.

Chapter 36

Luke still hadn't sorted out a new front door or the redecorating of the hall and porch. He decided it was time to let Amy take charge and suggested she might like to choose a replacement door and pick paint colours. "Might as well brighten it up as we have the chance."

Amy seemed surprised that he asked, but a couple of days later, she showed him a photo of a door she had found.

It was a beautiful old door, far nicer than the damaged one. And totally different from what he expected her to choose. "Where on earth did you find that?"

"Oh, Sheena took me down to a reclamation yard. They had some gorgeous stuff. I got quite carried away."

"You carried away by antiques?"

"Yes, no need to look so shocked. To be honest, living in a modern shiny glass box of a house has made me see things in a different light."

"Go on..." he prompted.

"Well, the way Mabel furnished the annex made me see old things can be beautiful. I never considered that space could be used, let alone make a comfortable home. Now, seeing the overlooked potential has made me understand why you loved this place so much. The old furniture that I used to despise has a beauty of its own. Sorry I gave you such a hard time before, wanting to change everything."

Luke accepted the apology with a quick nod and approved her decor choices.

The routine in the house settled into a comfortable pace without the girls disappearing for days at a time. They were happy to have both parents together and never asked about Rupert. Hard to believe they could adjust so quickly.

For the first time in years, they were doing things together as a family daily, and it felt good. But Luke wondered how long this would continue. He was not yet fit enough to return to work. And who knew what would happen if Amy's business took off? All he could do was enjoy it while it lasted.

Amy's business was back on track without Rupert's connections. A few loyal clients were happy for her to complete projects she had already started. Luke stayed out of her business dealings, partly because spending time with her was becoming increasingly difficult. He was finding it harder and harder to hide his feelings and was afraid that he would upset the calm atmosphere by announcing how much he loved her, and how much he wanted her.

DI Hughes called round to break the news of Moira Walker's trial date. They had intercepted a shipment of goods being imported by the bogus company in Amy's name and discovered a huge consignment of drugs. So, she was likely to get a long sentence for her part in that. With added time for the slavery charges. More charges were likely as the investigations are still ongoing. "Obviously, you can't publish the story yet. But it will be a big one when the time comes." Hughes had added.

Luke had agreed and was glad of the reminder that he had stories to write, and for the next week they skirted around each other in the house, neither wanting to talk about the next move. Amy threw herself into cooking, dealing with the girls, spending time with Mabel and Sheena. Charlotte and James popped round frequently, as did Tamsin and Owen.

Amy surprised Luke by asking how they could help Owen. "I've asked Tamsin to help me with my work. I assume there is no chance of Owen going back into the fire service after what he did. But there must be something he can do using his background."

"I am sure there is, but it might take a little longer to figure out what it is. Maybe Sheena can come up with suggestions."

"Good thinking." Amy said with a smile.

Luke wondered what plot they would hatch. He couldn't believe how well Amy had taken to having Sheena and Mabel around. He often wondered what scheme they might come up with for him if he couldn't go back to work.

Luke's arm was improving, and he was nearly fit enough to do his fitness training, but he wasn't sure he was mentally ready. He went to see Andrew Clarke. "I think maybe it is time I took a step back, but I don't want to give it up altogether. I'm considering going part time if I can get back in shape?"

"Good plan. We'd hate to lose you, and I know a desk job would drive you insane. Part time would give you the chance to carry on with your writing. But you will still need to pass the fitness test."

"Yes. It will give me the opportunity to see if it can bring in enough to keep a roof over our heads."

When he got home, he told Amy what he had decided. She flung her arms around his neck and kissed him.

She stepped back, looking as shocked by her own reaction to his news as he was. He didn't know what to make of it, and was too much of a coward to ask.

The evening progressed normally. Luke read more to the girls than usual. He couldn't put her kiss out of his mind. What had it meant to her? Was he over-thinking, and it had just been a spontaneous reaction, rather than an intimate gesture?

They sat and watched a film together to the end. He got up and said, "Goodnight."

She echoed him and gathered up their cups and followed him out of the room.

He showered and was about to cream his scar when Amy knocked on his door, and came in and sat on his bed. Without speaking, she took the bottle of cream from him and gently pushed him to lie down, and applied the lotion to his scars.

Her fingers skated over his skin so gently, so tenderly. He was struggling. Part of him wanted her to stop, but mostly he wanted her to carry on, but he wasn't sure how much more he could take. He wanted to pull her closer and kiss her, but didn't dare.

"Can I stay?" she asked, putting the lotion bottle down.

He silently slid across the bed to make room for her. How he had longed for this moment. But he was afraid of frightening her off with the wrong move. He had to be sure she was ready to resume their relationship. He certainly was.

Thank you for reading **Smoke Screen.** If you enjoyed the book, please leave a review. I hope you enjoyed it. Here is a sample of **The Missing Link**, a Detective Inspector Gavin McKay mystery set in Scotland.

One

Gavin McKay had been a Detective Inspector in Strathclyde long enough to recognize the smell of fear wafting towards him from the man huddled in the corner of the cell. The mud-splattered coat wrapped around his body was steeped in the stench of stale beer, vomit and cigarettes.

"Where's Gavin?" the man shouted. "I want to talk to Gavin."

"Your friend's been going on like this ever since he arrived," the duty sergeant said, as he pushed the heavy metal door wide open. "He was picked up for abusive behaviour. He appeared to be determined to get arrested, bringing him in was the safest option all round. With a bit of luck, now you're here, he'll shut up. I've asked Doctor Munro to come in and check him over."

Gavin stepped forward and touched the man's shoulder. The threadbare fabric of the scruffy coat was too thin to disguise the lack of flesh on the bones beneath. Lank wisps of hair, an untrimmed, speckled beard and the ravages of street life made Neil Gillespie look nearer sixty-eight than thirty-eight. Hell, it was only two weeks to their shared birthday. If Neil kept up his current lifestyle, they wouldn't be sharing many more. Neil's deterioration pricked Gavin's conscience. He could have been more supportive.

"I'm here, Neil." Gavin hoped there was no

hint of pity in his voice. Since Neil's son died from an overdose two years ago, grief had taken over. Neil's head lifted, the movement gave Gavin a brief glimpse of his split lip and the plum-coloured bruises circling his eyes.

"About bloody time..." Neil muttered, as he pointed towards the door. "Tell him to push off."

Gavin signalled the sergeant to leave. "It's OK, he's gone."

"Did you bring some fags?" Neil asked with a nicotine-stained, gap-toothed grin.

Gavin dug into his pocket for the cigarettes and matches he'd bought on his way to the police station. He handed them over and waited, thinking how hard it was going to be once the no smoking laws were in place. Neil's hands shook as he removed the cellophane wrapping, eventually putting a cigarette between his swollen lips. He lit up, choking as the smoke hit his lungs. "You must go to the house," Neil mumbled, "near Mal... Mal... you know..."

"No, tell me."

"Mal...Mallaig, yeah, that's the place." Neil spluttered, "The place where they keep the stuff... it all happens there."

"What? Drugs?" Gavin asked, guessing Neil's drug crusade was still on-going. Neil didn't respond. "You haven't a clue, have you? Why should I stick my neck out for you?"

"Find the bastards..."

"Who? The guys who beat you up?"

"You know..." he muttered.

"No, I don't." Gavin struggled to curb his impatience. Anger wouldn't help. He lowered his tone and said, "OK, you win. If you won't say who rearranged your face, tell me how to get to this place."

Neil seemed to consider this request, closed his eyes, took a deep breath and started reciting a precise set of directions. Gavin listened, picturing the route as Neil spoke, committing the details to memory.

Neil finished talking, slumped back against the wall and sighed. Gavin waited silently expecting him to add something. Nothing was forthcoming, so he asked, "What's the name of the house?"

Neil shrugged.

"Have you ever been there?"

Again, Neil shook his head.

"Stop mucking about. Tell me what's so special about the place?"

With a sly grin Neil beckoned him closer and whispered. "You told me you'd like to help me nail our old pal, Hector Sinclair... this is your chance."

"Sinclair? He's just been promoted to Acting Chief Superintendent."

"I heard. Could've been your job, if you hadn't lost it."

"Lost what?"

"Your edge. Watch out, you don't want to end up a sad case like me. Maybe Hector becoming your boss will shake you up. I bet he's lapping up the power."

"Revelling in it, but what the hell has he to do with this house?"

"You find out. You're the copper." Neil pulled the coat up round his ears. "Get out of here, I need some sleep."

Gavin retreated from the custody suite, too late to go back home on the outskirts of Oban and too cold and wet to make a run enticing. He decided to catch up with paperwork while the building was quiet. He made his way upstairs, passing the coffee machine on the way. A ribbon of light spilling out of the half-closed door of his department puzzled him. None of his team would be at their desks this early. He had enough trouble getting them in on time when there was a big investigation on. He stuck his head round the door to check.

Paula Dawson, the sole occupant leapt behind a filing cabinet. Her hurried movement sent her handbag flying off the desk, scattering the contents.

"Paula are you alright?" he asked, wondering why his newest recruit would want to hide from him, or anyone else.

The young DC had only been with the team for a couple of months. Her quirky hair style had nearly put him off choosing her, but her sharp wit and warm smile put her ahead of the other contenders. He bent to help retrieve her possessions while waiting for an answer.

Perhaps she was wearing something she was too embarrassed to be seen in. Unlikely, Paula was not the shy type, especially with regard to clothes. She liked to shock; one particularly short red suede skirt worn during her first week had every man in the station walking round with their eyes on stalks. Eventually one of the other women officers had a quiet word about the image needed for the job. Since then, to his relief, she had been more conservative and shown a remarkable chameleon-like ability to adapt to fit in.

"What got you in so early?" he asked, trying to put her at ease. He placed the retrieved pens and cosmetics on the desk, and spotted a large rucksack propped against the wall.

She stepped out from her hiding place, head lowered, holding a tissue to her nose, the front of her t-shirt covered in blood.

"Couldn't sleep," she mumbled, as she bent stiffly to pick up a lipstick he'd missed.

He stepped closer, lifted her chin with one finger to check where the blood was coming from. This was no simple nosebleed. Her nose was battered, both eyes were bruised and her lip split, but he was more concerned about the possible injuries to her body.

"Have you seen anyone about this?"

She shook her head.

"Come with me, I think the doctor is downstairs, he can look you over."

"No. I'm fine," she mumbled.

"Who are you trying to kid?" he said. "Sorry, I insist." He didn't often pull rank, but on this occasion, he had no hesitation. Her well-being was more important than his concern about being seen as a bully.

"I don't want anyone to see me like this."

This was the classic response of an abuse victim. He guessed the boyfriend was in the frame. Gossip was that she lived with a nutter. No doubt she'd refuse to press charges. He didn't care. What mattered was getting her checked over. "Fine, I'll get him to come up here."

Gavin didn't give her time to argue. He phoned the duty officer and asked him to send the doctor up to his office after he'd examined Neil Gillespie.

"Sit down," he said, pointing to her seat. He perched on the edge of the desk and pointed to her rucksack. "Been thrown out?"

"No, I walked out." There was a hint of pride in her response.

"Good. Any plans?"

"I could stay with my sister, but I don't want

him harassing her."

"Better she doesn't know where you're staying," he said. "I have a spare room you could use until you get sorted."

The moment he said it he had regrets. Would she think he was trying to take advantage of her? Of course not, he was nearly twice her age. What would everyone else think? Did it matter? Did they need to know?

The fire door banged; Gavin went out to see if it was Dr Munro. He led him into the office and introduced him to Paula.

"Can you check her over?" he asked. "I'll leave you to it, but I'd like a word about Neil Gillespie when you've finished."

There was a coffee machine down the corridor. He shoved in the necessary collection of coins and waited patiently for the hot water to fill the cardboard cup. He only managed a few sips before Munro emerged.

"She's been lucky. A couple of cracked ribs and a battered face, a few weeks rest should be all she needs. Shame she doesn't seem willing to charge the bastard that did it."

"I thought she'd say that" Gavin answered, "but I'd still like you to do a report as if she were. Hang onto it, you never know. I might be able to get her to change her mind."

"Persuade her to take a couple of photos, in case she needs them in the future. I didn't have any luck."

"What about Gillespie? Anything I need to be aware of there?"

"You mean apart from the beating? It didn't do anything life threatening. The liver damage caused by his booze consumption is another matter. But we've known that for a long time. He isn't interested in rehab so there's nothing I can do. He needs to get back into the hostel, rough sleeping is not doing him any favours."

"I'll do what I can," Gavin said and shook the doctor's hand.

He gulped down the rest of his coffee, threw the cup in the bin and went back to face Paula. She hadn't accepted his invitation to stay, but it was the best offer she'd get. He pushed open the door, and said, "Time to go."

She looked puzzled. "Where to?"

"My place... No arguments." He hoisted her rucksack onto his shoulder, pushed her bag into her hands and said, "We need to get a move on, unless you want to face the morning shift."

She glanced at the clock, and suddenly seemed more than willing to go along with his suggestion though she did put in a condition of her own. "Just until I find somewhere else."

He nodded. Now was not the right time to convince her to press charges. He'd work on that later.

Two

A flash of luminous orange bobbed into sight, distracting Jim Cullen from the breath-taking view of the distant Hebridean islands.

His first instinct was to ignore it, but curiosity won, and he found himself scanning the water to find it again. The object had vanished.

The climb to the viewing point on the cliff had been tough. He struggled to get his breath back and then bent to touch his toes and stretch his muscles.

The blob reappeared. The distinctive, unnatural colour made him certain this was a lifejacket. It vanished again, bounced back, being pushed closer to the shore by the surging waves. The harder he looked, the more convinced he became he was looking at a lifejacket, and someone was wearing it.

His medical training told him the chance of survival in these conditions was negligible. But negligible didn't mean impossible. Automatic reaction kicked in. Jim scanned the cliff face, searching for a safe path. The first route he picked showed evidence of a recent landslide, so he scoured the scene once more trying to find a safer route without having to go right round the sweep of the bay.

"Come on, Digger," he called. His sister's black Labrador bounded towards him with a well chewed stick firmly clamped between his teeth.

If only there was someone on the island whom he could call for help. Even if he'd been carrying his mobile phone, it would have been useless, since there was no signal here, and the sparse island population didn't bother with phones. They had a radio transmitter for emergencies.

He'd worry about that later, first he had to get to the shore and reach the lifejacket.

Jim concentrated on his route, getting down wouldn't be easy, climbing back up would be a real challenge. He checked the water again. The vivid orange lifejacket was still moving nearer to the shoreline, he must hurry before the tide turned and towed it back out to sea.

Clambering up and down this cliff had been a regular childhood pastime, but he hadn't been down there for over ten years, and never in conditions like this. Recent rain had loosened the surface stones; the soil beneath was soft and slippery. Slithering and sliding, he reached a shallow ledge, halted to draw breath and took stock. 'Insanity,' he thought, but as long as there was a faint chance of saving a life, he'd risk it. His foot slipped. He slid about ten feet, slowed and slid again, stopping on a little ledge with a sheer drop below onto the sand. Without warning, the soil beneath him crumbled, leaving him hanging onto a small protruding rock with his fingertips. He lost his grip and plummeted twenty feet to the seashore, somehow managing in the few seconds available to turn his fall into a roll to reduce the impact on landing.

Winded, but unhurt by his undignified descent, he got up and ran to the water's edge. The orange blob was still there.

Not wanting to be weighted down, he stripped off and abandoned his boots and clothes just above the tide mark and plunged into the icy water. The numbing waves hit his bare chest as he dived towards the lifejacket that bobbed tantalizingly beyond his reach. Each time he made a grab for it, a surge of water tore it away.

He swam on, gasping for breath as he lunged forward, catching hold of a tangle of trailing rope. He tugged hard, but it came free in his hand. He grabbed again at another strand, pulling it tight as the water surged around him, until the entangled mass was close enough to thump into his shoulder. A chunk of splintered timber was attached to the life-jacketed body keeping it afloat. Jim had no choice but to drag the whole lot with him to the shore.

Determination drove him through the pain of fighting the backwash until he felt sand beneath his feet. Once he could stand, he started to untangle the knots that held his victim to the makeshift raft. His fingers were too numb. Using his teeth, he got one knot open, then found a second knot. He undid that one and pushed the mast away.

Now all that hampered his progress was the bulky lifejacket and waterlogged waterproofs. He got a firm stance on the sandy beach, ducked down, put his shoulder under the body, and straightened up. With the next retreating wave, he lifted the victim clear above the waves. Water swooshed out of the sleeves and legs of the waterproofs, lightening his load. What he'd earlier thought to be a hefty trawler-man actually weighed barely more than a child.

He stumbled through the shallows, until he reached dry sand and gently laid the inert body down. He sank to his knees, dreading the sight that lay hidden under the hood of the over-sized waterproofs. He stared at the stiff garish fabric for a moment before he pushed aside the hood. Long wet hair masked the features. He carefully pushed the hair out of the way, revealing a young woman's face. The paleness of her skin, and her blue tinged lips were in sharp contrast to the dark red and purple bruises on her cheeks. A streak of crimson blood still oozed from a gash on her temple. The fresh blood gave him hope that he wasn't too late.

Jim searched for a pulse. At first, he could find nothing. The cold could be responsible for her body almost shutting down. He would not give up on her. He checked her airways again, they were clear. Then he felt the faint flicker of a pulse.

It was enough to galvanize him into action. Yanking off the lifejacket, he pulled open the waterproofs, revealing a tight black leather corset which was restricting her breathing. A voice in his head reminded him not to judge anyone by their appearance. Restoring air into her lungs was his priority.

He rolled her over to find double knotted silk cords lacing the garment from top to bottom down her back. Whoever tied them had not wanted them undone in a hurry. Jim tugged hard, ripping four of the eyelets out, giving enough slack to ease the worst pressure off her rib cage.

He rolled her onto her back, noting several round scars on her breasts which looked like cigarette burns. He leaned over her, held her nose and chin, and breathed life into her. He counted, breathed, counted, massaged, counted, breathed, on and on, until he was rewarded by a spluttering as her body took control again, expelling the water she had swallowed. Her eyes remained closed, and her limbs leaden, but she was alive.

A gust of wind on his semi-naked body reminded him of the dangers of hypothermia. He scrambled across the sand, gathered up his abandoned clothes and hurried back to where she lay. He pulled her up into a sitting position and started to dress her in them. He eased her lolling head through the neck of his shirt and jumper. Then pushing his arm up one sleeve, caught her hand, and pulled it through. The fabric stuck to her damp skin making his task harder. He repeated the operation, pulling the clothes down over her body, until they practically reached her knees. He laid her down and pulled his socks onto her feet.

He hastily tugged on his trousers and his coat and shoved his bare feet into his boots. He shook her waterproofs hard, wrapped her in them, and lifted her onto his shoulder, anchoring her by partially zipping one of her legs inside his coat.

All he needed now was to find a scalable route to the top of the cliff.

Faced with a wall of crumbling sand, he had no option but to head for the far end of the cove. The abrasive effect of sand on damp skin trapped inside his boots, made him regret parting with his socks. But his concern for his patient was too great to let discomfort halt his progress.

The winter sun was rapidly sinking below the horizon. The fading light would soon be lost.

He started upwards, zigzagging, back and forth and occasionally down again to find a better path. Halfway up he reached a dead end. An overhanging rock blocked his path. He inched his way back and heard a whimpering noise just above his head. In his rush down the cliff, he had forgotten all about Digger. If he could reach the dog, then they'd be safe. Digger would guide them to safety.

Speed was the only thing that mattered, perhaps the difference between life and death.

MHM Photograpy

Caro Ayre

A childhood in Kenya provided lasting memories of hot sun filled days, vibrant coloured birds and flowers, armies of insects, roaming wildlife in vast expanses of open spaces and warm waves lapping on silvery sands.

I now live in rural Somerset where family, gardening, painting and writing keep boredom at bay.

For more information go to: -
Twitter @AyreC
Facebook- Caro Ayre Author
www.CaroAyre.co.uk

The Mallaig Link

When you can't trust your boss, who can you trust?

When surveillance of a mysterious house in Mallaig exposes a weak link within D I Gavin McKay's department, he pretends to drop the case.

Will solving the identity of a woman with amnesia provide the cover needed to hide the fact that he has not given up on solving what went on in that house. Can he find answers before someone else dies? Will his personal relationships suffer because of his determination to get to the truth?

Buy the first book in the Detective Inspector McKay series now, the sequel is coming out soon.

www.amazon.com/dp/B01CH4FCBS
www.amazon.co.uk/dp/B01CH4FCBS
ISBN 978-0-9572224-3-4

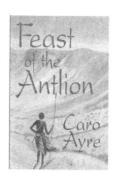

An action-packed novel with a touch of romance set in Kenya.

Poachers, plane crashes, blackmail and murder are not what Sandra Harriman expected to face when she took control of a huge wildlife conservation project.

Sandra feels like an ant in an antlion's trap as she struggles to protect her stepchildren's inheritance.

Uncovering her dead husband's secrets leaves her wondering who can be trusted.

http://www.amazon.co.uk/dp/B006PZBXCI
http://www.amazon.com/dp/B006PZBXCI
ISBN 978-0-9572224-0-3

A life-threatening illness within the family takes its toll.

Clare has battled for sixteen years to keep Hannah healthy while Mike, her husband, has never accepted that their daughter has Cystic Fibrosis.

The reappearance of an old flame and exciting challenges set by her children complicate her bid for a fresh start. Repairing the fragile bond between her children and their father is an uphill struggle, but worth fighting for.

www.amazon.com/dp/B00DFOT5VI
www.amazon.co.uk/dp/B00DFOT5VI
ISBN 987-0-9572224-1-0

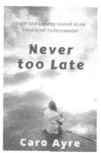

Friends forever, until one little lie shatters Fiona's dreams and hopes at home and at work.

Fiona's loyalty to Sally is tested to the limit. She can never reveal the truth, not even to silence a blackmailer.

One lie leads to more lies but Fiona stands fast. Events push the two women closer together, but Fiona still refuses to do anything that might hurt her friend regardless of who else suffers.

Read this heart-breaking emotional rollercoaster to find out if Fiona will ever find happiness.

www.amazon.com/dp/B0866BQXD6
www.Amazon.co.uk/dp/B0866BQD6
Paperback – ISBN 978-0-9572224-5-8

Printed in Great Britain
by Amazon